BEHIND THE VEIL

FATHER SPYRIDON BAILEY

Published in 2019 by FeedARead.com Publishing

Copyright © Father Spyridon Bailey.

Financed by the Arts Council of Great Britain

A CIP catalogue record for this title is available from the British Library.

To Guy and Tina – thank you for your stories of India.

Also by Father Spyridon

Journey To Mount Athos

Trampling Down Death By Death

The Ancient Path

Orthodoxy And The Kingdom Of Satan

Small Steps Into The Kingdom

Return To Mount Athos

Fiction

Podvig

Fire On The Lips

Vampire AD70

Lost Voices

Poetry

Come And See

Chapter One

While her gorilla of a boyfriend was in the toilets Nick leaned in close to the young blonde at the bar. She laughed at whatever he said and turned her head to get a better look at him. The gesture was enough encouragement for him to move closer so that he could almost whisper in her ear. James sat back at the table watching his friend go through his moves, keeping one eye on the toilet door for sign of approaching disaster. But to his relief Nick was moving back towards him with their drinks before the boyfriend returned, and as he slumped into the bench the two men exchanged glances: a smirk from Nick and a mock disapproving shake of the head from James.

"You're gonna get us in trouble, look at the size of him." The boyfriend returned to his place at the bar but clearly nothing was said about the blonde's encounter.
Nick grinned into his pint, "Nice though, isn't she?"
James gave a half-shrug, it wasn't something he wanted to think about.

Sensing his friend's reaction Nick tried to get him talking. "So when do you leave?"

"The day after tomorrow," James paused, "I can't believe it's finally here."

"I hope you're doing the right thing Jim, it's a big step."

"I'm done here, there's nothing left to keep me."

"Oh thanks mate," Nick pretended to be hurt and laughed.

"You know what I mean, I need to get away and start again."

"Well at least the money's good, you don't need to stay long, put some cash away and keep your options open."

James shook his head, "No, I'm not coming back. No matter what happens I don't want to live in Sheffield again."

"Listen to yourself, it's not that bad. She can't have spoiled the whole city for you."

James looked at his friend and fell silent, he couldn't find the words to answer, he took another drink and said nothing

Nick watched the blonde wander over to the jukebox and make her selection. The boyfriend had his back to them and was oblivious to Nick's interest. Two of his mates had joined him and they were deep in conversation. Feeling a little uneasy at Nick's behaviour James tried to alert him to the reality of their situation.

"Look at the size of them lot," he threw a glance at Nick to check if he was listening.

"I know, I've seen 'em before, bunch of thugs. She's wasted on them."

The response only added to James' unease, "Get ya eyes off her then, we don't need any trouble."

This seemed to snap Nick away from his primitive urges, he laughed, "There's only three of 'em."

"Okay Bruce, take it easy." James laughed for the first time since they'd come out, the beer was beginning to relax him, and he sensed he'd pulled Nick back from inviting danger.

Suddenly the opening bars of Tears Of A Clown filled the room and Smokey Robinson took everyone to a better place. "The scooter club used to meet here every week, they had this stuff on all the time. Do you remember?"

"Yea," James nodded, "it was great."

6

The blonde was half-heartedly dancing behind her boyfriend who continued to ignore her, and as she moved she threw Nick a furtive glance. The man listening to the boyfriend looked their way, it may have been nothing but James was anxious again.

"Shall we drink up and go somewhere else?"

"You're kidding, it's raining, let's settle in here for the night."

The man at the bar looked their way again and this time the boyfriend also turned to look over. It was a momentary thing, but even Nick got the message. "Maybe you're right, I think we're on their radar."

"Shall we neck it and get off?"

"Okay, but I need the toilet."

"Wait until we get to the next place," said James, "don't walk right past them. They'll think you're challenging them."

"This isn't With Nail And I," laughed Nick, "and anyway, I'm not wearing perfume."

"I see you didn't try denying being a ponce though!"

Nick laughed as he got to his feet, "Wish me luck."

The group of men paid him no attention as he left, but almost immediately after finding himself alone, all three of them began throwing glances towards James. He avoided looking back, but even staring ahead he could feel their eyes aimed at him. He began to wonder if they had mistaken the blonde girl's attention as being for him, and began willing Nick to return to even the odds. But even then he knew they didn't stand a chance. He imagined turning up for his new job bruised and swollen, and this might be if all went well.

Nick appeared as the toilet door swung open and immediately he began grinning at his friend. The expression didn't leave his face as he came across the room, "You gonna get another in?"

"No come on man, let's get off."

7

But Nick sat back next to him, "Go on, get a round in, you'll see why I'm laughin'."

James pursed his lips and grabbed the two empty glasses, he walked as casually as he could to the bar, not daring to check whether his approach was being observed.

"Two pints of butty please," and as the barman replaced the dirty glasses James turned to look back at Nick. On the wall behind him was a TV screen now showing the football, the interest hadn't been in them at all. A wave of relief swept through him, and as the barman lifted the second pint onto the bar James ordered a couple of shots of Jack Daniels.

On his return Nick laughed at him, "Bit vain to think everyone was looking at you wasn't it?" James manoeuvred the drinks onto the table, "You trying to get me drunk Jim?"

"Why not? We could do with a blow out."

They lifted the shots and in unison said "Cheers." The undiluted bourbon cut through to the back of their throats and they both quickly took a swig of beer to soften the impact. "Do you mind me asking you something?" James said.

"No, go ahead."

"Why do you still give the come on to all these girls? You're not gonna follow through with anything, so why do it?"

"It's nothing Jim, I'm just messin' around. You know I wouldn't do anythin' like that."

"You wouldn't want Lucy doin' it though, would you?"

"No of course not, but blokes would get a different idea if a woman did it. As soon as they give you the eye you know you've got a chance, that's just the way it is. Although, if I'm honest, none of these girls are gonna give me a chance, it's just a bit of fun."

"You sure Nick? Especially when you've had a drink."

"Oh come on Jim, what you doin'? Don't get all serious on me, I don't need it. Have you ever thought if you could lighten up a bit you might not be on your tod?"

James shrugged, "That's not why she left, but you might be right. I am turning into a miserable sod."

"No, I'm not sayin' that, but you do carry the world round on your shoulders at times, you weren't always like this."

"I know, it's true. I don't know what's the matter with me lately, and it's not just since Emma went. I can't explain it really, I just have a lot of stuff goin' round my head. I can't put it to rest."

"What sort of stuff?"

"You'd laugh if I told you, it sounds daft."

Nick shook his head, "No I wouldn't, what stuff?"

"You know how Emma goes to church, well she always wanted me to go with her but I couldn't see the point."

"Too right, I didn't know she was tryin' to convert you."

"No, it was nothing like that, she used to say she wanted to be able to share things with me, but I wouldn't be able to understand. It sounds bad when I say it like that, but she didn't mean it to. And the more I realised there was a big part of who she is that I can never know about, the more it all seemed to go wrong. Does that make any sense?"

"I dunno," admitted Nick, "Lucy has got her hobbies and I couldn't care less about 'em. In fact if she ever tries telling me about her night classes I shut down and smile politely." He laughed a little at his own observation.

"It's more than going to pottery classes Nick, Emma had something that I couldn't be any part of. It wasn't just something she did, going to church on a Sunday, it stayed with her all the time. I'm not sayin' I wanted that, but I did want to know that part of her. Does that make sense?"

9

"I suppose so, but if you don't believe what she believes, how can you?"

"Exactly, and that's why it all started going wrong."

"You mean she broke up with you because you didn't want to go to church?"

"That's not what I said at all, she never put pressure on me. It wasn't the church thing, it was the God bit." James stared down at his feet for a moment, lost in thought.

"Can I be honest with you?" Nick said.

James looked up at him, "Yea of course."

"You won't want to hear this, but I think you're better off without her."

James shook his head, "I don't agree."

"Come on, think about it, she never wanted to move in with you, and she got you all serious about stuff. And now look at you, she's left you in a right mess."

"I didn't mind not living together, that's just something she thought was the way to do it. But I don't know, you might be right about how I've changed." Even as he said it, he didn't believe it. There was no desire in him for an argument, and he knew Nick could never know what Emma had brought to his life. So he tried to move the conversation on. "You and Lucy still look happy, so you might be right about some things."

"Well, once we got the baby there wasn't a lot of choice. I can't say I wake up every morning clicking my heels, but it'll do. She nags the ass off me, but she always has."

"You need to hang on to her Nick, you're punchin' above your weight."

Nick laughed, "I don't deny it, but let's be honest, child bearing has taken its toll." They laughed again, "I'm only jokin', and anyway, as far as I know I'm responsible for getting her pregnant so I shouldn't complain if it's left its mark on her."

James hesitated, "Are you serious?"

"What, about being the dad? No, I had a few doubts, but to hell with it, what does it matter. He'll grow up calling me daddy and like you say, I'm not going to get many better offers than her."

They shared a few more rounds and the combination of alcohol and loud music brought them escape from any further meaningful thought or conversation. As the bar began to thin out Nick said "Do you fancy coming back to ours for a drink?"

James checked his watch, "It's a bit late, Lucy won't be happy."

"You're kiddin', one last chance to say goodbye, she'll be pissed off if you don't."

"I've had enough, do you fancy some chips?"

"Yea, I'll walk back along London Road with you, the beer's given me an appetite."

The silence of the cold air hit them both as they stepped out into the street. The rain had stopped and the cloudless sky looked vast, even from beneath the streetlights. It wasn't something he would normally have asked, but with a belly full of beer James said "Doesn't it bother you at all that you might not be the dad?"

"No, why should it? It's not about DNA is it? You can have biological fathers who couldn't care less about their kids, but I love being a dad."

"What if some bloke turned up wanting to be in on it?"

"Are you kidding?" Nick laughed, "Most blokes would run a mile. And how would they know?"

"So it's not someone still around?"

"I wouldn't know Jim, I haven't asked. I don't want to know, and Lucy's not interested either. And unless I need a kidney transplant in twenty years' time there's no reason why any of it should come out one way or another. To me it's about what we do as a family, none of the rest matters at all."

11

"I'm impressed Nick, seriously, I think you're right." It was true, he respected his friend for adopting this approach, but knew he could never act this way himself. Maybe Nick was just a better man, he thought, or maybe he was just more willing to settle.

There was an all-male queue at the chippy and as Nick and James entered a few hostile glances came their way. Everyone shuffled forwards in silence, looking up at the menu board or reading advertisements, avoiding unnecessary eye contact. More refugees from the pubs piled in behind them, and by the time James was at the counter there were another dozen men now waiting. As the little Chinese woman took his order angry voices erupted behind him. He instinctively spun round to see two of the thugs from the pub yelling at another group. Without warning two of the men began punching each other, fists like rapid pistons snaking back and forth. A heavy blow caught one of the thugs to the side of the face and he staggered back out into the street. His opponent lurched forward and grabbing him around the neck swung him to the ground. Before anyone could intervene he began kicking the man as he lay on the floor, the toe of his shoe making heavy contact with his victim's rib cage. The second thug rushed him and pushed him out into the road, swearing as he did it. There wasn't any traffic, and so he stood rooted to the spot waving his arms in invitation, screaming "Come on then!"

But the man who had pushed him bent down to his friend, "Are you okay?"

"Yea," he mumbled from the floor. He helped him to his feet while their opponent continued taunting them and shouting abuse. By now two other men had moved out into the street and it was clear that the thugs from the pub were in over their heads. They exchanged a few insults, promised further retribution if they ever saw them again, and walked away defeated. The victors re-joined the queue, loudly boasting and laughing, their chests swelled with pride and adrenalin.

James paid for his food and was glad to get out. He stood a few yards away from the shop front waiting for Nick, and once they were together they moved off quickly. Nick turned and smiled, "They didn't get their chips."

"That's it for me," said James, "I'm done with this place."

"Come on, no one got hurt. You get nutters everywhere. You were the one who told me those statistics, Sheffield is one of the safest cities in the country. You'll get a lot more of that in Brum."

By the time they reached the junction Nick had torn open his bag of chips and was greedily eating them. He wiped his hands on his jeans and extended his arm, "Look after yourself Jim."

It was an overly formal gesture but it felt right. They shook hands, "Cheers Nick, I will."

"You planning to visit any time soon?"

"No, I doubt I'll have any time before Christmas, but I'll get in touch and arrange something."

They released one another's hands and stood looking at each other for a moment, Nick patted him firmly on the arm. Without another word they turned and headed off in opposite directions, James still carrying the chips which he now pressed against his stomach for warmth. Away from the pubs the streets became even more still, and as he walked James tried to imagine how Nick could so easily take on the responsibility of a child without being sure he was the father. But then he admitted to himself that Nick was heading back to a family, and he was alone. The thought prompted a morbid mood which began to inhabit him, and by the time he reached the front door of his flat he had given in to melancholy. He stepped into the darkness of his hall and placed the chips on the shelf with his keys. He had lost his appetite for anything but more booze. He went through to the kitchen and pulled a face at the empty fridge, regretting not having stocked up on beer. He made himself a coffee in the semi-darkness and went through to the living room where he finally turned on the light. Slumping into the settee he cupped his drink with both hands and realised his ears were ringing from the music in the pub.

He glanced up at the mantel piece over the unlit gas fire where his eyes rested on a small framed picture of Emma. Her eyes looked serene and there was a quizzical smile on her lips. Placing the coffee on the low table in front of him he stood up and reached for the picture. He remembered the exact moment he had taken it, and how it had felt to have her smile at him like that. He knew he would give anything to go back to that moment, but then became annoyed at himself for such foolish thoughts. She was gone. Even keeping her photograph like this was stupid, but he couldn't bring himself to hide her away in a drawer. With almost everything else now packed for the move he hadn't been able to bring himself to consciously choose whether to take the picture with him, and now it was one of the last things that gave any sign that he had lived here. He felt the sting as tears welled up. He began running through what had gone wrong, and remembered snippets of what she had said, but it was a waste of time, he knew it was over for good.

He lay the picture face down and sat back in his seat. The coffee was too strong and bitter but he swallowed it regardless. Looking around the bare room he considered what was left to pack and decided he was on top of it. He could sleep in tomorrow, spend a few hours in the afternoon saying goodbye to his mother, and then he was ready for Birmingham. This lifted his spirits a little and he reached over for the newspaper he had dropped on the table earlier. He skimmed a few stories on the sports pages until he had turned to the horoscopes. He didn't believe in them, but it was a habit he had picked up from his mother. Emma always criticised him for reading them, but she wasn't here to say anything now. It promised him good things, and he was happy to think for a moment there might be something in it. He lobbed it back towards the table and wandered through to find his bed.

Chapter 2

With the car loaded with everything he owned James drove from Sheffield City centre up to Mexborough. The grey miserable town brought back memories of why he had left. As a child he was warned by his father that the mines were going to close and that he should look for some other kind of work. One Saturday afternoon James and his mother were visiting family near Rotherham, and from the top deck of the bus he had looked out over regiments of riot police waiting to confront striking miners. The sight of the silent rows of men in riot gear left him with a fear of their power, and even as a schoolboy he shared in everyone's anger at how the BBC portrayed their victims. Six months after the strike his father had been called up for jury duty, a case of a miner accused of assaulting a policeman. James remembered his father's delight in the copper's reaction when the jury pronounced a not guilty verdict; the policeman's word had been called a lie. It was a story that his father repeated many times, and it was always greeted with approval from his audience. As James pulled up outside the same house his mother still lived in he felt the familiar comfort of home, something he couldn't explain. Locking his door he wondered how safe his belongings would be out in the street but decided that in broad daylight even here no one would break in. He had his own key to the house and let himself in, "Hi mom, how are you?"

"Hello love, do you want a tea?"

He followed her voice down into the kitchen where potatoes were cooking in the pans. She was already filling the kettle as he walked in, and turned to smile as he offered her the flowers he had picked up at a petrol station. "Oh beautiful, thank you." She took the flowers and pressed her face into them, "they smell lovely." But then looking at him added "You look terrible."

"I know, I was out with Nick last night, it'll wear off in a few hours."

She shook her head, "Go and sit down, I'll bring your tea through."

On the coffee table next to her favourite seat was an enlarged photograph of James' father taken on holiday in Spain. James gazed at it for a moment, reflecting on how lonely his mother had been since he'd died. Her widowhood left him feeling guilty, but there wasn't anything he could do about it. As she came through he said "I like the picture of dad, I haven't seen that one before."

"He looks handsome in it doesn't he? I've always liked that one of him." She placed the cup of tea in front of James and stood with hers in the doorway.

"Are you going to be alright when I'm gone?" He said.

"Of course I am Jimmy, I've got Cath and Mary, they'll keep popping in. Anyway, I'm only a few hours up the motorway if I need any jobs doing." She laughed, but there was a certain element of truth to it. "I'm more worried about you, how are you gonna be down there?"

"I'm looking forward to it, it's a good job, it could lead to all sorts of other things."

"I know Jim, but work isn't everything." She paused and added "Have you heard from Emma lately?"

"No, not since she went to Bath."

"I did like her Jim, she was a sweet girl. It's a real shame it didn't work out."

"Well that's what happens sometimes." He was a little irritated at the pointlessness of her comments, he had heard it all before and nothing she had to say could help.

17

"Are you sure it's just a hangover? You don't look well."

"It's nothing your dinner won't fix, it smells good."

"I've got a Marks and Spencer roast, beautiful bit of meat."

He smiled at her habit of announcing where she had bought the joint, she'd done it all his life. They sipped at their tea and finally taking her seat she flicked through the TV stations while the food cooked. He was grateful for the mindless distraction of a gameshow, and they spent the next fifteen minutes seeing if they could answer the questions before the contestants. Eventually she disappeared into the kitchen and the sound of plates and cutlery being arranged let him know dinner was on its way. He glanced at the clock and felt an urge to set off, but there was no getting out of spending a few hours covering the same old ground with his mother. He wanted to be there, but he felt a growing pressure to hit the road.

After lunch James escaped to the kitchen to do the washing up, despite his mother's protests; it felt good to at least be able to do this small thing for her. He made them another tea and joined her one last time. "I need to get off before three," he announced.

"Yes, before it gets dark, especially in Birmingham."

"I'm not in the city centre, I showed you on the map mom, it's a nice road. You'll have to come down and see it."

She didn't acknowledge his remark, she had no intention of travelling so far. "You going down the M1?"

"Yea, then cut across to Birmingham, it's an easy run."

James sat watching the clock for another hour and then got to his feet. "I need to make a move, thank you for lunch."

"Oh that's a shame. Be careful down there Jimmy, let me know how things go."

"I will, and if there's any problem just give me a ring."

"I'm alright here, don't worry." She walked him to the door, "That car looks ready to burst."

"I know, I didn't know if it would all go in. I need to give myself time to unpack."

"Don't worry, you get yourself off. It's been nice having you." She gave him a concerned look and grasped his arm, "Are you sure there's no chance of getting back with Emma. Why don't you give her a call?"

"It's done mom, I told you. Don't start going over that again, please."

"I'm sorry love, you just seemed so happy together. I always liked her."

"Right, I've got to go, it's been lovely seeing you."

"Thank you for my flowers," she offered in the hope of not parting on bad terms.

"Okay, see you soon." The engine turned over on the first attempt and he waved as he pulled out from the curb. He regretted feeling so resentful towards her but he was frustrated at her comments. He couldn't admit how he was feeling, and if she knew the truth it would only worry her.

He followed the series of dull roads down to the motorway and joined the Sunday afternoon traffic. Contending with car-shaped images of strangers was easier than talking to real people, especially with an ache behind the eyes that wasn't shifting. He turned on the radio but immediately recoiled from the artificial voices of a Radio Four drama. He found a football commentary and let the next couple of hours drift by. As the road signs assured he was getting close he sensed how alien this new city was, and he found it impossible to imagine ever feeling like this could really be home. He had only visited his new flat once before and now had to use the same road map he had drawn himself from that first visit. But spotting a few familiar landmarks he eventually pulled up outside his new front door. The small rectangle of lawn outside the front window had recently been mowed, and he convinced himself it didn't look too shabby. He carried a box with him up the three steps and dumped it in the hall. He didn't want to leave the car open and unguarded, and so created a pile of his belongings just inside the flat before locking up the car and closing the front door behind him. The air was a little musty, but he was pleased to finally be here. With his boxes secure he did a quick check of each of his three rooms to remind himself of how it looked, and again he was pleased with it all. He was getting it at a good price and he could be in work in less than twenty minutes.

The rest of the evening was spent hanging clothes in the wardrobe and deciding which picture frames looked best where. The familiarity of his nick knacks quickly turned the flat into something he could call his, and at a little before nine o'clock he sat at the two-person sized dining table to assess his handiwork. He was pleased with how it looked. Tomorrow morning he started his new job and he was a little nervous. It wasn't anything he couldn't handle, in fact accountancy for a firm this size was something he could do in his sleep, but the prospect of new people and a new boss created enough uncertainty to unsettle him. Maybe there was an attractive colleague who might catch his eye, but then even the thought of this depressed him. In anger he blurted "Oh come on!" He knew he had to shake himself out of this state of mind, Emma wasn't the first girl he had loved, but there was a sense of regret that went further than simply losing a girlfriend. He tried to analyse his feelings and decided he couldn't understand what was going on inside himself. It wasn't something he had known before, and he couldn't see a way of correcting what was wrong.

He plugged in his laptop and found a few emails he had no interest in reading. On Facebook a few people from work had wished him well but he couldn't be bothered responding. He considered checking out Emma's homepage but decided it could do him no good. Almost against his will he dug out Emma's picture from his bag, knowing it was the wrong thing to do. He stared at her face and felt the emotions returning, the simple, understandable emotions of loss that made sense to him. But before self-pity could take hold once more he strode into the kitchen and dropped the frame in the bin. It was such a melodramatic move that he laughed at himself, it felt foolish to behave this way, but it brought him relief. It was a final, decisive act, and he knew it meant letting go of any hope of her return. He was pleased with himself, Birmingham was a fresh start and he had to make it happen. Invigorated by this new attitude he decided to find a local corner shop and get some basics in: he needed a cup of tea. There was enough cloud cover to keep the night air warm and as he walked through the dark he managed to turn his nerves into excitement about what lay ahead.

Chapter 3

The anticipated twenty minute drive to work turned into forty minutes of nose to tail traffic. James arrived on time but stressed, and was glad to escape the car. He went into reception and approached the young woman behind the desk, "Hello, I'm James Harris, I'm meeting Mr. Stone at nine." The receptionist gave a practiced smile and asked him to take a seat. She rang through and a few minutes later a short, middle aged man in a blue suit approached him.

"Hello James, good to see you again." He extended his hand and they performed the formalities. "If you'll follow me through I'll introduce a few of our team before you get stuck in." He led James down a series of glass corridors to an open plan office where a few people were already working. James was introduced to a man of about his own age, "This is Liam," said Stone, "he's doing a very similar job to you, so if you have any questions he's the guy to go to." James sensed he was being offloaded by someone who didn't want to be bothered by any problems he might have, but Liam seemed friendly enough. "I know they went through the operating system with you James," Stone explained as they walked to a vacant desk and computer, "but before you get thrown in at the deep end I'd like to just run through a few things."

For the next twenty minutes James endured Stone's explanation of the departments he would be working with and how he was to use the company's policies when it came to the accounts. It was all unnecessary, it was almost exactly the same system he had worked with in his last job, but he nodded politely and with some relief thanked him for his help when it was over.

"There's just one final thing," said Stone, "you must lock your computer down whenever you leave your desk; even if it's just for a minute or two. It's a disciplinary matter if you leave an open computer unattended." The warning felt very heavy handed and already James was getting a sense of the man.

As Stone walked away James looked around at the now busy office, he exchanged smiles with a few people, and began opening files to see how much work they needed. To his relief most of them were in good order; his predecessor had done his job properly. He pulled up a few spreadsheets and buried himself in the figures, immediately feeling at home in what he was doing, and the next few hours drifted by. One or two friends used to pull his leg about being an accountant, and he often made out to them that he knew what a boring job it was. But the truth was he enjoyed his work and he felt good at it. He liked the numbers and he liked working alone. There were team meetings and there were clients who needed advice, but on the whole he enjoyed being able to get on with his work without too much interference from a boss. So long as he got his work done he knew they wouldn't interfere with him. Emma jokingly accused him of being on the autistic scale, to which he always claimed every man was somewhere on it, but it was true, he was happiest when people at work left him alone.

At one o'clock there was a lot of movement around the office as people began making their way to lunch. At the one end of the work space was a seating area and a few of the women congregated there to eat their sandwiches. As Liam passed his desk James said "Is there anywhere near here to buy some food?"

"Yea, I'm heading down there now."

James tagged along and the two men asked the usual questions to get to know each other. James was struck by how thick Liam's Brummie accent was and he became aware of his own alien Yorkshire voice. By the time they were back at their desks James had concluded that this was not someone he would want to spend any length of time with: it wasn't anything specific, they just didn't click. But he'd broken the ice with someone and it was a start. He only hoped that this early connection wouldn't get in the way of meeting people he liked.

As the afternoon rolled on more work appeared in his inbox and by five o'clock he realised he'd taken on more responsibility than he'd realised. It wasn't anything he was concerned about, but they had definitely sold the job to him without revealing the full picture. As people began drifting away he exchanged a few more smiles and nods, but continued working until six. By the time he was shutting down his computer he felt he'd made a good start on things and walking out to the car he felt confident about making a success of the job. At the interview they had assured him of potential promotions, and even after this first day he was already fantasising where it might lead.

The traffic home was a little easier and he stopped off at Morrison's to pick up some provisions. As he pushed his trolley down one of the aisles a woman's voice behind him said "How was the first day?"

He turned to find one of the women from his office smiling at him.

"Oh hello, yea, it was fine thanks."

"I'm Pauline, I'm part of the sales team."

James introduced himself and they stood for a moment sharing pleasantries, until she eventually said "Well, better get the dinner on."

There was nothing really in the exchange, and James wasn't attracted to her, but a simple human encounter was enough to make him feel more at home. The supermarket was on his route, and he made a mental note to make it his regular.

Back in the flat he cooked himself a frozen ready meal and listened to the radio. The last thing he wanted after a day in front of a screen was to mess with his laptop, and so with Radio Three providing Mozart, he ate his food looking around at his new flat. He knew he would have to send a few emails later just to confirm with friends that all had gone well, and later in the week he would give his mother a call to put her mind at rest. After a busy ten hours he sat back and drifted with his thoughts. He ran through the events of the day and began remembering some of the women in the office. But this line of thought brought him back to Emma and he became annoyed with himself. He took a shower and after checking his messages was in bed by ten.

The rest of the week was much like the first day and James quickly settled into his new routine. He picked up a few names and started eating his lunch with his workmates. They were friendly enough, but like Liam, he sensed they weren't the kind he would naturally be drawn to. Within the first month he had fallen into the habit of drinking a few glasses of wine most evenings and at the weekends he tried a few of the local pubs. The result was always him sitting alone at a table and leaving without having met anyone. It wasn't intolerable, but within three months he was struggling with the loneliness. He told himself he just had to get on with it, and when his monthly wage appeared on his bank balance he was reminded of why it worth sticking it out. He bought himself a better sound system and upgraded his laptop. Around the flat appeared a few luxuries that felt good to buy, but pretty soon merged into the background. He was pleased with himself that he at least had not contacted

Emma in fourteen weeks, but a day didn't go by without thoughts of her filling his head. The intensity of his feelings for her hadn't subsided, and he began reading articles about how to deal with bereavement. Some of it made sense, but none of it helped, and by the end of November he began to harbour real concerns about his mental health. In the evenings he became restless and moved between rooms looking for something with which to occupy himself. His concentration at work was beginning to suffer, but he could do this stuff in his sleep and no one commented on his effort. He recognised in himself a lack of interest in almost anything, and even a healthy bank balance was losing its buzz.

James stood next to the kettle in the lunch room, as he waited for the water to boil he absent-mindedly scanned the posters and adverts that staff had pinned to the notice board. His attention settled on a bright yellow piece of paper on which was printed the invitation to "FIND YOUR INNER PEACE THROUGH YOGA". Beneath the headline was a brief summary of some of the benefits yoga could bring, and the assurance that no prior experience was necessary. The next meeting was tomorrow night where an introductory talk was being given. He didn't have a pen on him to jot down the address and so after furtively looking around pulled the poster from the wall and folded it into his pocket.

After lunch he returned to his files but felt excited at the thought of what the poster had promised. He knew he needed something, and if it didn't work out he wouldn't have lost anything. Through the remaining hours of work he watched the clock slowly advancing in the corner of his screen until he was finally able to escape from his desk at exactly five. He drove directly home and heated up a can of beans for dinner. As he ate he reread the poster he had unfolded beside his plate. It didn't seem to have been written by a nutter, and he didn't think there were any real cranks in the office. He wondered who might have been the one to stick it up, and concluded it must have been one of the women. After dinner he watched a few Youtube videos of people explaining the physical and psychological benefits of yoga, and the more he learned the greater his enthusiasm grew. It didn't hurt that some of the yoga instructors were very attractive young women, and by the time he was in bed the fantasy of meeting someone at the class was taking hold of him. Something positive to get him out of the flat was enough in itself, but if there was the possibility of finding a sense of peace he knew he had to investigate it.

Chapter 4

The venue was a community hall owned by the local Anglican church. Three quarters of the car park was empty as James pulled in, and as he climbed from the car he looked in from the dark evening to the brightly lit room where a few people had taken their seats. He could see a few of the usual hippies he expected at this kind of event, but on the whole everyone looked what he considered normal, which he found reassuring. As he entered a man in his early twenties stepped his way, "Hello," he said, "welcome."

"Thank you," James replied uneasily.

"Have you studied yoga before?"

"No, I thought it sounded interesting. I've read a bit about it but never tried it"

The man's smile broadened, "I'm sure you'll get a lot from the meeting, please take one of these." He offered an A5 leaflet which James took to his seat. A middle aged couple smiled at him as he sat, and he used the chance to read as a means of avoiding chit chat. The booklet was a brief history of yoga, which he found interesting, but it was really nothing more than he had learned from Youtube. As he finished reading he looked up to see a beautiful woman in her late twenties enter. Her skin was dark and James struggled to identify her race, and as she glanced around the room James quickly looked away with embarrassment. As she sat down a couple of rows in front of him he gazed at her again for a moment, becoming aware of how attracted he was to her. He studied her should-length hair which was thick and almost completely black. But a minute later a man of a similar age entered and sat beside her, leaving James disappointed.

By 7-30 about half the seats were filled and the young man who had greeted James at the door stepped up in front of them. "Good evening," everyone immediately fell silent, "it's good to see you all tonight. My name is Aaron and I'd like to introduce you to Robert Evans who is going to be speaking to you tonight." At this a man who had been quietly sitting on the front row stood up and made a small wave to everyone. He had an unassuming presence and James had barely noticed him. It was difficult to judge his age, he was whip thin and there was something still youthful in his face. Aaron continued "Robert has been teaching yoga for thirteen years I think," he turned for confirmation and Robert nodded. "He studied in India before returning to Britain, and from personal experience I can testify that he has been a great help to many of us in this country who have wanted to know more about this wonderful practice. So without further ado, I'm going to hand you over to Robert."

There was a brief, polite applause and Robert looked around into the various faces before him. "Thank you Aaron, and can I please add my welcome to you all tonight. Some of you I know well, and some of you are here for the first time. In a short while I'm going to invite you to try out a few yoga postures for yourselves, it's far better to do it than talk about it, and hopefully you'll get something immediately from what we do tonight. After we've finished there will be drinks available and an opportunity for everyone to chat and ask questions. There are a few people here tonight who have been studying yoga at least as long as myself, so hopefully we can find someone who has the answers." There was a murmur of supportive laughter, a group signal that they were on his side rather than a reflection of his wit, and as Robert sat on the edge of a table where everyone could see him James glanced across at the woman again: there was a stillness about her that was very attractive, and despite the man next to her James hoped for the chance to speak to her later.

"The first thing I want to tell you about yoga is that it is entirely scientific. In fact Oxford University has made a study of the benefits of yoga and found that it reduces blood pressure and lowers stress. They showed that it can help us sleep better even if we practice it for just a short period each day."

An older woman raised her hand, and Robert said "Yes?"

"How long each day would we have to do it to get these effects?"

Robert nodded, "About twelve minutes a day will produce incredible results. It can increase flexibility, and make us more present in our daily lives."

Once more the same woman raised her hand, "What does that mean?"

"By present I mean we can become aware both of our physical and inner state, we can clear away the clutter that so often distracts us."

The woman raised her hand yet again, much to James' amusement who smiled as he watched Robert demonstrating as much patience as he could muster. "Does it matter if we're a bit older?" She asked.

"Not at all, if I may, let me run through a few things which may answer your questions." He smiled and nodded at her again. "I came to yoga through studying exercise and its effects on the body. I actually wrote my masters dissertation on the effects of exercise on the skeleton. I realised that through yoga we can focus on different muscle groups, and since everyone's body is

30

different, we can adapt the practices to suit our individual needs. If you have any particular health concerns it's always best to consult your G.P. first to put your mind at rest. But this is just a precaution, there's not anything we teach that can be harmful."

James liked what he was hearing, his concerns were leaving him and he wanted to know more. Robert took a drink of water and said "Yoga is a mind-body practice rooted in ancient Indian philosophy which enables a greater positivity within us. Western science is only just beginning to understand the benefits of yoga which have been enjoyed for thousands of years in India. It's really a meditative tool which can help us to control our stress response through control of our breath and conscious movement of the body." Robert paused and looked around to assess how closely his audience was following him, and was pleased to see such attentive faces. "Some of the things we describe in yoga may at first sound odd because we are translating ancient knowledge into words and a mind-set that is very different in twenty-first century England to the time and place from which the teaching comes. It's true that the stretching of the body increases strength, which is what most people seem to have heard about yoga, but so much more is actually going on inside us. There are flows of energy that yoga unblocks so that we are literally energised in ways we couldn't have thought possible. There are studies in America being done that show that yoga affects us at a molecular level, it enables a flow of energy like information through us, even at this most basic level of our existence. This can change not just how the brain operates but the physical structure of the brain itself. And the important thing is that we're introducing a positive, conscious change, one that we choose, rather than being affected in a passive way by the world around us and our life experiences."

A man in his mid-forties raised his hand and Robert looked and smiled at him. "I'm not entirely sure of everything you've said, but can you tell us how it relates to Hinduism?"

Robert shook his head, "Don't worry, I'm an atheist, you don't have to have spiritual beliefs to practice yoga. My approach is entirely scientific, that's the world I come from, and the evidence of its benefits was enough to convince me without any religious baggage. I don't mean to be disparaging about anyone's beliefs, I just want to make it clear that we won't be trying to convert anyone to any religion through our classes."

The man looked satisfied with the response, and Robert continued: "There are many different types of yoga, coming from different schools and parts of India. But we can identify four common components they all share. First we have the physical realm, which is where my interest lies, which is concerned with physical postures and breathing. Second is what is seen as self-regulation; this means we start to take conscious control of our emotions and reactions. Third there is a level of mental observation that is developed, some people call this mind-body awareness, and it's this conscious sense of being in the present that I was talking about. We hear a lot in the media today about mindfulness, and this is where it comes from. And finally there is for those with the religious beliefs what they believe to be deeper spiritual states, this isn't anything I have any interest in, and it's more to do with mediation and lifestyle than the yoga itself." There was a brief look of unease on his face as he said these last things, "I think we should really just focus on the health and wellbeing that undoubtedly comes from yoga. There is a sense of power that can be unleashed and directed within us, but I wouldn't in any way describe this as a religious thing. As I say, I'm certainly not religious."

He pushed off from the table and stood up, "I'm sure there are more questions you want to ask, but how about we dip our toe in the water and see how it feels. Can we push the chairs to the side of the room please?" Everyone got to their feet and cleared away the chairs to create a space in the middle of the room. "Right," continued Robert, "we'll do a little warm up first, it's very important to warm up and cool down when we do any kind of exercise, but with yoga we can do both these with some yoga postures. We'll try some stretching that comes under what is called warrior poses, they are proven to help with our general balance and movement. Please spread out so you have some room. Now watch as I place my feet wide enough apart to form a secure base. Now I raise my arms slowly up and stretch to push my hands into the space above my head." He did this twice and then invited everyone to join him. James felt a little self-conscious at first but everyone was so caught up in following Robert's lead that he quickly relaxed into it. For the next half hour Robert led the group through various postures and stretches, it was all fairly gentle, but by the time they had finished James could feel his muscles glowing beneath the skin. With the cool down movements completed Robert congratulated everyone on how well they had done.

"This has been a very brief introduction, but if you'd like to learn more we'll be meeting here every Friday and you'll have a chance to meet more of our regulars. There's tea and coffee on its way," he pointed to the large boiler which was beginning to rattle as its contents boiled, "and if there's anything more you'd like to know please ask. For our regular classes we charge five pounds to cover the cost of the hall, but tonight has been our gift to you."

This last line ruffled James' feathers a little, it sounded fake, but he'd already decided he liked the teacher, and he'd heard enough to convince him it was what he needed. A short queue was forming at a table laden with empty cups, and as James joined it the woman he had been observing stood next to him. "How did you get on?" She asked.

"Yea, good thanks, I enjoyed it." He was pleased to discover her eyes were darker than her hair as they fixed on his.

"Do you think you'll come again?" She said.

"Yea, I think so. What about you?"

"Oh I've been coming for a while now."

"Really? How long have you been practicing?"

"Oh it must be over ten years at least," she smiled and her dark eyes flashed with a hint of amusement, "I'm getting on now."

Not being sure how to respond, he said "I'm James by the way."

"Good to meet you, I'm Rachel." She was well spoken with barely anything of a detectable accent.

"How did you get into yoga? You must have been quite young." James said.

Rachel smiled and let the compliment go, "It's a long story, we all have our own personal path." She fixed her eyes on him, "Can I ask you something?"

"Yes of course."

"When you go home tonight, think about what you were thinking before the yoga, and what came into your mind while you were doing it. We're preoccupied with a conversation right now, but reflect on what thoughts the yoga has left you with. Sometimes it's not just the physical impression yoga makes on us, we can be touched pretty quickly at the level of our mind."

It sounded more than he had anticipated doing, but he said "Okay, I will."

As they edged closer to the boiler the man who had been sitting next to Rachel approached them.

"This is Jacob," Rachel said.

"Hello; James," said James holding out his hand.

"Hi," Jacob said without warmth before immediately looking at Rachel, "Do we have time to stay for a drink?"

She glanced at her watch, "I suppose we should get off, that's a shame," she said to James. "It was lovely to meet you, hope to see you again."

As they walked away Jacob gave a cursory "Bye" and didn't look at James as he said it. Watching them leave James wondered if they were a couple, the way they had spoken to each other certainly gave the impression they were more than friends, but in hope he embraced the possibility that she wasn't his. He found himself at the front of the queue where Aaron was serving drinks.

"Hope that wasn't too strenuous your first time, James."

"No, not at all, but I think I've used a few muscles that have been dormant for a while."

"What Robert said about setting a little time aside each day is worth remembering. The benefits only really come when we practice daily. And that way the muscles don't get too much of a shock either."

He handed James a cup, "It's been good to meet you."

James smiled and moved away, glancing around at the various groups in conversation he realised there was no one he recognised from work and wondered who could have left the leaflet in the office. This left him with some relief as he realised that anyone from work might figure out he took the poster from the wall. He noticed that the older woman with all the questions had cornered Robert who was patiently listening to her, and James smiled again but felt a little sorry for him. A tall man in his mid-thirties turned and saw James alone. "Hello, I'm Rupert."

"Hi, James."

"Have you studied yoga before?"

"No, you?" James said.

"Just over a year now, Robert's a terrific teacher."

"Yea, he seems to know his stuff."

"So you'll try it again?"

Without hesitation James said "Definitely." He finished his drink, "I've got to get off, but I'll see you next week." He returned the cup and slipped out and as he started his car he was already thinking about Rachel. He went over their conversation, looking for something he might have missed, and remembered her comment about remembering what he had been thinking about. He tried to recall his thoughts, and decided that before the session he had only felt uncomfortable and unsure of himself. During the yoga he had been so preoccupied with where his arms and legs were that he hadn't really given much thought to anything else. And if he was honest, at the end of the session he had been distracted by her. He tried to analyse what this might reveal, but concluded he hadn't been operating on a sufficiently meaningful level for any of it to be significant. He smiled at how foolish he felt for expecting some great insight after only half an hour of stretching, and brushing aside any further attempts at self-analysis slipped a CD into the player. The music immediately soothed his thoughts and he felt a deep sense of relaxation fill his body.

Chapter 5

The following week was a process of passing time before the next class. James was relieved to see in himself a genuine enthusiasm for something, and this affected everything he did, including work. He tried not to allow himself to obsess over Rachel, he knew it was unhealthy and could lead to massive disappointment, but when his thoughts did drift her way he enjoyed the feelings they brought him. He wondered how he could still be feeling such loss over Emma while simultaneously entertaining these thoughts about Rachel, and a part of him suspected it revealed how superficial his feelings really were. It was a difficult realisation to accept, and he wanted to brush it aside, but still it persisted.

Each evening he spent time stretching and repeating some of the postures Robert had taught them. They became more natural as the week went on and he was convinced that he could detect an improvement in his balance as he did so. He felt a little frustrated that he only had a small repertoire to work on, and resisted copying some of the demonstrations online. He couldn't explain why, but the sense of himself as someone who did yoga began to create a different mood within him, the beginnings of a new identity as a person who practices something outside the ordinary sphere of western life. He began reading more articles online, ordered a few books and watched as many videos as he could find. Other interests began to lose their appeal and he felt a growing desire to talk to someone about what he was learning. He wasn't sure if it was a result of his improved mood or something directly resulting from the yoga, but he found it easier to sleep and other than the one night didn't feel the need to open a bottle of wine.

By Friday he was genuinely excited about the class and after work drove to a local sports shop to buy a soft rubber mat. He had seen them in the videos and decided it would be good to have a space in the flat permanently set aside for yoga. He also selected a red ADIDAS tracksuit identical to the one worn by Bob Marley in the late seventies. It didn't hurt, he decided, to look good while he was doing it.

At seven-twenty he was at the centre dressed in his new gear. He spotted Aaron sitting cross-legged at the back of the hall but other than Robert didn't recognise anyone else. As seven-thirty approached his anticipation of Rachel's entrance caused him to keep glancing at the door, but she never appeared. After initially feeling a little deflated James made a conscious decision to focus on the real reason he was there, and once Robert began the class he forgot about any distractions. The session was for an hour, and James was pleased to learn more postures and stretches. Robert was careful to sensitively correct anyone who was misinterpreting his instructions, and a few times he came over to physically move one of James' arms or legs to the right position.

After sixty minutes the muscles in his stomach and thighs were newly present to him, he could feel parts of his body to which he had previously been a stranger. There were nearly thirty people in the group and everyone treated the class with great respect and seriousness. James could detect a certain degree of deference towards Robert when anyone asked a question, and it wasn't anything he thought out of place.

At the end of the session each person rolled up and gave their mat to Aaron and while the tidying up was going on

Robert made a point of approaching James. "I'm glad you managed to make a full class, how was it?"

"Very good, thank you. I've been doing the stretches you showed us all week, and I'll have a go at some of what you showed us tonight."

"That's really good James, you'll feel the benefits. Excuse me." Robert went to help Aaron carry the mats out to his van, and James decided it was time to leave. He exchanged farewells with a few people and passed Robert and Aaron who were standing in the car park discussing the meaning of one of the postures they had practiced. As he drove away James thought about Rachel for the first time since the class started, and decided it was probably important that he didn't confuse any feelings he had for her with his interest in yoga. He concluded that it was for the best that she hadn't showed up, and he was pleased that the evening had affected him so positively regardless of her absence. His attention turned to how much yoga he could do over the next few nights, and he was keen to extend his evening sessions a little. He felt more confident about what he was doing, and the response he was getting from his body told him he had found something helpful.

On Saturday night he met up with a few of his workmates and they went clubbing. In his late thirties he felt too old for these environments and he hated the music. But they drank too much and managed to have a good time. James had had more hangovers than he could count, especially when he was younger, and he woke on Sunday morning with another for the collection. By mid-afternoon he was still feeling the effects of the alcohol. His head was tight and no matter what he ate or drank he couldn't settle his stomach. He decided to do some yoga but found the movements he had been doing for over a week now felt awkward and his whole body was stiff. He made himself another cup of tea and sat at the table staring at the yoga mat on the floor before him. The night out had been fun, but it wasn't worth the price he was now paying. He had damaged himself, he knew it, even if it was short-lived, and this wasn't a healthy state he had left himself in. Yoga was already too important to him to allow anything to prevent him from practicing it, and he decided he would never get so drunk again. It was a big decision, and knowing how deeply he meant it gave him the feeling that he had reached some kind of turning point in his life. How he would avoid the beer when he was back in Sheffield with Nick and the rest of them would be a higher hurdle to leap, but for now he had set himself a new path. For the rest of the day he gave up on doing anything physical and took one of his new books to bed. He buried himself in his quilt and began reading a history of yoga philosophy.

Chapter 6

Rachel's entrance impacted on James more than he wanted to admit. He was already standing on his mat, preparing himself for the class with various stretches. She was wearing loose fitting cotton trousers that looked Indian in design, and even in a baggy T shirt James noted how beautiful she looked. She acknowledged the people around her and took her place at the back of the hall where James would have to turn to see her: he controlled himself enough not to do it.

At the front of the hall Aaron was fiddling with something at the table that always sat in front of the class, and as he moved to his mat James could see it was a small Indian statue. It wasn't anything he recognised, and when Robert took his position to teach the class James thought no more about it.

"Hello everyone, tonight we'll be moving on from the warrior poses to a range of postures that I think you'll find useful. This means that some of you will be learning quite a few new movements all at once, and I'll do my best to help you learn them, but for those of you more accustomed to them, I want to extend our range tonight and explore the different combinations of postures and how they work together."

James was pleased to hear this, he wanted to learn as much as he could as quickly as he could, and he was determined to take as much new information home as possible. Robert demonstrated the first posture of the night, which involved arching the back while lying with the stomach on the floor. James pulled himself into position and could sense his body resisting the alien movement. It took great focus to hold the posture, and as his mind abandoned all other mental activity, James felt the familiar stillness that he was becoming accustomed to. Robert wandered round the class, checking everyone was correct and comfortable, and returned to his mat to introduce the next posture.

All of his inhibitions had now left him and James followed his teacher's instructions without hesitation. Robert explained "We're going to build on the mountain pose we used last week as the basis for aligning different parts of our body, from the feet up through the torso, the shoulders and then the neck, head and arms." He adopted a pose and began explaining the specific positions of each part of his body from the ground up, and again James attempted to copy him. As he lifted his arms he felt someone's hands take hold of his hips and gently pull them back slightly. He turned to find Rachel standing behind him.

"Ease your hips back slightly so that you hold in your stomach," she said.

James did as he was told, "That's better," she said, "now hold that as you lift your arms. But don't let your torso relax." She smiled as he did it, and with a single nod moved back to her own mat. James' mind began racing with excited thoughts, he wasn't sure how to interpret her actions. Other people were helping the beginners out when necessary, it wasn't such a strange thing to do, but he clung to the fact that she had chosen to help him as a sign of something more.

The rest of the lesson passed quickly and James was trying hard to retain all that he had learned to apply it to his home practice. As he rolled away his mat Rachel approached him again, "I hope you didn't mind me showing you where you were going wrong."

"No, thank you, I appreciate the help."

"It's very easy to miss what is happening with these postures, when we see them for the first time there are certain parts of the pose that we may not notice at all. Even when we hear the teacher describe them, it is different to actually moving our body in this way. When we do it for the first time we feel the difference, do you understand what I mean?"

"Yes, definitely, when you pulled me back it felt very different."

"Even a slight movement like that changes our whole balance, and once the centre of our gravity moves every part of our body is affected. So when we take our weight back like that it pulls on different parts of the stomach and chest and has an entirely different impact on us."

James was impressed with the way she spoke, he was interested to learn more but didn't know enough to even ask the right questions. He didn't want to bring up what he had been reading for fear of sounding silly, but was desperate to keep the conversation going. And so he had to hide his enthusiasm when she invited him for coffee. "There's a coffee-bar next door, Jacob isn't picking me up for half an hour; do you fancy it?"

They said their goodbyes to everyone and she led him to the little café where they were the only customers. She refused to let him buy her drink and they took their cups to a table near the wall.

"Have you been practicing at home?" She asked.

"Yes, it's becoming a part of my routine." He watched her slowly stir her drink and delicately return the spoon to its saucer. Her movements were very controlled and deliberate, and he noted again the sense of stillness about her.

"That's important, we cannot make real progress unless we practice daily." She looked across the table at him and her face took on a serious expression: "Do you remember what I said to you when you first came?"

"What about?"

"About recalling your thoughts before, during and after yoga. Did you manage to do it?"

James was a little flustered, he had remembered to do it, but the results hadn't been impressive. "I did, and I suppose the main thing I noticed was how my thoughts were replaced with a sense of my body during the class, replaced with a kind of stillness." He wasn't lying, but the bit about stillness came straight out of one the books he'd been reading.

"You should do it regularly, I wasn't just talking about the class, but when you practice at home. Take a few minutes to reflect after your yoga, give your mind time to incorporate what you have done to it." She paused to look for his response.

"I will, thank you." After a moment's hesitation he asked "What do you find when you do this?"

Her serious expression returned, "It all depends on what kind of yoga I have been doing and what other practices I have been working on. With yoga it is very much as you describe, but the further we walk along this path the deeper the stillness becomes so that we are able to not only turn off the chatter in our head but begin to hear something from deeper within ourselves."

James had a number of questions, "Do you mean an inner voice?"

"Something like that, but not necessarily our own voice, in the sense of our mind. It's not easy to sum it up so casually."

"And what other practices do you mean?" James asked.

"I learned yoga at the same time as mediation, for me they are two sides of the same coin. There are different arts I have tried to learn, but to remain at peace I cannot live without yoga and meditation."

"I don't really know anything about mediation," he admitted, "I'm not looking for anything more than the physical change."

"I understand," she smiled, "when we first encounter yoga it brings great rewards. It is natural that you should feel content with this if it is something you have not known in your life before. But there comes a point for many people when they thirst for something more, and the deeper they move into yoga the more they realise that they are only practising a small part of something beautiful. Yoga and meditation are not two separate practices at all, they are streams flowing from the one source."

Only now did James begin to pick up the slightest hint of an accent in her voice, but it was so subtle he couldn't identify it. Hearing her speak about these things he said "Where do you come from originally?"

She laughed to herself, "I was born in Kent, but my mother is Indian and believe it or not my father is German. I'm a strange old mix. I've lived most of my life in the U.K. but we travelled a lot. I don't feel I belong to any one place, I know it sounds a bit flaky, but my mother always encouraged me to see the whole world as my home."

Jacob appeared at the door and looked at the two of them sitting together. He watched for a moment and then entered, his face remained expressionless, as though he were keeping something back. "How was the class?"

"Hello Jacob, yes, it was good." Rachel said.

James smiled and nodded at him, unsure of how he might react to finding them here like this. But Jacob continued to give no sign of his feelings and pulled out the chair from beside Rachel. He sat down and leaned forward, clasping his hands on the table. "There's only so much you're gonna get from Robert, he's good enough at what he teaches, but it's all a bit limited."

"As a beginner I have to say it suits me," James said. Up close he realised Jacob was much older than he had first thought and his red hair was thinning at the front.

Jacob snorted beneath his breath, "I don't want to criticise what he does, I'm sure there are plenty of people who make a start through classes like this, but there are a lot of western fakes around who have learned a bit of yoga and set themselves up as experts."

"Jacob, don't be so negative. You know there are people in the West making enormous progress," Rachel's voice was calm but it was clear she was a little annoyed with him. "You know enough to not make comments like that."

"I know, I'm not saying that, but unless they're rooted in something more, how can these people assume to teach others?"

Rachel glanced across at James and smiled, "He's had a taste of India and thinks he knows a guru when he sees one."

James hoped her comment was only referring to the country and not their relationship, and asked him "When did you go to India?"

"I've made a number of visits, I started going about eight years ago, an incredible place." He had calmed down a little, and for the first time forced a smile. "I'm sorry to break things up, but I have to leave for London early tomorrow, so I need to get back and sort things out."

"Yes, of course," Rachel rose from her seat, "It's been good to talk to you James. Remember what I said about your thoughts, take a moment to reflect on them. If you can do this after each yoga session, you might be surprised." Her face filled with warmth and her eyes lit up with a smile, "See you next week."

"Yes, it's been good, see you both again." As the word "both" left James' lips he resented any suggestion it might have made, not that anything he said could change things, but there was still no indication of what the nature of their relationship might be. Even as they left he looked to see if they held hands or stood closer than friends, but there seemed no particular closeness. Finding himself alone he bought another coffee and returned to the table. Her empty cup still sat before him, and this physical proof of her presence brought him pleasure. He knew it was wrong to allow these kinds of feelings to grow if she was involved with Jacob, and decided he would have to find some way of learning the truth. He turned his thoughts to what she had said, and knew he was conflicted about it. Mediation didn't appeal to him, he had no desire for any kind of religious beliefs, and he wondered whether she was right about its link with yoga. He reassured himself by remembering Robert's introduction class, and how he had been adamant that his interest was purely scientific. This was an approach that James felt at home with, he wanted the physical and mental benefits; this was all he needed.

Chapter 7

In his first session of the week at home James attempted to incorporate as many of the new postures and movements that he had learned as he could. He discovered he couldn't remember exactly how to perform some of them and became frustrated at not having someone to ask for help. When he finished he was surprised to discover he had been working for nearly an hour, and sat on his mat to think about what he had done and what had worked best. It would be useful to have his thoughts organised by the next class so that he knew exactly what guidance he needed. He traced the successes and difficulties he had had and recognised which parts of his body he hadn't moved correctly.

He remembered Rachel's advice from the café and tried to reflect on where his mind had been and how the yoga had affected him. Before the session he recognised that his thoughts had been consumed with work, and in fact there had been an endless stream of meaningless concerns which amounted to nothing. As he expected, he saw that during his yoga session he had been focussed on the postures and for the bulk of the time he had been free from all concerns for the outside world. As for now, after the yoga, he saw in himself a certain pride at how he had maintained the pattern of sessions and he felt pleased with having used some of the new postures so well. With this realisation he wanted to do something more, but wasn't sure what. He didn't want to return to his worldly self and start worrying over the tiny demands of his life, but he couldn't think what to do next. He sat still on the mat for a moment, and as he closed his eyes he tried to enjoy the sense of peace that the yoga had brought him. But as soon as he became conscious of the feeling it seemed to evaporate and his mind was invaded with the little tasks he had to perform for work. He got up from the mat and decided to take a shower, it always helped him to relax after a session.

By ten o'clock he was sitting in bed with his laptop open in front of him. Some of the usual sites he visited now looked a little empty to him, and once more he recognised how superficial so many of his interests outside yoga really were. He concluded that though the flat was silent his head was filled with noise. He typed into his search engine Indian Meditation and was rewarded with countless sites to choose from. He began clicking through a few of them, encountering new terminology and ideas, but his eyes began resting on the photographs of various holy men. They looked out at him with relaxed smiles and their clothing and long beards seem to promise something very different to the world of which he was growing tired. He lay reading for a long time until he forced himself to close down just before midnight. As he lay in the dark he thought about Rachel's claim that meditation and yoga are two sides of the same thing, and wondered if there really was something more he should seek out. That feeling at the end of his session was a need for something, but nothing physical. Within himself he could feel a yearning being brought to life, but he didn't have any idea what it was he wanted. At the same time, the reality of that feeling told him there must be something that he was missing, a piece of the jigsaw that would have filled the hole he was becoming aware of.

Each night over the following weeks he continued to expand his repertoire and took from the classes everything he could retain. Rachel and Jacob attended intermittently, and she was always friendly, but an opportunity to talk at length never presented itself. By mid-December James' life outside of work was focussed entirely on yoga. He had amassed a bookshelf of publications and had adapted his diet to what he had read was not just healthy, but to a combination of foods that promised to energise the body and mind. He was acutely aware of the physical impact it was all having on him, he had lost weight, his stamina had increased, and at work when meetings became tense he consciously controlled his breathing and avoided the stress that would once have afflicted him.

His sleep had improved and he was aware of certain images that had begun to appear to him in his dreams. He had dreamt a few times of Indian statues about which he knew nothing, and he put it down to the books he was reading. Many of them contained illustrations and photographs of various Indian temples, and though these were normally the parts of the books he skipped over, it made sense to him that what his eyes had seen would be recalled by his subconscious mind.

One Friday night James entered the hall to find Rachel already there. He had often thought about her, but the initial intensity of his feelings had been replaced with an acceptance that nothing could come of it. Accepting this gave him a new confidence to speak to her, and as he approached she gave him her usual smile.

"Hello Rachel, how have you been?"

"Good, thank you, and you?"

"Yea, I'm good thanks. Do you remember that time we had a chat about yoga, and you mentioned meditation?"

"Yes, of course, in the coffee bar."

"Is there any chance we could talk again some time, I've been reading quite a bit and I've been wondering about its connection to yoga, like you said."

"It's not just a connection James, there cannot be the one without the other. It is inevitable that if you are taking yoga seriously these questions should arise. Would you like to meet up tomorrow?"

"That would be great, thank you."

"What about the coffee bar again, since we both know it, how about five tomorrow?"

"Great, thank you, I'll see you then."

He walked over to the usual place he used and began his warm up routine. The old feelings about her had returned, and he hoped he wasn't just getting her alone under false pretences. By the time Robert began the class James was filled with excitement and it took him a while to calm himself down to participate properly. His paranoia suggested to him that his inner state would be revealed through his movements and he didn't want Rachel realising what might be his true motivations.

The following morning James did a little shopping and spent the afternoon trying to read, but he was too distracted to settle to his book. He monitored the progress of the day with increasing excitement, all the time telling himself he had no right to allow these feelings to develop. He picked out a change of clothes that he thought looked good but didn't give the impression he had thought too much about them, and at last was able to drive over to meet her. He used the centre's car park which was almost full, and took his time walking to the café. Through the window he could see most of the tables were occupied with shoppers but there was no sign of her. He went in and ordered a coffee and found the only available table was the one they had used last time. He sat down and hoped that she didn't think he had deliberately chosen the same place, and then dismissed his concerns for the nonsense they were.

Sipping at his drink he watched the crowds passing by the window and wondered how many of them practiced yoga. He had begun to divide the world up in terms of the two groups and often when he saw Asian people he wondered about their experiences before coming to Britain. Most of the shoppers looked flustered and unhappy and he was pleased to see in himself a genuine concern for them. Suddenly Rachel was at the window reaching for the door, and James felt relief that she was alone. As she entered she smiled at him and walked to the counter. James wondered whether he should get a refill but decided to sit where he was. As she approached the table he awkwardly stood to be polite, and she waved him to sit down.

"Hi James, I'm sorry I'm late."

"I've only been here a few minutes myself," he said, and then realised his half-empty cup revealed something different.

They exchanged a few pleasantries about the weather and how busy town was today, before Rachel said "It's good that you want to know more about yoga, it isn't just physical exercise, a lot of people miss this."

"I don't really know what to ask," he admitted. "I suppose I was starting to get questions about how it was making me feel, not just physically, but everything else."

"Yoga means union, the union of mind and body, so it is not surprising that you should have these questions." She said.

"It might sound stupid, but I'm not even sure what you mean by that kind of unity."

"Well you've been doing it already when you practice yoga, even if you haven't been using these terms. You've been focussing your mind while moving your body, think about how that has been affecting you."

James nodded, "But I don't know what to do with my mind. I mean, I don't know what I need next. I sometimes finish my session at home and it's like I've left things half done."

"The yoga traditions of India show us that meditation is integral to yoga, the next steps in yoga for you are all about focus and concentration. They are really the same. It is a shame that many western teachers strip yoga of what it can do for us by reducing it to gymnastics. The goal in all of this is purification of the mind."

"That sounds attractive, and I can't imagine you'd find many people who wouldn't admit they need to sort their head out, but if I'm honest I'm still unsure about meditation."

"I like to think of yoga as a kind of technology, an ancient technology that goes beyond anything we think of in that way."

"I don't understand what you mean," James said.

"By technology I mean a kind of inner-engineering, a way of evolving human consciousness."

James laughed a little, "That's as impenetrable to me as the first thing you said." He hoped the humour with which he said it would avoid sounding like he was mocking her.

"Maybe we should try something, instead of trying to describe it, we should do it." She looked around and said "There's too much distraction here, is there somewhere we could find some quiet?"

"There's a little park round the corner, I think there's some benches there."

"Right, let's go," she left half of her tea and moved to the door.

James followed her out into the street and pointed up the road, "It's just down here."

Already the crowds of shoppers were thinning and the sky was darkening. The park was less than five minutes' walk away and James was relieved to find it empty. "Shall we sit up there?" He pointed to a wooden bench beneath a huge oak tree.

As they sat she turned and said "I'm not suggesting we start meditating, but there are a few things I can show you that you can try at home. First, uncross your legs and flatten your feet on the ground."

He looked down to copy her, and she said "Now straighten your back a little, don't slouch." He laughed at her abruptness, and sat up. "Now look ahead of yourself, find a patch of grass to focus on. Right, just look at it for a moment, sense how far away from you it is, and how perfectly contained it is within the whole lawn. Now slow your breathing down, slowly take in a deep breath, hold it and now exhale, slowly. Pause for a moment and then repeat it."

He followed her directions and became aware of the air as it moved in through his nostrils and into his lungs.

"Now allow each breath to fill your chest, and feel your body drawing oxygen before rejecting the carbon dioxide. As you slowly breathe you are filling yourself with goodness and pushing out the poison." She allowed him to do this for a few minutes, and then said "Now let your conscious mind enter and leave you with each breath. Allow your mind to move freely so that it doesn't matter whether it feels contained in your head or is moving in and out with the air."

As he concentrated on his breath his sense of himself began to move and for a brief moment he even felt his mind move beyond the physical limits of his body. The realisation startled him and he immediately returned to his normal state of being. Rachel looked at him, "Did you experience something?"

"Yes, briefly, I felt like…I felt like I was moving out of my body."

"That is good, don't be unsettled, if you could continue with this exercise you can learn to control that movement so that you ebb and flow with the rhythm of your breathing. This is enough for now. When you practice your yoga, make time to follow it with ten minutes of this breathing exercise. You will find it becomes a powerful feeling as you learn to control it."

She smiled again and James allowed himself to be overcome by her warmth. In the fading light she looked almost fragile, and yet there was a great strength that was emanating from her.

"See how this makes you feel after a week or two, and then we can look at something else. I am happy to meet like this if you want."

"Thank you, I really appreciate it Rachel. You look cold, are you shivering?"

"A little, after living in warmer places winter in Birmingham isn't easy to adapt to."

She gracefully stood up and brushed away what the bench had left on her skirt. The night was coming quickly and the darkness made it feel later than it was. "Are you parked up by the centre?" James asked.

"Yes, I saw your car there."

"I'll walk you back."

As they strolled through the little park he imagined that they would look like any couple to a casual observer and he was pleased with the thought. The passing cars bathed them in their headlights as people headed home from the shops. They chatted briefly as they walked and James thanked her once more as they stood beside her little Citroen. "It's been really good of you to spare the time like this," he said.

"Not at all, I've enjoyed it. And it's so important to share this knowledge with as many people as we can, it will have an effect on the whole world as people begin to change."

Pulling out from the car park into the evening traffic he glanced into the rear view mirror and caught himself smiling. The smile broadened as he recognised how content he felt. He was especially pleased with himself that the greater cause of his contentment was the experience of the breathing exercise, and not just infatuation with a pretty girl.

Chapter 8

A Christmas alone in the flat wasn't an appealing option, no matter how at home he felt there, and so James made arrangements to visit his mother for a couple of nights. He messaged Nick and a few friends and arranged to meet up for Christmas Eve; the rest of the trip would consist of watching his mother's television and force feeding himself from the boxes of treats she would have stocked up on. Christmas day fell on a Tuesday, so he had the best part of a week off work before even thinking about New Year.

In the days before he left he followed the same routine of work and then yoga. By now he was aware of how flexible he was becoming, how the energy he had first felt growing was now a tangible strength within him, and how everything else in the day was just treading water until he could begin his sessions. He practised the breathing exercises Rachel had shown him and had begun to extend the feeling of moving beyond his body until he felt almost entirely outside himself. At first he had questioned whether this was just his imagination, but as he progressed he began to understand it as a real phenomenon. At these moments he seemed to lose himself to a new reality, an inability to distinguish between anything around him, so that he was absorbed into an experience of himself as inseparable from the world beyond himself.

The opportunity to talk further with Rachel didn't occur, she attended only one more class before

Christmas, and on that occasion Jacob had been with her. James sensed an undercurrent of hostility from him and assumed she had told him about their meeting, and this he was disappointed to conclude was evidence of the nature of their relationship.

As he pulled up outside his mother's house in Mexborough he spotted her at the downstairs window watching for him. He waved but she had already gone to the door to let him in.

"You've lost a lot of weight Jimmy, aren't you eating?"

"And hello to you too," he laughed, "yes, I'm fine." He gave her a hug and noticed how the bones of her shoulders felt like a frail chicken skeleton, and once more he felt concern about how vulnerable she was.

"What's that?" She was looking at his rolled up yoga mat.

"It's just an exercise mat mom, that's why I've lost weight, I'm trying to stay fit." She seemed satisfied with the explanation and led him through the house. She had hung tinsel around some of her picture frames and James was glad to see a long line of Christmas cards across her mantel piece. They shared a few hours catching up, she wanted to know what he thought of Birmingham and whether he had met anyone at work.

"No, I'm afraid not, you'll have to wait a little longer for grandchildren."

"That's not why I asked, I just want to know you're happy."

"I am, I've met some good people at an exercise club; I feel really settled."

"And how's work?"

"Everything's fine mom, it's been a good move."

She sensed he was being honest and allowed the television to absorb her attention. James glanced at the clock, "I've promised to meet Nick and George in Sheffield in a while."

"I thought you might, are you staying the night there?"

"No, I'll get a taxi back, it'll be late, so don't wait up."

"Is he still with that blonde girl?"

"Lucy? Yea, they've got a kid now, he seems happy."

"Oh that's nice, I'm glad he's settled."

James knew it was what she wanted from him too, but didn't admit to her that it was going to be a long time before he gave her that pleasure.

The Pakistani taxi driver was determined to talk as he drove James into town. He was insisting that the England cricket team was overrated, and as he chatted on James thought how strange it was that two peoples could be so close in so many ways and yet be so different where it mattered. His view of India was now over-romanticised, he knew it, but he couldn't connect with anything about Islam or the obsession with cricket. Pakistan might as well have been on the opposite side of the earth from India as far as he understood it, and he made little effort to respond to the driver's ramblings. James tipped him with the minimum possible amount and crossed the road to The Crown. The atmosphere was already loud and animated as he entered, just as it was every Christmas Eve. Nick waved from a table near the windows and James pushed his way through the drinkers.

"How you doin' Jim boy?" Nick enthusiastically shook his hand, "what are you drinkin'?"

At the table were George and two other friends from school. James grinned to see them, "How are you then? Yea I'll have a pint of Stella, thanks Nick." He slid along the bench.

"Great, thanks," George said, "haven't seen you for ages." The others nodded their greetings.

James explained where he was living and touched on his new job. But he could see they'd already had a few and the last thing they wanted to hear about was work. Nick returned balancing a new round on a tray, "Come on ladies, drink up, or Father Christmas won't be leaving any presents."

"No worries, he's been stalking my kids for years. No matter how many times we move he keeps finding them," shouted the friend next to George.

It was the first beer James had drunk for a long time and it tasted good. He sank it in four gulps, "Bloody hell Jim," laughed George, "don't they have beer down in Brum?"

James squeezed past Nick and took his empty glass to the bar. He could feel the effects of the first pint immediately and the combination of alcohol and the mood of the crowd around him was by-passing any intention to drink sensibly. He carried the drinks over in two runs and flopped beside his friends. "Where's Lucy?"

"She's not feeling well, a shame to catch something at Christmas, but I think she wanted to spend it with the little one."

"That's a shame, but she'd only be countin' how many beers you had."

They laughed and Nick said "Well no one's countin' tonight. You're lookin' well Jim, a lot better than last time I saw you."

"Yea, I feel it, it's surprising what a bit of time can do."

"Have you heard from Emma since you went down?"

"No, and I'm not fussed."

"Oh yea," Nick grinned, "you got something on the go?"

"I don't know yet, it's early days." He regretted saying it, it felt like a betrayal but he didn't know who he could have betrayed.

"Do you think you'll settle down there?"

"I haven't thought that far ahead yet, but I'm happy for the moment."

"I'm glad it's worked out for you, I was worried when you left."

James pulled a mock look of concern, "You're such a caring man Nick, what would I do without you?"

"Glad you're seeing my feminine side Jim, I've always been much deeper than you realise."

As they laughed George said "Is this turning into Oprah Winfrey? Take it down a notch lads."

They avoided anything more serious for the rest of the night and by midnight the women in the pub were bombarded with kisses from any man who could reach them. Christmas Eve was the one night guaranteed to be trouble free no matter how drunk everyone became and by one o'clock the merriment spilled out onto the pavement as people began heading home.

"You comin' back to ours?" Nick asked him.

"No, thanks, I'm only here for a short while and I've promised my mom I'll be there for the day."

"Fair enough."

"Yea, I'm gonna head up the taxi rank and get a lift home."

"The bastards will try and charge you double tonight," George chipped in.

They parted with drunken hugs and James began walking under the council Christmas lights past loud revellers who sang and shouted into the night. Being alone sobered him up a little and by the time he was queuing for a taxi he began observing the party-goers with a little disdain. It wasn't that he thought he was really any different to them, but the excessive joviality looked forced and he saw how desperately everyone needed this night. In a few days they would be back at jobs they hated with only the conviction that they had had a good time to keep them going. James tried to control his breathing and relax, but he was still too intoxicated and he realised that this was the first day in many months that he hadn't practised any yoga. He'd had a good time but the day felt wasted. By the time he was climbing into a taxi the frivolity of it all left him miserable and he knew he had let himself fall back into his old self. He didn't blame his friends, this was entirely his own doing, but he understood that if he wanted to pursue other goals he would have to make conscious choices about who he spent his time with.

The taxi driver had had a long night and other than the occasional exchange over the radio he drove in silence. James noticed the price on the digital counter climbing quicker than it should but felt no resentment. Outside his mother's house he paid and tipped without complaint and tried to make as little noise as possible as he entered. His mother had placed a few presents beneath a little tree she had decorated, and seeing them made James feel sad for her. He wished he'd spent the evening giving her a bit of company, and imagined her sitting there all evening alone in front of the television. He convinced himself he'd make up for it over the next couple of days and with a belly still straining with the beer he collapsed into his bed.

Christmas Day had its own routines and each seemed to bring his mother great pleasure. After dinner they sat in front of the television, and James studied the BBC's output like an anthropologist seeing things for the first time. He was struck by how superficial the programmes were and how the secular references to Christmas were empty of any spiritual meaning or message. He tried to imagine how Christians might react to their festival being treated this way and concluded that most of them were probably happy with it. He couldn't recall many opposing voices, not even from Emma who was always quick to identify where the media was misrepresenting her faith. With his stomach now stretched from an excess of food he began to long for the ascetic peace that he knew was being experienced at that very moment by followers of other traditions. It didn't help that he had a crippling hangover and his body seemed to have aged decades overnight.

He left his yoga until bedtime, partly to give himself time to recover and also so as not to abandon his mother again. He could hear her moving around preparing for bed as he unrolled his mat across the floor. He began with a few simple postures before pushing himself a little. After twenty minutes he sat down and began his breathing exercises. He felt himself begin to move with his breath, his single point of focus becoming his place of being. As he exhaled he moved out with the air and could sense his physical body just behind him. The moment was filled with such an intensity of awareness that it felt like he had entered a new space within the physical space of his room. Into the darkness before him there suddenly appeared a vision of an eye staring back at him. It was acutely detailed as he stared into it, he examined the lashes and the glaze across its surface and knew that it was gazing back at and into him. James blinked his physical eyes and was aware once more of the dim light in his room and the shadows of objects all around him. He couldn't explain what had happened but knew it was more than an imagined picture in his mind. The eye had appeared real, not just physically real, but a reality that went beyond physicality. He sat staring into space trying to understand what had happened, or what it could mean, but no explanation came to mind and it wasn't something he had read about. The house had no Wi-Fi or he would have made an internet search, and his 'phone was low on data.

Climbing into bed he determined to look further into the experience, and without trouble his exhausted body gave in to sleep.

Chapter 9

As everyone completed their cooling down postures James turned to check that Rachel was finished. Seeing her rolling up her mat he took his chance to catch her while Jacob wasn't around.

"Rachel, is there any chance we could speak again?"

"Hello James, how are you? Yes, of course, what is it?"

"Can we take a seat for a minute? I need to ask you about something that happened to me that I'm not sure how to understand." He waved his hand toward the plastic seats piled at the back of the hall.

"What is it?" She said.

James pulled a couple of seats from the stack and as they sat said "I've been practicing the breathing exercises after my yoga at home. It's been helping a lot, I really appreciate you introducing me to it."

"I'm glad to hear it."

"Yes, well I was experiencing a different perspective on myself, outside myself, when I saw an eye."

"You've seen the eye? That's wonderful." She said.

"It keeps happening, every time I do the breathing exercises after yoga I see it. But I don't know what it means. I've tried to read up on it but I can only find general stuff, philosophy and religious stuff, but I want to know what this experience means and why it's happening."

Rachel looked at him with a serene smile, she reached forward and placed her hand on his. "I have some friends who can help you with this, would you like to meet them?"

The physical contact pushed aside any reservations he might have had, "Yes, thank you."

"As you know I don't always make this yoga class, but I'm part of another group that meets to practice yoga and meditation. We only meet once each month, I'm sure you'll find your answers there. They can explain things better than me."

The sensation of her hand touching his consumed him, and as she pulled it away he didn't know how to interpret the gesture. Other than a few drunken kisses at Christmas this was the first woman to touch him this way since Emma had left. He struggled to manage his feelings and focussed on what he should say. "I'd like to very much, thank you."

"We meet on the second Tuesday of each month, so we have a meeting next week. I'll let them know you're coming, you'll be very welcome; they're very friendly people."

"Where do you meet?"

"It's a flat just the other side of Birmingham, I could pick you up if you want." She laughed, "If I try to give you directions you'll end up in Coventry."

The other members of the class were leaving and Aaron was throwing impatient looks at James and Rachel. "I think he wants to lock up," she said, "we should go." They stood and she turned to look up into James' face, "Don't worry about what you are experiencing, it is a good sign. I can't begin to explain things here, but trust me, you are making progress. You just need to guide your efforts properly to know where to go next. I'm so happy for you James, it will all make sense to you soon. Keep doing what you are doing and be patient."

James restacked the chairs and they followed the rest of the group out into the night. At her car Rachel said "Wait a minute, let me give you my email address, if you contact me I'll get back to you with the arrangements." She bent and leaned in through the open door and scribbled on a scrap of paper.

James took it and stood back as she pulled out from her parking space, she wound down the window, "I'll see you soon," she said and drove away.

In his own car James turned on the cabin light to check what she had written; in an elegant style it read rachelaashna@yahoo.co.uk and satisfied that he could make out every letter he slipped the paper into the breast pocket of his shirt. As he drove home his thoughts kept returning to her hand on his, and as he juggled with the prospect of meeting the group and what her gesture might mean, he grew tired of how infantile his emotions were. He began to imagine how they would react if they knew the truth of his feelings, and how Rachel would feel if she knew what he was thinking. He shook his head with disappointment, he had to take control of himself, discipline his thinking; he knew these adolescent fantasies could threaten what might be an important relationship to him. And he knew it wasn't fair on Jacob to harbour these feelings, whatever he thought of him.

In the flat he ate a little food and sat quietly at his table for a while. Rachel's reaction to what he had described gave him encouragement and he was keen to meet these other people. The Friday night yoga group was already reaching the limits of its usefulness to him. There was still plenty of yoga that Robert could teach him, but what had at first appealed to him, seeing yoga purely as a form of physical exercise, was now too restrictive. He went over to his mat and began to gather himself. He focussed on his breathing and began to follow its movement in and out of his body. Almost immediately the eye appeared before him in his mind and he gazed into it without any anxiety. The sense of looking and being observed created in him an awareness of himself that seemed to come from the perspective of the eye. It was as though he were observing himself while the eye itself remained other to him. His breathing slowed and as the air moved through the channels of his body down into his lungs he recognised the oxygen moving out into his entire system and felt the positive transformation that each breath brought to him.

He sat like this for a long time, all other thoughts were excluded, until he opened his eyes and fixed his attention on the wall opposite him. The room around him came back into focus and once more it was a Friday night in Birmingham.

Chapter 10

At work on Monday morning James pulled out a copy he had made of Rachel's email address and sent a brief message to confirm his contact details. For the rest of the morning and on into the afternoon he kept checking to see if she had responded and each time was disappointed. By late Monday evening there was still nothing from her and it began to agitate him. He wished she had given him a telephone number so that he could at least make contact directly, and as the evening went on the gaps between his checks shrank. Catching himself about to open his email just twenty minutes after he had last looked he grew a little resentful of her, and decided he wouldn't check again that night.

His mood affected his yoga session and eventually he went to bed without any breathing exercises or attempting to reflect on his thoughts. He knew exactly what he was thinking and didn't need her advice to see it. He slept fitfully, and throughout the night kept reaching over to look at his alarm clock. The hours stretched on until four when exhaustion took over and the rest of the night passed painfully quickly.

The alarm was a shock to his tired head and after he turned it off he slumped back into his pillow. As tired as he was his thoughts immediately turned to Rachel and he quickly climbed out of bed and stumbled into the living room to turn on his computer. As it warmed up he filled the kettle and spooned instant coffee into a cup. He wandered back to the screen and typed in his password, peering through thin creases where his eyes normally would be. Tiredness quickly left him when the system opened and he experienced a physical reaction in his chest when he saw Rachel's name beside an email. He pulled a chair across in front of his laptop and clicked on her message:

Hi James,

I will pick you up at 6-30. Send me your address, postcode and any directions you think will be useful.

See you tonight,

Rachel.

It didn't matter to him that the tone was completely neutral, he reread the brief collection of words and then looked at the time it had arrived: four in the morning. He was slightly troubled at the thought of her sitting at her computer so early, it didn't seem to fit with what he knew of her. But then he decided there may have been a technological glitch somewhere that had delayed it reaching him, until he realised she had said "tonight", so it must have been written that day. He told himself it wasn't important, she had written and he would see her tonight. After sending her the details he finished making his coffee, took a quick shower and without eating anything headed out to work.

By the end of the afternoon the bad night's sleep left him tired and a little unfocussed. For the last couple of hours he got very little done and his mind repeatedly wandered back to the coming evening. He risked looking up a couple more articles on meditation and sat reading at his desk, occasionally moving his mouse around to give the impression he was earning his pay. He worried that he would be out of his depth if anyone at the group asked him about what he believed, but knew it would be even worse to come across as someone trying to throw in the odd fact or name to impress them. He relaxed with the thought that he knew no more or less than was true, and that he was attending because he wanted to learn.

A few minutes before she was due James had his jacket on and was standing in his dark bedroom watching the road. He was glad there wasn't any parking space available immediately outside the flat, it meant she wouldn't have time to leave her car and come in. He felt that if she saw his private world something of him would be exposed; some secret that would reveal his inauthenticity. Finally headlights paused in the road and he recognised the Citroen. She gave a short beep of the horn but he was already half way across the road to meet her. As he approached he noticed that she was alone.

"Hello, did you have any trouble finding me?"

"No, not at all, jump in."

She smelt of oils, a musky smell that filled the whole car. They made small talk for a few minutes, catching up with what they had been doing over the weekend, until Rachel said "Have you been continuing with the exercises after your yoga?"

"The breathing? Yes, every day."

"Have you had any further experiences when you've done it?"

"I've seen the eye every time, but it's changed."

"What do you mean? The eye has changed?"

"No, the eye looks the same, but I've looked into it more, allowed myself to accept it instead of reacting and stopping the breathing exercise."

"That is good James, you have an instinctive wisdom."

He was flattered by her comment, "I don't know about that," he said, trying to conceal the pleasure he got from it, "it just felt right."

"That's what I mean, wisdom isn't a matter of rationalising everything. There are great intellectual thinkers who have no wisdom at all. This goes against the western idea of intelligence, but there is a way of knowing

70

that is not contained by rational thought. Having a sense of the right thing to do is part of that. Don't ignore this in yourself James, it is a valuable part of who you are. When it comes to these kinds of experiences we have to trust our insight because the logical part of our brain hasn't encountered this kind of thing before. So unless we're going to react with fear or confusion, we have to go beyond what our logic or our past experiences tell us. It feels like a step into the unknown at first, but the more often we do it the greater our sense of judgement grows, and the more confident we become in trusting this part of ourselves."

"It is a big leap," James agreed.

"Don't worry, only we make the decision whether to take it or not, no one can force us. We don't have to take any steps at all if it doesn't feel right. That's part of it, part of what I'm talking about." She turned and smiled briefly to reassure him, and he saw the street lights flash in her eyes. He liked to listen to the sound of her voice, there was a softness that was grounded in a certainty, a confidence that he rarely recognised in women of her age.

The traffic had thinned out and they cut across Birmingham without any difficulty. She took the A38 and headed towards Rednal and then turned off into a wide street of tall, impressive buildings.

"This is nice," was all he could say.

"It is, we've been meeting here for a long time. And they were here long before I found them."

"Who is it who lives here?"

"None of us are here permanently. I lived here for a few months until I found my own place, and Richard is here at the moment."

"So you rented it and passed the lease on?" James asked.

"No, we have a friend, David, he owns the building. He owns a couple on this street. He lets us use the rooms whenever we want and if anyone is caught short he lets us stay for a while. You'll have to meet him, he's an interesting man; I think you'd like him."

James tried to imagine the kind of wealth that enabled someone to own a second property like this, "What does he do?"

"He runs a business down in London, that's why he doesn't make the group so often."

She pulled into a space not far from the house and they walked through the cold night to the stone steps leading up to the front door. She led the way and pressed the button beneath the small speaker in the wall. A voice crackled "Hello?"

"It's Rachel," she announced.

There was a buzz and she pushed open the heavy wooden door, "Come on, it's the second floor."

The hallway was elegant with a high ceiling and a large carved banister up the stairway. She skipped ahead, and as they climbed the steps an electronic sensor turned on the lights. James found himself at the end of a surprisingly long corridor, the narrow frontage of the building was deceptive, it extended back a long way. Rachel opened the first door they came to. A cloud of sweet smelling incense wafted out to envelop them and she led him into a low lit room where half a dozen people sat chatting. There were a few framed paintings on the walls and enough chairs for at least a dozen people. The group was made up of two women in their thirties, and four men who looked to range from their late twenties to their early forties: Jacob wasn't present. They all smiled as Rachel and James entered and he watched as they exchanged kisses and hugs. "This is James," she finally said, turning and pointing his way.

As they each stepped forward Rachel introduced them and James desperately tried to remember their names. Richard was one of the younger men and he made a special point of declaring that James was welcome in his home. The oldest man in the group was Simon, as he shook James' hand he said "Rachel mentioned you on the 'phone, if you want we can have a talk later about what you've been experiencing."

"Thank you, that would be good."

"Now that everyone's here," Simon said to the whole group, "let's move next door and get started." He led the way back into the corridor and into the next room and everyone removed their shoes before entering. As James went in he found himself in a bare room except for mats laid out in rows on the floor and a low table at one end of the room on which sat a small statue. Incense sticks were burning either side of the figure but James couldn't make out what the statue was. The group began to sit on the mats and Rachel invited him to do the same. Simon sat on a mat at the front of the room, and with his back to everyone he invited them to close their eyes.

"Take a moment," he said "to become aware of the people around you. Hear the small sounds of the world outside, let go of all your worries and concerns."

There was silence for a couple of minutes and James could feel himself beginning to relax. Simon continued "Now focus on your breath. Slow your breathing down and pause between breaths. Receive your breath and feel it penetrate deep into your body, hold it, and now let it out beyond yourself. Again, allow the breath to move down to your diaphragm, hold it there, and now move out with the breath, out beyond yourself, beyond the walls of this room, out into the reaches of space. And as your breath now returns feel the distance of the universe returning with it, entering your body. As your breath leaves you, this time let it flow out beyond the limits of physical space, travel with your breath beyond space, beyond the breath itself, sense yourself dispersed into a place of infinite peace, so that you become nothing and all perception is of infinite stillness."

Simon led them through a series of exercises, and with each one James felt himself drawn deeper into the meditation so that when Simon finally asked everyone to open their eyes it felt like a burden to return to the reality of limbs and eyes and ears. No one moved or spoke, and for another minute everyone allowed their conscious minds to incorporate the effect of the meditation. Still without speaking everyone stood and went back into the other room.

As James was tying up his shoes Simon took the seat next to him. "Is that form of mediation familiar to you?"

"No, I haven't done any real meditation, only the breathing exercises that Rachel showed me."

"If you have been doing those then you have been meditating, you just didn't use the term or think of it that way."

Richard interrupted and asked who wanted coffee, one of the young women went with him to help and everyone began to chat informally. Simon turned back to James, "Would you feel comfortable telling me about your experiences?"

"Of course," James was pleased to be addressing what he had hoped to ask about, and told him everything he could recall.

As he came to the end of his account Simon said "If we are persistent yoga and meditation will always open our perception to new things, particularly subtle energies we haven't known before. We can become aware of our own imbalance, tell me, have you been experiencing headaches?"

"Nothing serious, just the usual tiredness from work."

"Good, have you heard of Descartes?"

"The philosopher? Yes, of course." James said.

"One of his realisations was that there is a point in the brain that can be affected, stimulated into life. We've since come to understand a lot more about the pineal gland, but meditation is one of the tools that Descartes highlighted as doing this. It's a very western, scientific approach, but even from that perspective Descartes was on the right track."

Where once, just a short time ago James would have needed the reassurance of hearing that it was all scientific, now he wanted something more. "But what about the eye?" He said.

"You must cherish what you have seen James, it isn't something to be taken for granted. In Indian philosophy we are told that there is a seeing beyond seeing, a form of sight that is beyond sight. Through yoga and meditation we can open the gate to our soul's perception, a higher form of perception than the physical senses allow."

"Perception of what?" James asked.

"Of other realms James, of a new form of wisdom where even the physical senses can be transformed. We mustn't struggle against the natural will of the universe, neither can we force it to our own ends, we must feel and embrace the natural intention of the cosmos and within it recognise our deepest desire, which is for peace and connection. Yoga is the first step to achieving unity with our inner self, a unity that has no beginning or end." Simon fell silent and as he looked at James he began to laugh, "I'm sorry, forgive me. I completely understand why you should look at me like that, does it sound like mumbo jumbo?"

James shook his head, "No, not at all. I'm sorry, I didn't mean to pull a face. I just need time to think it through. Some of what you've said connects with the things I've been doing straight away, but some of it is beyond me."

"Only for now," Simon reassured him, "we must walk before we learn to run. And run before we fly. If I was to give you any advice at this stage it would simply be to notice. Try to be aware of everything that's going on in your mind, and notice how you are seeing the world. Within this, try to notice if anything is changing, if the way you are seeing is different to how it used to be."

Richard returned with a tray of cups and Simon began talking to him about the flat. There was some issue with one of the neighbours and Richard was seeking his advice. James caught Rachel's eye as she glanced across at him and he smiled to let her know all was well. None of the group gave him the impression they were intent on converting him to anything, and listening to their conversations it was clear they were bright and friendly and James was satisfied they weren't trying to pull him into some cult.

Later Richard walked Rachel and James down the stairs to the front door, "It's been good to meet you James, do you think we'll see you again?"

"I'd very much like to come back, if that would be alright with everyone."

"Of course, we'd love to see you." He kissed Rachel's cheek and after their farewells pushed the door shut behind them. A light rain had begun to fall and they darted across to the sanctuary of the car.

She made a turn at the end of the street and as they headed back towards the north of Birmingham she said "What did you make of it?"

"It was good to speak to Simon, I need to take some time to think about what he said."

"What about the meditation?"

"Very useful, thank you for bringing me."

"Do you think you will meditate more regularly?"

"I would like to try, I felt the impact even of that one session."

"I can send you some texts which will help, little exercises that are good to start off with. I've got some videos I can send links to which are pretty amazing, there's plenty of material you can use."

"I'm really grateful Rachel, the group was very welcoming."

"There are a few more people who normally come, they're a good lot when you get to know them. We lose people when they move away or travel and don't come back, and new people like yourself pop up. It just naturally replenishes itself. Simon has been there from the beginning, a few of us have been going for a good few years, and Richard is the latest before you, he's only been there a few months."

"What are all the other rooms used for?"

"One of them is David's room when he visits, there's a kitchen and a living room; the others are kept locked. I think David stores things in there, but I didn't see inside them while I was living there."

After a brief pause James asked "What does aashna mean? It was in your email address."

"It was the name my mother often called me when I was small. Aashna is a term of endearment, a bit like darling, it was her special name for me. She used to say it means honesty, and told me I must always be truthful if I'm to live up to it. I sometimes wonder how well I have done at this."

"That's very sweet, were you an only child?"

"No I had an older sister who died when I was only seven, she was very beautiful and she loved me very much. I cried for a long time when we lost her."

"I'm sorry to hear that."

"Yes, there is great sadness in the world, we must find the way to overcome it."

By the time they arrived outside his flat the dashboard clock said it was nearly eleven. The lack of sleep had finally caught up with him and he'd felt himself drifting off over the last few miles. With little fuss she said goodnight and drove away, and James' thoughts turned to his bed. Alone in the flat he moved around without turning on the lights, enjoying the sensation of moving through the darkness from memory. Without checking his computer he splashed a little water into his face, threw his clothes over the chair beside his bed and let out a groan of pleasure as he pulled his quilt tightly around himself and sank into his pillow.

Chapter 11

A few days after meeting the group James was sitting at his desk, staring at a spreadsheet which was so badly organised that he was tempted to make a telephone call to complain. He leaned back in his chair and looked at the black rectangular shape of the screen, its geometrical presence seemed as important to him as the lists of numbers he was meant to be struggling with. As his eyes focussed on the shape, he became aware of the same black form on each desk around the room, everything else seemed to fade from his vision. He then noticed the sharp straight edges of tables and door frames, and the room became a series lines cutting across each other at various angles.

The sensation was nothing like anything he had known before, and he closed his eyes for a moment to shake it off. As he opened his eyes the greens and blues in the room had become vivid, almost shimmering, inanimate objects appeared to be vibrating with energy. James gazed into the convergence of shapes and colours and the everyday meaning and use of the world around him was replaced with a sense of the simple reality of their presence.

One of the women in the office walked past him and the moment was lost. Once more he could see the columns of figures on his screen and he felt the urgency to return to his task. He printed off the spreadsheet and decided to start the whole thing from scratch, it would be quicker than working with this mess. He forgot about what had happened and immersed himself in his work.

It wasn't until he was back in his flat, sitting on his mat after his yoga session that he remembered the experience in the office. He knew it had been more than tiredness in the eyes from staring at a computer screen for so many hours, there was a sense of meaning behind it. As he had seen the room so differently, he had understood that he was seeing a reality that he had normally been blind to. In the act of seeing he had understood something. It wasn't an understanding that could be expressed in words, but somehow he had been aware of a truth that changed the way he existed in the room.

He began his breathing exercises and followed the pattern shown to them by Simon. It had become a daily routine for him and the experience of reaching out beyond the room into a different space was becoming much stronger. He was feeling in control of the movement so that he felt himself directing the breath wherever he wanted it to take him. He continued for half an hour and then sat listening to the world around him. Silence was no longer empty and he allowed the slightest ripple of the air to wash over him.

Over the next few weeks James attended yoga class and continued to learn more postures. Neither Rachel nor Jacob attended and James resisted the desire to email her. A week or so before the mediation group was due to meet James was sitting on his mat early on a Saturday morning. There was little sound from the traffic and he began to listen to a sparrow singing outside his window. As he focussed on the birdcall it seemed to rise in volume and significance. James was aware of the little bird's throat as it warbled, he could sense the little rush of air as it left the beak, and within the sound was the mind and intention of the living bird itself. Each deliberate change in pitch and rhythm of the call communicated the presence of the creature's will, and James recognised a unity between his own consciousness and the tiny life force within the bird's skull. It filled him with elation and he had to stop himself from becoming emotional at the sweetness of the feeling. A rush of joy passed through him and he became grateful for the bird's presence.

He spent some time reading a new book he had bought on the history of mediation in India, but there were so many schools of thought and different kinds of teaching he couldn't trace what he was doing to any one tradition alone. At lunch time he checked his emails and was pleased to see Rachel had contacted him.

Hi James, I hope all is well.

I don't have the car on Tuesday and so can't pick you up. I will see you there if you make it.

Rachel

Although he enjoyed the chance of talking to her alone in the car he was relieved she wasn't making a special journey to give him a lift. He sent a message back assuring her it wasn't a problem and shut his laptop down.

He decided to take a walk and headed up to the local park. There were a few couples pushing prams around but the cold weather had kept the crowds away. As he walked he began running through the timeline of how he had met Rachel and all that had happened since then. It had all occurred at a tremendous pace and he felt exhilarated to think how his life was changing. As he lost himself in his thoughts he approached a young couple sitting on one of the benches. They sat in silence and it was clear to anyone that cared to look that they were unhappy. As James drew near he felt the weight of their loneliness pressing down on him and as the young girl looked his way he was almost overcome with sadness for her. He forced himself to look past them, he didn't feel he had control over his reaction and didn't understand why he should feel such intense empathy at this moment. His rational mind was telling him they were young enough to start again, that kids their age start and end relationships all the time, but still he couldn't shake the terrible reality of their emptiness. His reaction left him uncomfortable and he tried to assert some control over himself, and walking back to the flat he began questioning whether these feelings were good for him.

He emailed Rachel and asked her to ring him on his mobile number. He trusted her enough to be honest about his concerns, and he didn't know anyone else he could speak to. Within a couple of minutes of sending the message his 'phone rang.

"Hello James, are you okay?"

"Thanks for ringing me back, I'm not sure. I needed someone to talk to and hoped you wouldn't mind."

"Of course not, what is it? Are you sure you're okay?"

"I think so, I'm just experiencing a few things which aren't like me."

"What kinds of things? Do you mean in meditation?"

"No, not necessarily, although I feel like they're linked to it. My perception of things is shifting, I can't explain it, I'm getting moments when things suddenly change perspective without warning and I feel like I'm seeing things differently."

"In a negative way?"

"No, not necessarily. In fact some of it is very beautiful, just the sounds and sights of things, but I wanted to know if this is normal."

"Not for everyone James, some people remain closed off even after all kinds of disciplines. You're opening yourself up, it's a real thing, it's going to affect you in ways you don't expect. It's going to be something that affects your whole being, every part of you, even your emotions and thoughts, don't let it panic you."

"I'm not panicking, don't worry, maybe I've made too much of it. I just needed to speak to someone about it."

"Speak to Simon next Tuesday, he can explain things much better than me. I'll drop him a line and let him know you'd like to talk to him again, he'll be happy to help."

"Thank you Rachel. Can I ask, did you go through these kinds of things?"

"My experience was very different, but I know there are people in the group who would identify with what you're describing."

James noticed there was a hesitancy in her voice that he had never noticed before. "I'm sorry," he said, "I didn't mean to ask about anything you're uncomfortable with."

"No, don't be silly. I'm not uncomfortable talking about it at all, but it's been such a long time since I began the process and I was a very different person back then."

"Well, thank you again for calling me back, it's good to know I'm not going crazy."

"No, you're going sane, which is far more dangerous." There was no trace of humour in her comment and it caused James to frown.

"Well, thank you Rachel, I'll see you at the group."

"Okay, but feel free to ring me back on this number if you need to, don't feel you're going through this alone. Bye for now." She hung up before he could respond and her abruptness left him wondering if he'd said something to upset her. He felt better for talking to her, she had managed to lift his anxiety and he realised that describing his experiences to another person made them seem far less of a concern than when they were just in his head. He was also pleased to have her number, it was one more line of connection with her that brought her that little bit closer.

Chapter 12

Pulling up outside the group's house James was surprised to see Rachel's Citroen a little further down the street. He wondered if she had lied about not having it so as to avoid picking him up, and the thought troubled him. It would be out of character for her not to say straight out that she wanted to drive directly to the meeting, and he questioned whether his image of her was entirely secure.

Trying to put aside the impact this made on him he locked his car and walked up to the imposing front door. Richard answered the buzzer and pressed the switch to let him in. The hallway was in darkness as he climbed the stairs but the landing light came into life as the censor detected his presence. He recognised the smell of incense and being there already began to feel familiar. He wasn't sure whether to walk straight in and hesitated at the door before giving it a couple of raps with his knuckle. Jacob was standing the other side of it as it opened, "You don't need to knock, come on in."

Everyone from the last meeting was there again and they all greeted him warmly. In addition to Jacob another middle aged woman who hadn't been there before introduced herself as Susan, she was prematurely grey and her long hair was tied back in a pony tail that almost reached her waist.

Rachel stepped over to him, "I'm glad you remembered the way."

"Yes, no trouble," James remembered her car and couldn't shake his suspicions. The group chatted for a few minutes before Simon invited them through to the other room. They slipped out of their shoes and followed him in, and once more he led them through a meditation session. James found himself too distracted to settle properly and though he could feel the benefit of what they did, his mind was jumping around too much to repeat the depth of meditation he had known at his last visit. The time dragged a little for him and he was relieved when Simon announced that the session was finished.

As they returned to the other room James noticed that Jacob avoided any eye contact with him and he assumed the 'phone call with Rachel must have been unwelcome. Simon invited James to sit beside him. "How have things been going?" He asked.

"I think they've gone well. Did Rachel mention to you about what I said to her?"

"Yes, she told me everything, you mustn't worry about anything. Everything you described to her is perfectly normal, in fact it's good that you are going through them so soon."

"Rachel thought you might be able to help me understand it a bit more."

"I will try to help James, but if I say anything that sounds strange or you don't like the sound of, please feel free to stop me. I don't want to say the wrong thing and leave you with a negative impression just because I've used a clumsy way of saying something."

"Thank you, I will," James assured him.

"When we speak of reality, we normally assume we are talking about the world that is present to us through our five physical senses. As we begin to develop our ability to sense things in other ways, sense the world around us in other ways, the old material reality loses its importance. Loses it in the sense that it is no longer the only way of seeing things. This is what I was hinting at last time we spoke, the new reality that we begin to encounter can often be more intense and more real to us when we encounter it. But we mustn't imagine that this higher sense of meaning is just because it is new to us. This isn't just a psychological reaction to a new experience. In fact the truth of the new reality reveals itself to us as greater than anything the five senses can show us because we are perceiving it with a deeper, more powerful part of ourselves." He paused to give James time to absorb what he had said. "Rachel mentioned your experience when you saw the young couple, would you be happy to tell me about it?"

James related how he had felt. Simon listened carefully until he had finished, and said "The energy you have been sensing that moves with your breathing isn't just your point of focus, it is something more, more than yourself. If you develop this energy you can direct it at people. If you experience anything like that again, allow your breathing to carry the positive energy out from you to whoever you are focussing on. It can bring many kinds of healing." Satisfied that it wasn't troubling him Simon continued "As you practise the exercises you have learned here, you will begin to experience these changes much more. Let them come over you and allow yourself to experience them without concern. The more you can embrace them the deeper you will allow yourself to go into them. Each experience will lead you to the next as you become more open, and when you are ready we can try some different strategies for your meditation which will give you the capacity to direct these experiences in ways that you do not yet know about. It is a positive journey and you have begun to make progress."

"Thank you Simon, I needed to hear that."

Simon patted him on the arm, "Embrace and cherish what is happening to you."

As James nodded back to him thoughtfully, Susan stood and in a loud voice said "Can I have everyone's attention please." The room fell silent, and James caught Simon smiling to himself at Susan's manner. "I have some good news to share," she continued. "David is going to be able to be with us next month, he wants to talk about this year's pilgrimage, so can you all please make an extra effort to attend. Could the message be passed on to those people not here please?"

"Yes," said one of the young women, "I'll send an email out to everyone."

"Good, thank you, please go back to your coffee," she laughed, waving her hand before them.

Simon turned to James again, "Have you heard much about David Munro?"

"A little, I understand he owns the building."

"Yes, but I mean about the man. Has Rachel told you anything about him?"

James shook his head, "Not really, only how generous he's been letting people use the flat."

"He's a truly wonderful man James, I don't just mean his material generosity, which has helped many people all around the world, but the man himself. He has taught me so much about meditation and yoga, my life would be on a completely different track if it wasn't for him. Do you think you'll be able to come?"

"Yes, I'm sure I will," James said enthusiastically.

"That's great, I'm so glad you'll get to meet him." Simon's eyes lit up as he spoke and his zeal was all over his face.

They finished their drinks and a few people began to leave. James checked his watch and got up to go, just as Rachel and Jacob got to their feet. She smiled at James before saying goodbye to everyone. James thanked Simon once more for his advice and followed Jacob out. They descended the stairs without speaking, but once outside

Rachel approached James. "I'm glad you're coming to the group, you are ready for this."

He shrugged at the comment and said "Is everything alright with your car?"

"It's not my car," she smiled, "it belongs to the group. David lets us use it, that's why I couldn't give you a lift, Jacob took it to London this morning and only just got back in time to pick me up."

James felt foolish for all he had been thinking, but more than that he felt relief. He hoped she hadn't picked up on his attitude to her all night, and without thinking bent and kissed her cheek. "Good night," he said.

Jacob drove up alongside them and threw James an openly hostile look which he pretended not to notice and waved them both off before climbing into his own vehicle. He sat quietly for a moment before turning on the ignition. His relief had turned to shame as he recognised how suspicious he had been and how quick to jump to assumptions about her. He knew it was all coloured by how attracted he was to her, and he was determined to control his thinking in a more conscious and directed way. He was allowing emotion to dictate his responses, and he knew those particular emotions could only lead to misery, so he told himself to remember Rachel as a friend and resist anything else. The confusion he had felt all evening had robbed him of the chance to participate fully in the meditation, and he was determined to make the most of every important opportunity that the universe placed in his path.

Chapter 13

A few days later James was sitting at his desk at work comparing spread sheets and deciding how he was going to inform the head of marketing that his current rate of spending was going to leave him without any further budget for the last month of the financial year. He had no interest in listening to the usual excuses and chose to drop the bad news on him by email. As he finished typing he sat back from his computer and imagined the distress that was currently being experienced in the office on the next floor. It wasn't his problem but he knew it would have a major impact on the whole marketing team, and as he began imagining how they would deal with it he found his breathing slowing and he began to meditate. His concern for them grew and as he felt himself moving with his breath he imagined it carrying him to the office where his email had arrived, he saw a figure bent over his desk and he embraced him. The sensation was a tangible movement in his own chest, and as he found himself back in his own chair he sensed the energy moving between himself and the object of his focus. It was like light but with some form of substance, and it emanated not from his mind but his chest. As it moved he believed it was bringing some kind of healing, but he had no concept of how.

He opened his eyes and saw that no one in the room had paid him any special attention, he hadn't behaved in any way that was out of the ordinary, and yet he had experienced something powerful. He overcame the urge to rush up the stairs and see how the marketing manager would react at seeing him, and told himself he didn't need that kind of evidence to know something profound had just taken place.

Over lunch he sat alone on a wall in nearby side street, contemplating what had happened. He remembered what Simon had said to him and tried to recall every detail. He began to wonder how many other people had experienced this, not just in the group but all around the world, and he realised how shut off he had been through most of his life. He looked around at the parked cars and curtained windows, the façade of western life appeared to him like a straight jacket, preventing people from discovering their true potential. The insistence that we spend our lives focussed on material gain and attending to superficial goals that ultimately have no meaning was a giant con, one that he had fallen for just like everybody else. Even as he thought these things the nagging anxiety about having a comfortable retirement and enough money to buy his own place started eating away at him, and he let out a groan of frustration with himself. He had tasted something beyond any of this and it gave him a sense of reality and meaning that none of the material pursuits he had been trained to value could touch. He checked his watch and walked back to the office, resenting the demands on his time his job was making on him.

A few days later he was sitting in the lunch room nursing a cup of coffee. Two of the secretaries were standing near the boiler and he heard one of them say she was feeling unwell. James began listening to them and though his feelings were only shallow, he felt some concern for her. Closing his eyes he consciously tried to reproduce the experience he had had earlier in the week, he controlled his breath and felt the energy leaving his chest and surrounding the sick woman. Being so close to her the energy seemed much stronger and James felt he could almost pick her up and move her. He gave as much positivity to her as he could, and it brought him a deep sense of joy to be doing it. As he opened his eyes the women were still talking but the one who was ill turned her head and glanced over at him with a smile. It was confirmation that James didn't need but he was grateful for the sign that she had felt the connection between them.

At home that evening he cut his yoga session short and moved on to his meditation. Knowing that he could achieve such things at will filled him with enthusiasm and everything else felt like a waste of time. He began the breathing exercises and took his time, he wanted to enter into a deep meditative state and knew he needed patience. His breathing slowed and his mind entered deep down into his being, there he found a stillness where he was utterly at home and wanted to remain. The eye appeared before his closed eyes and as his breath left him he felt the sensation of hurtling upwards, as though he were physically travelling out into space. Like the shapes he had seen in the office he became aware of endless geometrical patterns that moved and exchanged form so that reality became a kaleidoscope of colours and movement. He tried to watch but his attention was caught by the sense of another living being somewhere out of sight. He turned and searched the shapes before him but the presence remained out of view, always at the edges of his vision. Just as he began to question what was happening he felt himself hurtling down and back into the physical world where weight and temperature were real again. He sat without moving, trying to commit everything that had happened to memory. He considered writing it down but when he thought about what he could say he realised he didn't have the words to express it. His peace was replaced with excitement and he wished he had someone to talk to. He didn't want to try and describe it in an email and if he rang Rachel at this hour it might cause trouble with Jacob.

And then, with a clarity that cut through his uncertainty, he knew he didn't need to record or say anything. There wasn't any need to tell anyone about any of it, the experience itself would lead him into an understanding. He had to trust what was happening to him, not chase after explanations, but allow the experience to reveal itself to him as much as he was able to receive it. This realisation calmed him and he was pleased he had enough wisdom to see it. This reminded him of what Rachel had said, and he accepted the little flash of wisdom for what it was.

At 3am that night he was sleeping deeply. He was dreaming about climbing a steep mountain and found himself looking out over a great plain from a high cliff. As he enjoyed the view the presence that he had experienced while meditating approached from behind. Without words or sound it instructed him not to turn around, but unable to resist James half turned to see who was there. The presence immediately rushed him and with a tremendous force pushed him forwards over the edge of the cliff. James bolted up in bed, and though the dream was over he felt the presence still with him in the room. He became afraid and grabbed at the lamp beside his bed and turned on the light. Everything was as it always was and in the light the sense of presence had vanished. He rearranged his pillow and leaned back on his bed, the fear had gone and he wasn't even sure he could remember what the dream was about. He closed his eyes and with the light still on quickly went back to sleep.

Over the next few weeks James tried to practice the technique he was developing at every opportunity. He even sat at his bedroom window at night trying to imagine the people in each of the houses across the street, he watched their brightly lit curtains and reached out to them. He felt that the force of the flow of energy was increasing and he learned to manipulate its direction and impact so that he could select people out of groups and crowds and target them without any effect on the people around them. He began to wonder how much positive change his actions were having and wished he could know more.

On the Monday before the next group meeting James was again at his desk going through some old files to prepare a new folder. As he studied the numbers Mr. Stone appeared at the desk next to his. "Liam, I've just been in a meeting with your line manager, we were going over some of your files and we found multiple errors." Stone made no attempt to disguise his disdain.

"What? I'm sorry, which files?" Liam was nervous and Stone had caught him off guard.

"The Crown files, the whole lot has got to be rechecked. You'll need to have it done by Wednesday, I'm arranging a department meeting and I want you to present what you've done."

"I can't do them by Wednesday, I've got too much on."

"Are you serious Liam? Do you have any idea how much this could cost us if you don't put this right? Between you and me, if you don't get on this quickly I don't think your job is safe."

Liam was fighting back tears, "Do you want me to leave the files I've been working on?"

"Don't be ridiculous, and mess them up as well? Do your job Liam, that's what you're being paid for. And do it quickly. Am I making myself understood?"

"Yes, I'm sorry, of course."

Stone looked satisfied with himself as he strode away. James pulled his chair a little closer to Liam's desk, "Are you okay?"

"Oh yea, thanks," Liam was still struggling with his emotions.

"There wasn't any need to talk to you like that, if there's any way I can help just ask."

Liam looked at him, "There's just so much of it," he said.

"I'm ahead with my stuff, I can give you a few hours tomorrow if it'd help."

"Thanks, I really appreciate it. I'll sort it out and let you know what you can do tomorrow then."

"No problems, we're meant to be a team, he could have called the meeting and got us to share it instead of turning it into a trial."

"Thank you," Liam said in a trembling voice.

James moved back in front of his computer, his anger still simmering. He could see Stone standing by one of the young women's desk giving fresh orders. James closed his eyes and tried to calm himself, he controlled his breathing and began to meditate. The energy began to move but instead of the positive light he was used to feeling, a dark, malevolent force snaked out from him and he sensed it wrap around Stone's throat. In the moment before he willed it to contract he opened his eyes and the energy was gone. He raised his hands and rubbed his eyes, disturbed at what he had done. He went to the bathroom and splashed cold water into his face and looked at himself in the mirror. He could still make out the anger he had felt and he knew he had lost control. It was as though the energy that he felt was really a part of him and not the neutral force he had imagined. Although he was surprised, and even shocked at what he thought he might be capable of, the moment had been exhilarating and he knew there was a deeper power to what he was doing. He could still feel it in his chest, and as he returned to his desk he became simultaneously aware of every living being in the office. It was as if some invisible thread were connecting him to every person around him, and all he had to do was pull hard and they would react. He understood that its potential wasn't just for healing.

Chapter 14

At 6am on the morning of the next group meeting his 'phone began vibrating on the bedside table. Half asleep he looked to see who was contacting him and all annoyance evaporated when he saw it was Rachel.

"Hello, is that you Rachel?"

"Yes, I'm sorry to call you so early, but I wanted to be sure to catch you before you set off for work."

"What is it? Is everything okay?"

"Yes, don't worry, there's two things. First, I just wanted to confirm you are definitely coming tonight. Are you okay for transport?"

"Yes, I'll be there."

"Good, the other thing I wanted to ask is how your meditation is going. We haven't spoken for a while and I wondered how everything is."

James was surprised that she would telephone at such an hour when she could ask this sort of thing at the meeting. But he appreciated the opportunity to mention some of the things he had been experiencing; though not all of them. He described the sensation of energy moving with his breath, and how he had been directing it and she accepted his descriptions in a matter of fact way.

"I understand," she said, "this is nothing unusual. We can speak more tonight, have a good day, bye."

Barely giving him time to respond she hung up and he stared at his 'phone for a moment before dropping it back on the table. He still had an hour before the alarm would go off and he curled back into his quilt in the hope of getting some more sleep. But his mind was now racing and he lay there thinking about Rachel's call. Despite all the questions it left him with he was amused at her quirkiness and was glad she had made contact.

That evening as he climbed the stairs to the meeting he could hear voices he recognised laughing and chatting. The door to the meeting room was open and as he entered he saw that everyone was present as well as a young Chinese girl who he hadn't met before. Sitting at the far end of the room was a man in his mid-fifties, his greying hair was cropped tight and he had a deep tan that gave him a look of health and vigour. As he saw James enter he stood and approached him, and extending his hand simply said "David Munro."

"Hello, I'm James."

"It's good to meet you, I've heard lots about you, how are you?"

"I'm well thanks, and I've been hearing you mentioned a few times, it's good to put a face to the name."

Munro smiled, he let go of James' hand, he was average height and very slim, and it struck James that he looked like a middle-aged Paul Newman. There was a charisma to him that left James feeling he was meeting someone of significance, and there was a strange excitement just from being around him.

"Shall we go through to the meditation room now that everyone is here?" Munro asked.

As they traipsed in Rachel made a point of greeting James and squeezed his arm as she passed him. He instinctively looked to see if Jacob had noticed but he had his back to them. They took their places on the mats and Simon led the session. He began with the breathing technique and guided everyone's focus into a sense of movement in and out of their bodies. James quickly saw the eye and before he could begin his usual response he felt a wave of energy flowing into him. It was similar to what he had directed at people over the previous weeks but felt more complex. There seemed different elements to the flow of energy, it was no longer the simple essence he had known before. As it engulfed him he lost track of his breathing and allowed his consciousness to be consumed with this new sensation. And then, at the source of the energy he recognised Munro. He opened his eyes, expecting to see him looking back at him, but like everyone else he was still sitting motionless, his back to James, still apparently focussed on Simon's words.

James was reluctant to re-enter a deep meditative state and ignored Simon's guidance. He kept opening his eyes to secure his connection with the room and keep his conscious mind there in the physical world. His reluctance came from an awareness of the intensity of the energy he had felt, it was something he knew he couldn't control and he didn't want to succumb to it until he was sure he understood it.

As Simon finished the session James waited before following everyone into the other room. He slipped into the back of the meeting and found a chair that enabled him to be unobserved by most of the group. Simon stood up and addressed everyone: "It's always good to have David with us, welcome to you David, and tonight is doubly special. David has some exciting news he wants to share with us. Please David," Simon gestured for Munro to take the floor.

"Thank you Simon, and it's always special to make the meeting here. As most of you know, we have a number of these groups in different cities, and I don't always get to see everyone as often as I would like. So again, it's good to be with you." He paused for a moment, and then said "I do indeed have some exciting news. I believe this year's pilgrimage was mentioned to you last month, well the good news is this year the bulk of the cost is going to be covered from my trust. There will be ten places available by invitation, and the only costs that the pilgrims will need to cover will be for the flight. All other transport and accommodation will be taken care of. Those of you who have been in previous years will know how special Rajasthan is, and how beneficial the experience can be."

"That's wonderful David," Simon took it upon himself to speak for the group. "Thank you for your generosity which we all benefit from just being here in this building."

"Those people who have been selected for the trip will be notified soon," Munro continued, "it will take place in just over two months' time. There will be more practical details available closer to the time, but this year is going to be a very special trip for all sorts of reasons, which I'll go into another time." He looked around at the group and smiled, he could see the impact his news had made. His eyes met James's and his smile broadened, it was such a look of warmth and acceptance that James regretted his reaction to the experience during the meditation; he feared his suspicion had once more been a barrier to being open to something positive.

Everyone stayed longer than usual and Richard was kept busy supplying refills of coffee. Jacob barely seemed to notice James was in the room who took it as a good sign and was happy to talk to the Chinese girl who wanted to know all about him. When people started to leave James decided to do likewise and as he headed for the stairs he heard Rachel behind him. "James, wait."

He turned to watch her coming after him, "Is everything alright?" He said.

"Yes, I just wanted a word, I'll walk down with you." As they descended the wide stairway she said "I have some amazing news, but I was asked to wait until after the meeting to share it."

"What is it?"

"David spoke to me about the Indian trip, and he wants to offer you a place. Isn't that fantastic?"

It was completely unexpected news, and James stumbled over his response. "I.. I don't know what to say."

"You don't have to say anything, it isn't a decision you have to make now. David will be in touch with you some time over the next couple of days to talk it through. This could be a once in a lifetime opportunity James."

"Why is he offering it me? I've only been in the group a few months."

"He normally selects someone who is new along with a more established member. That's just the way he likes to organise it. Also, he thinks you would benefit from it."

"How would he know that, he's never met me before?"

"I know, but he keeps in close contact with some of us, and when I told him about you he wanted to know everything. He's very interested in your development, it's such an opportunity."

"What sort of things did you say about me Rachel? Is that why you rang me this morning?"

"Don't worry, just the things related to our meditation. Part of the purpose of the pilgrimages is to develop members up and down the country. It's a way of sharing the teaching and bringing more people into the reality of what is possible in life. But for the individual pilgrim it's the chance to learn more about meditation than you could from years practising here in England, straight from the people who know it as a way of life. A few hours each week is one thing, but being immersed in the experience is something completely different. No one returns unchanged, it's the chance to grow. David recognised in what I said about you someone who was ready and would make the most of what it can do for them."

Her answer didn't satisfy him and as they reached the front door he stopped and turned to face her. "I don't know if I'm ready for a trip to India, and I don't even know if I can get the time off work. It all sounds good, but there's no way I can commit myself to anything tonight."

"You don't have to James, there's no pressure on you of any kind. I completely understand your situation. It's easier for me, I said yes as soon as he offered me a place."

James had to catch his breath, "You're going?"

"Yes, David thought we would make a good pair, to help each other, as we've become friends."

This changed everything and James' feelings about the trip were suddenly filled with possibilities. "I don't want to sound odd, but what about Jacob?"

"What about him? He went two years ago, it's too soon for him to go again."

"No, I mean, won't he have a problem with you going, or with us going?"

"Why should he James?" Rachel frowned, unsure of what he meant.

"I don't know, I know it sounds ridiculous, I just get the impression he thinks I'm trying to steal you away from him."

Rachel laughed, "You know he and I are just friends don't you?"

"No, I thought… I assumed you were a couple. You come to the yoga classes together, and you share the car."

"I told you that belongs to the group. I'm on his route, that's why he gives me lifts. Oh David, I can't believe you've been thinking this."

As she spoke James found himself in an entirely changed world, every reason he had given himself not to fall in love with her had vanished, and every possible sign of how she felt could be newly re-examined. He tried to hide his reaction, "I'll have to give this some thought," he said, "two months isn't long to sort things out."

"It's long enough if you want to come James, the only possible thing that could prevent it is you. Think about it, and talk to David. He'll answer all your questions. I hope you come, it could be amazing."

They stepped out into the night air and she held his arm, "I'll speak to you in a few days when you've made up your mind." She drew near and kissed his cheek, her warm breath on his face was intimate and close in the cold, dark street. She turned and walked to the Citroen. Before climbing in she turned to wave and smiled once more, and then disappeared from view before driving away. James waved to the back of her car in the hope that she could see him and leaned against the roof of his own. He looked up at the stars and grinned to himself.

Chapter 15

The following day James was preoccupied with the possibility of making the trip. He oscillated between excitement over time in India with Rachel and the reality of booking leave and abandoning his accounts when many of them would need his attention. He knew the kind of reaction the request would receive from his boss and even the rest of the department would be displeased at having to cover for him when their own workloads were already so demanding. But still, it was tantalising to think of being there and his imagination conjured up all kinds of fantasies, most of them involving his co-traveller.

Later that evening he was standing in front of the kettle waiting for it to boil when he heard his 'phone ringing in the other room. It was a number he didn't recognise, "Hello?" He said.

"Hello James, this is David, David Munro, how are you?"

James felt a wave of excitement pass through him, "I'm good, thanks for ringing. Rachel told me about the trip."

"Yes, and I understand you're unsure about it."

"The trip sounds like a great opportunity, I just don't know if I can arrange things in such a short time."

"I understand James, it's not something you make a quick decision about. Can we talk? I mean in person. Would you be able to come over, I'd like to go over it all, I'm not trying to persuade you into anything, I just think it would help you to come to a decision if I could explain what's possible."

"I'm working all week, would some time at the weekend be okay?"

"No, I have to return to London on Friday, can you come over after work tomorrow?"

"Yea, I suppose so, what time?"

"Whenever suits you James, I'll be there all evening. Show up when it's convenient."

"Okay, I'll see you tomorrow."

"Good, see you then James."

Munro hung up and though James felt he had been a little pressured into agreeing to meet after work he was pleased to be offered the chance to talk further with him. He returned to making his coffee and as he stood in the kitchen the possibility of going to India became more real to him.

The following day would have been like any other tedious work day that merged into every other like it except that at every chance he got James anticipated his meeting with Munro. There were still files that he needed to work on as people began leaving at the end of the day, and it was almost six before James was finally able to get away. He decided to eat after his meeting and drove straight down to Munro's building. There were still traces of sunshine across the sky as he strode to the front door and a little nervously he pressed the doorbell. Munro's voice came over the intercom, "Come on up, James."

Munro was waiting at the top of the stairs, "I'm glad you could come, would you like a drink?"

"No I'm good thanks, I had one just before I left work."

"Come on down to my office, you haven't seen this part of the building before." Munro led him down the corridor where one of the doors was open, "Please, come in."

One side of the room was lined with bookshelves, on the opposite wall hung a large painting of a mountain. As soon as James saw it he knew it looked familiar but couldn't place it. There was a large desk in front of the tall window and three armchairs took up the remaining space.

"Take a seat James," Munro gestured towards them.

As they sat James said "It's funny seeing the inside of another room here, it's an impressive building."

Munro ignored the comment, "Let's get down to business. You've had a day of work and I'm sure you need to get back and rest. I chose to offer you a place on the pilgrimage for a number of reasons. First, I always like to offer it to new members, they very often get the most from the experience. I also like to pair them up with someone who knows the ropes, it's good to have a trusted guide in these things. Second, I think you are particularly suited to taking advantage of what this trip can offer."

"Why is that?"

"I know from what Simon and Rachel have said that you are making progress in all kinds of ways. Not everyone responds to meditation the way you have, not everyone is willing to respond this way. You know that you have begun to experience an awakening within yourself; this is too important to allow to go unfulfilled."

"I don't really know what it is I'm experiencing David, but you're right, it is something important to me and I do want to allow it to continue. But can't that happen here? Why do you think going to India would be so beneficial?"

"You can learn a great deal from people like Simon and Rachel, but they'll be the first to admit that they're still only at the foothills of a very high mountain. In order to climb it we need someone who has been to the top who can show us the way. Our pilgrimages to India include intense training in meditation as well as sessions with masters in this field. There's nowhere on earth we can find these teachers, nowhere else we can achieve our true potential. I think this is what you want, am I right?"

"Yes, I do. I know how it sounds, but I'm worried about how it will impact on my job, I probably could get the time, but it wouldn't go down well."

Munro laughed a little, "I understand, I operate in the world of business, my head isn't completely in the clouds. I couldn't afford buildings like this if I didn't take my work seriously. You mustn't feel embarrassed about paying attention to your other commitments, we all have to walk in more than one world at times. All I would say is that the experiences you have already had are just the tip of the iceberg of what is possible for you, and what you will definitely come to know if you go."

James took a deep breath, he felt a strong desire to accept the offer, but still he hesitated. "I just don't know, I'm sorry."

"We are probably going about this the wrong way," Munro pulled his chair round to face James. "We talk about using more than our rational mind and here we are trying to make a huge decision with nothing but good old reasoned arguments. How about if we try something else?"

"Yes, what are you thinking of?"

"Would you be willing to meditate with me now?"

"Yes, but what do you think it will achieve?" James tried not to sound too dismissive.

"When we were meditating in the group last night, did you feel something different to normal?"

"I did," James admitted.

"The energy you have been experiencing is something much bigger than your experiences up to now have led you to believe. If I told you honestly what I have seen you would think I was making it up. It is something we have to experience to believe. Would you let me show you something?"

"Okay, what do you want to do?"

"First, let's meditate a little, use our usual breathing exercises, just for a few minutes."

They closed their eyes and began to control their breath. Less than a minute in and James saw the eye before him, not just looking at him but watching, seeing into him in a way that made him feel he could hide nothing. As the experience intensified he began to feel the energy flow out from him with his breath. He directed the energy towards Munro and tried to communicate to him a positive, healing impact. As he began there was a wave of energy that came back towards him and engulfed not just him but everything he was trying to transmit. His thoughts, fears, everything he was feeling was suddenly drowned in this new energy that filled him with light. Once more he could sense Munro's presence as the source of it and as the intensity increased so Munro's presence grew until it seemed to fill not just the room but James himself. The two men were somehow flowing into one another at a level beyond conscious thought, and James recognised an impulse of what he thought was positivity and love.

Slowly the energy withdrew and James was alone within himself once more. He opened his eyes to see Munro sitting opposite him smiling. His entire body was shimmering with a light that was gradually fading until just his face remained illuminated. As the light dimmed Munro's eyes finally shone as the last two points of entrance into this source of energy. Finally Munro looked back at him from a face that looked as it always did, where ordinary worldly light from the room reflected off hair and skin, and James understood that all had returned to normal. He felt overwhelmed by what had just happened, and Munro could see the emotion in his face.

"Don't allow yourself to become agitated when you experience things for the first time James, maintain the peace you know from your meditation."

"I'm trying, it's just that… I don't know what to say. That was incredible."

"Not really, as I said, the tip of the iceberg. There is great consolation in what is to come, but nothing will take you by force. Every step on this journey must be freely chosen, you must want and agree for everything to come."

Though he felt reassured by Munro's words, he took in very little. James was still recovering from the experience, desperately trying to make sense of it from his own perspective, the terms Munro was using still felt abstract and alien to the reality that had touched him.

Munro continued "We are learning to reject false information, the learning that has been imposed on us from our birth. We are taught to divide everything up into neat compartments but it all connects and so much of what you are learning is really different faces of the same jewel. Let us take meditation and devotion for example, they are both forms of worship and both are necessary for us to purify ourselves. What may feel alien because we have learned to see it as such is in fact a natural part of each of us. So many Hindu names and images lead us into something much closer to home."

"I'm not a religious man, David, I don't want anything like that."

"Like what? Didn't you just experience the power of our connection? Wasn't that real to you? You don't need religious words to know what just happened. The language of Hinduism is a way of communicating ancient truths, the teachers of these truths come from a particular culture, don't let the externals shut you out from the inner truth. Haven't you understood the reality of yoga?"

"Yes, I felt that immediately," James admitted.

"The wise men sold yoga to westerners as "scientific" because they understood that that was the only way it would be accepted. But every Indian yoga teacher knows that there is no yoga without Hinduism, and there is no Hinduism without yoga. This could never be revealed to a people full of prejudices. And now they are teaching yoga classes in English schools: do you think the school teachers and the parents understand how utterly inseparable yoga and Hinduism are? Every one of those teachers is a missionary for Hinduism, they just don't know it. They even run yoga classes in their church halls, as you know. None of this would be possible if the whole truth were declared openly. The impact of this great practice is only possible if its messengers are wise with their tongues. For those, like yourself, who advance beyond some simple stretches and gymnastics there is an infinite realm of possibilities. Of course, even the children who adopt the postures are performing worship, but they cannot understand this yet, and the word itself would frighten them away if they heard it."

"I don't understand what you're saying, you mean that yoga is like worship?"

"No, yoga is worship. Each and every posture you adopt is an act of devotion. Regardless of intention, like burning incense before a statue, if the action is completed then so too is the worship. I can see you're uncertain about this, don't worry. You've found the yoga to be beneficial, right?"

"Yes, definitely."

"So discovering the philosophical language behind it shouldn't trouble you. We're just talking about how it's explained, how ancient people communicated this truth. Maharishi Patanjali lived over five thousand years ago and his teaching is the basis of what you've been practicing. Krishna and many others taught yoga, as the means by which we find unity within ourselves, but also unity

109

between all of us. You experienced that connection when we meditated, it is powerful, healing, it overcomes barriers. Yoga and meditation bring harmony within us and between us, the physical postures are only a snapshot of something that we become. The wonderment you have felt today is necessary before we can embrace the source of life, it is childlike recognition of seeing something for the first time."

"When you say source of life, what do you mean?"

"The word Yoga refers to reconciling ourselves with our true self, our god self, it means to yoke our self to the universal spirit which is Brahman. Again, you see, I am using these terms, but look beyond them, don't let the names get in the way. If we can transcend the falsehoods we have learned we may transcend the bonds of this world, the bond to rebirth, the bond to our unreal self. So we mustn't be thrown when we hear words we think we know. Words like religion, magic or even evil. The goal of yoga is to see within ourselves the higher self, and there we see all, everything, good and evil, because we cannot deny the truth of ourselves."

James sat in silence, overloaded with the torrent of information. He frowned slightly and admitted "I think I'm out of my depth."

Munro laughed, he leaned forward and playfully tapped him on the knee. "Of course you are, we all are. Coming from the West we have a lot of catching up to do. But don't let that worry you, what are your choices? You can say it's all too much and I can't try, and opt to paddle in shallow waters, or you can embrace what you have begun to experience and set out for the deepest water you can find. What have you got to lose James?"

Munro's eyes fixed on him and for a moment the two men stared at each other as James' mind whirled with it all. "If I can swing it at work, I'm in."

"Excellent, this is good news." Munro looked at his watch, "It's getting late, and you have work again tomorrow." He stood and James checked his watch. It was later than he expected and he climbed from his seat.

"Thank you David, I really appreciate this opportunity."

As they walked out and along the corridor Munro began describing India to him and finally they reached the front door and Munro offered him his hand: "Any change in you is a change for the whole world. Don't think you are being selfish in wanting this, we all benefit from it."

Briefly shaking his hand James smiled and repeated his thanks. The night had turned dark and regardless of what happened, he realised how hungry he was and his thoughts turned to food.

Chapter 16

A few days after his meeting with Munro, James was listening to the radio as he cooked dinner. He was muttering under his breath at the latest BBC misrepresentation of the facts when his 'phone rang. He smiled when he saw who was calling, "Hello Rachel."

"Hello James, David told me about your decision. I am so happy for you."

"Yes, thank you, I think I should take the opportunity."

"Most definitely, this will be an amazing experience for you."

It didn't escape his notice that she made no reference to how much it meant to her too, "There's a lot to sort out before we go," he said.

"Oh, the usual little things, don't worry about them. Whatever is necessary, the important thing is you're coming. It might sound silly but I wanted to check your passport is up to date and remind you to look into getting your shots. Don't leave it too late, you know how long it can take to get an appointment."

"I hadn't thought of that, I'm not registered with a practice down here. I can ring my doctor back in Sheffield. I'm still registered at my old address. I'll have to visit my mother before we go so I can kill two birds with one stone."

"I'd love to come up and meet her, would that be possible?"

James Hesitated, he hadn't expected her to suggest it. "If you want, but it'll be a flying visit. I'll go and come back in the same day."

"That would be better for me, just let me know when it is. I've never been that far north."

"Sheffield is barely past the Midlands, but at least you'll discover there are other people with my accent."

She laughed. "I'd like that. Are you going to yoga on Friday?"

"Yea, I've not been for a while, what about you?"

"Okay, I'll see you then. I'm really happy about India James, bye."

Returning to his cooking he allowed the sound of her voice to stay with him, but his smile vanished when he thought about how his mother would respond to her. He would have to ring her first and insist that she didn't ask any embarrassing questions, she was bound to jump to conclusions; perhaps the same ones he was allowing himself to jump to.

As he pulled into the car park that Friday he was happy to spot the Citroen already there. He quickly walked over to the hall and inside looked around for Rachel. His heart sank a little when he saw her talking to Jacob at the rear of the room. She had her back to him and didn't see him approach and Jacob ignored his presence until he was standing beside them.

"Hello," James said, "how are you doing?"

Rachel gave him a broad smile and kissed his cheek, "Hello James." Jacob gave a jerk of the head but said nothing.

"Are you alright Jacob?" James was determined to challenge him head on.

"Fine, why do you ask?"

"Nothing, you just don't seem too happy."

"Leave it, this isn't the time."

"Time for what?" James felt confident knowing Jacob wasn't involved with Rachel, and wanted him to acknowledge whatever it was he was feeling. He suspected it was still jealousy even if they weren't a couple.

"Perhaps we should talk after the class," Jacob said as he walked away to find his mat. James looked at Rachel for reassurance but she seemed oblivious to what had happened and moved to her own place.

James performed the yoga with little enthusiasm, he was too focussed on how things would develop after the class. He avoided looking back at either Jacob or Rachel, and by the time the class ended he could feel the adrenalin in his chest as he anticipated the confrontation. He rolled his mat away and looked around to see what would happen next. Rachel was chatting with one of the older ladies and Jacob was heading for the door. James followed him out into the night and found him waiting in the car park.

"Is there a problem Jacob?"

"Let's not play games, I don't have time for it."

"So what's wrong? It's not just tonight, you've been giving me funny vibes for a while. Is it Rachel?"

"Rachel? What do you mean?"

"I don't know, I'm just guessing, are you unhappy because we're getting close?"

Jacob sneered, "You idiot. I'm not involved with her, do you really think we all operate on your level? I know you've been hanging around her, and maybe that's why you've joined the group, but believe it or not some of us think about other things."

"So what is it then?"

"Look James, I don't think you're the right person to go to India. You're just not ready. Somebody else could go who could really take advantage of the opportunity. Not just waste the time chasing skirt."

"What, someone like you? I'm sorry if you think David's made a mistake choosing me."

"I do think it's a mistake, but no, you see, once more you interpret other people through your own selfish worldview. I went two years ago, but Richard has never been and he's a genuine seeker."

James shook his head, "I'm sorry you feel like this, and you may find it hard to believe but I do want to go for the right reasons. Don't you trust David's choice in this?"

"Don't play that card James, I've known him much longer than you. I used to work for him. Yes I trust him, but I don't think he knows you fully enough. I'll be honest with you, when he rang to ask my opinion I was completely against it being you, but Simon and Rachel got their way. It's a mistake, you're not the right person. Maybe in a while, but not now, not before others."

James could see the anger in Jacob's face and he wondered if he would throw a punch. He stepped back from him and allowed the energy in his chest to push out and forwards to block him. As though he could see what was happening Jacob stood motionless and closed his eyes, and James felt the strike of a wave of energy hit him. The impact forced him to take a further step back and left him slightly unsteady on his feet. He felt afraid and this fuelled his anger.

Jacob opened his eyes and stared at him, "Don't persist with this," he shouted.

"What are you doing? What is this?" James said.

"You're not ready," his voice had calmed, "look at yourself. Don't go to India, tell David you've changed your mind. You're a long way from understanding any of this. It's not what you think."

As they spoke Rachel emerged and before she could hear what they were saying they both turned to face her in silence. She stopped and looked at them, "What is it? What are you two doing?"

"It's nothing," Jacob said, "we were just talking about India."

"She threw James a quizzical look, "Are you sure everything's alright?"

"Yes, definitely, don't worry."

"Alright then, we'll see you again soon." Once more she kissed his cheek and as she did James saw a look of anger in Jacob's face. He immediately knew that all of Jacob's talk about the trip was just cover for his real feelings and he enjoyed the brief moment of affection from her all the more because of it. The two men nodded their farewells for the sake of appearance and James watched them climb into their car. He resented Jacob being alone with her and turned and quickly started up his own. Without glancing back at them he pulled out and turned for home. The conflict left a strange trembling sensation in his chest which he put down to adrenalin.

James ate a small meal and was in bed by just after ten. He never had trouble sleeping on Friday nights, the week's toll enabled him to slip away within a few minutes of hitting the pillow and even the scene outside the yoga class no longer disturbed him. His dreams were fast and vivid, images streamed through his mind so quickly that his waking mind would never remember them all. He was startled from his sleep and lay grasping at what had passed through him. He vaguely saw himself climbing a mountain once more and as he struggled he became aware that something had been around his waist. Behind him Jacob had been pulling him back and somehow he had cut the rope and raced forwards towards the peak of the mountain. There had been something else there too. The shadowy presence he had dreamed before had multiplied. James couldn't recall any details about them but he knew they had threatened him. Their presence was filled with hatred for him, and it was feeling their loathing that had woken him. He lay for a moment staring at the

116

shadows of his room, trying to recall more details but everything was just beyond his reach. He rolled over and remembered the smell of Rachel's hair as she had kissed him, and filling his mind with her presence he went back into sleep.

Chapter 17

James stood up from his desk and Liam said "You knockin' off already?"

"No, I've got a meeting with Stone."

"Oh lovely, have fun."

James pulled a knowing face and made his way to the door of Stone's new office. He knocked and was called in.

"Take a seat," said Stone, "I'll be with you in just a minute." Without looking up he continued to type into his computer and took his time reading through what he had written. Eventually he lifted his glasses from his face, "How can I help you?"

"I've been given the opportunity to visit India, but it's in five weeks. Is there going to be a problem with me taking some holiday time at such short notice?"

"Impossible. I'm sorry James, but there's no way we can lose you without warning. And when you say your holidays, do you mean all four weeks?"

"No, I'd be away for two weeks, so I'd need a little more than that, maybe sixteen days. I know this isn't the best thing for the company, but it's a once in a lifetime opportunity, It means a lot to me to be able to go."

"No James, like I've already said, it can't be done. I can see you're disappointed, but that's just the way it is."

"Can't you look into it, see if anyone can help? There may be ways round it."

"There's little point continuing with this, I don't know any other way of saying it. We can't lose a member of the team at such short notice, you know how much work is coming up. This is a busy time."

"It's always a busy time Mr. Stone."

"Thank you, I really don't need to be told that." Stone was becoming impatient.

"I'm sorry, I wasn't trying to be funny, I just meant we're on the go all the time."

"Was there anything else you wanted to discuss?"

"Oh, is that it? There's no way of trying to arrange anything?"

"James, please, you're not listening to me. There really is nothing I can do to help."

"Alright," James stood to leave.

"Your work here is appreciated James, I don't want you to go away feeling we don't know what you do."

"No, okay, thanks." James returned to his desk crushed with the realisation that none of his plans were going to happen. He took out his mobile and called Rachel.

"Hello James, where are you?"

"I'm at work. Listen, I've just been told I can't have the time off for India. I'm gutted. I'm so sorry to let you down."

"That's ridiculous," her voice was filled with annoyance. "They can't manage for just a few weeks without you. Are you sure there's no way of persuading them?"

"No, I'm sorry Rachel, it looks like I won't be coming."

"Listen, don't do or say anything just yet. Will you trust me on this?"

"Trust you on what? There's nothing to be done."

"Seriously James, get your head down for the afternoon, forget about all this. We'll see what can be done."

"Whatever you say," he shook his head, "I'll speak to you again soon."

"I'll ring you tonight. Don't worry."

She hung up and James leaned forward onto his desk. He opened a file and stared at the columns of numbers. He resented them, he resented the screen, the desk, the room, it was all he could do to stay seated and not walk out. He thought of Jacob and how pleased he would be to hear the news, and his feelings grew worse.

He made it through the rest of the afternoon and drove straight home as soon as it turned five. He dumped his suit jacket over a chair and sat on the edge of the table. He felt helpless, there was nothing he could do to make the world give him what he wanted. His thoughts turned to Mr. Stone and his anger began to rise. From his jacket pocket he heard his 'phone vibrating and considered ignoring it. Only the possibility that it might be Rachel was enough to make him answer it. To his surprise it was Munro.

"Hello James, I've heard what's happened."

"I know, I'm sorry David, there's nothing I can do."

"Okay, take a moment and listen to me carefully. How much does this job mean to you?"

"I suppose I've got mixed feelings. It pays well and it may lead to other things." James was unsure where the questions were leading.

"Right, well I have an opportunity in one of my London branches. I know you're serious about your work, Rachel has painted a good picture of you. Give in your notice and come and work for me. I'll beat whatever your current salary is and I'll pay you a bonus to cover the move. I know this is a big step James, but it's a positive one. You'll have your foot in more doors than you ever could in Birmingham. Hand your notice in and I'll start paying you from the day your present contract ends, and I'll give you a week after India to move down."

"I don't know what to say, it's so out of the blue." James was overwhelmed at what was being offered.

"I've got people down here who can help find you accommodation. But I need to know now. What do you say?"

"Thank you, yes, I'll do it." James could barely believe the words coming out of his mouth.

"Excellent. I'll get a contract sent up within two days. Take a look at it and if you're happy to sign up, welcome to the team."

"Thank you David, this is so generous of you."

"Not at all, you'll be earning your money, but most importantly, you'll make the pilgrimage."

James felt a little light headed, he grinned as he repeated his thanks and hung up. Before he could think anything through he rang Rachel.

"Well," she said, "is everything sorted?"

"David's offered me a job, in London, I'll start after India."

Rachel shouted with pleasure on the other end of the line. "I'm so happy for you James, I knew he would make everything right."

"I'm going to hand in my notice by the end of the week. I'll have to work out four weeks and then I'm done. It'll give me time to prepare for the trip."

"We'll talk more when we meet, have you made your appointment with the doctor?" She said.

"No, I'll do it tomorrow. Thank you Rachel."

"What are you thanking me for?"

"None of this would be happening if you hadn't stepped in. I'm really grateful to you."

"It's David we should thank. And anyway, it means a lot to me that you'll be there, in India."

"It's happening then, we're definitely going. I can't believe it."

"Let me know when your appointment is. Have a good night James, I'll see you soon."

He made himself a coffee and sat at the table trying to bring order to the chaos of feelings he was experiencing. He returned to imagining the weeks with Rachel, and decided that he was right to be willing to do anything to make that happen – even if it meant resigning with no other job waiting, but now he had something to go to. He considered briefly what moving to London might mean and concluded that one strange English city was much like the next. And with great satisfaction he smiled to himself when he pictured how the faces of Stone and Jacob would look as he delivered the news.

Chapter 18

James followed the sat nav's directions to a narrow side street in an affluent area of East Birmingham. He was surprised to discover Rachel was living in such an upmarket part of town and worried how she might react when she saw the humble setting for his own background. He pulled up not far from her house and as he walked to the door she appeared and trotted out to him before he could reach it. She was wearing a long cotton skirt and an Indian print blouse.

"Morning James, what a beautiful day." She slipped her arm through his as they walked back to his car.

"I hope you're going to be warm enough without a coat," he said, remembering the weather in Yorkshire.

Five minutes later they were out of Birmingham and heading up the motorway. The traffic wasn't too bad, but either way James didn't care; he was happy to be alone with her for the duration of the journey.

"I have something for you James." She reached into her bag and pulled out a CD. "It's a compilation of different tracks, I think you'll like it."

"Stick it on if you want."

"No, not now, wait until you're alone. It's not the kind of stuff you want to talk over."

"What kind of music is it?"

"It's different Indian tracks, some of it is chanting, some of it is more classical Indian instruments. You'll have to listen and make up your own mind."

"Thank you, I will. Is that the kind of music you normally listen to?"

"I don't listen to anything too much, but when I do I like to give it my attention. I don't like a lot of modern stuff that just slips into the background. I'd rather have the silence. What about you?"

"I like music, always have. I used to go to all-nighters with my scooter club, you know, old Northern Soul and Motown." He glanced across to gauge her response.

"I've heard of Motown, but I don't know much about the other kind. I can't see you in a scooter club." She chuckled to herself at the idea.

"Oh yea, I used to ride a Lambretta, a real jack the lad I was. I don't think you'd have liked me very much back then."

"I don't think that's true James. These things are all surface, you're still the same man beneath it all. The things we fill our time with can be pleasurable, but they're just distractions at the end of the day. Mostly people need distractions from themselves."

"What makes you say that Rachel?"

"I think most people are unhappy deep within themselves because they've settled for the lives they've been taught to accept. But deep within every person there is the potential for so much more, and so long as it's left unfulfilled they feel empty. Look at all the rubbish people buy, the gadgets, the cars, but none of it changes anything. Marriages keep failing, families break up, people take their own lives, it's an ongoing tragedy. And it could all be solved if people were shown how to discover the real depth to themselves."

"Do you think people are any happier in India?" It wasn't meant to catch her out but as he said it he sensed she took it seriously.

"There is great unhappiness everywhere, and it has many causes," she said. In India millions of people are hungry and afraid, their basic needs aren't met, like fresh water and secure shelter. But even within this situation they can find comfort from what is within them."

"What was your childhood like?" James asked.

"I told you about my sister. So I know what it is to suffer. My search for truth was helped by having friends who pointed me in the right direction. I have been very blessed all my life to have special people around me."

"What about work? I've never asked you, what do you do?"

Rachel hesitated before answering, she looked out of the window for a moment and then said "I suppose you would say I have an independent income."

"Independent of what? Of having to work?" He laughed.

"Yes, in a way, but it doesn't sound very nice when you describe it like that. I receive a monthly income from a trust. I know how fortunate I am, I don't take it for granted, but it means I'm free to pursue what's really important to me."

"That must be great," James said honestly, "I'm a little envious."

"I'm sorry, it isn't good to create envy in other people. Forgive me."

"There's nothing to forgive, really, I'm glad for you. At least you're using the time to try and do something constructive, there's plenty of people who'd take it as a green light to do nothing with their lives."

"What a terrible thought," she said. "That is the consequence of a damaged culture. Instead of producing people who find every moment of value in their lives it creates victims who just want to run away and escape reality. David was talking about this the other day, how he so often has to help his staff reorientate themselves not just for work, but for living."

"Do you think he'll have to reorientate me when I work for him?" James was trying to make a joke but she sensed a genuine concern in his question.

"Not at all, you've shown how much you desire the truth of yourself. That's why he thinks you'll fit in. Don't worry, you'll be a great success for him."

"How did you meet him?"

"It was through friends. They introduced me to him when I was living in Germany. I attended a group there and one thing led to another."

"There are groups abroad? I didn't realise it was international. Does he finance them as well?"

"Oh yes, Munro money is benefitting people across the world. He's trying to bring change on a global scale. But it happens one person at a time. He says it's like ripples on a lake, all the tiny ripples start to meet and before you know it the whole lake is different."

They made good time and reached the doctor's surgery a little early. Rachel sat waiting in the car while James was inoculated, and as he came out he gave her the thumbs up sign that all had gone well. He climbed back into the car and said "Nothing to it."

As they approached Mexborough Rachel went quiet and glanced back and forth at the buildings around them. "It's all so lifeless," she eventually said.

"I know, just one big mass of concrete. As Doncaster and Rotherham expanded, the gap between them shrank away, and now you can't tell where one place ends and another begins."

"I can't imagine how people stay sane living in such a place."

James laughed, "They don't. Every other person here is as mad as a hatter. It's the only way they can cope."

"What about your friends?"

126

"Oh yea, they're the maddest of the lot. I don't know how I remained so normal." He laughed again and was relieved to see her smile.

As he followed the familiar roads to his mother's house he saw it all through her eyes and felt embarrassed. "Here we are," he announced as he pulled up. "I hope she's in."

"Didn't you tell her we were coming?"

"I'm only kidding, she wouldn't miss this for the world."

He let them in and called down the hallway, "Hi mom, how are you?"

"Oh James, I'm in the kitchen."

"Where else," he whispered as he led Rachel through to meet her.

"No, go on through to the living room, I'll be there in a minute," his mother shouted as she realised they were coming in.

James dropped into the sofa while Rachel stood looking at the photographs on the mantelpiece. "Is this you as a boy?" She held up a small frame to show him.

"Yes, I was still in primary school, I can't believe she's got that one out."

"You were very cute, you look mischievous." His embarrassment swelled but he enjoyed how interested she seemed.

James' mother appeared with a tray of cups which she set on the coffee table where she had laid out a lace cloth. "Here we are," she said, "I've brought the milk and sugar." She looked carefully at Rachel as though examining her, "Hello, it's nice to meet you."

"Hello, and you too," Rachel said smiling. "These are beautiful photographs."

"That's my husband there, he's not been long gone."

"James takes after him," Rachel observed.

"Yes, both handsome chaps."

"There you go," James said, "a mother's biased opinion of her son."

"Would it be alright if I used your bathroom?" Rachel asked.

"Of course dear, I'll show you where it is." The two women disappeared for a moment before James' mother returned looking serious.

"You didn't say she was... you know," she said.

"She's what?"

"You know, dark."

"She's mixed race mom, why? Did I need to warn you before bringing her to the house?"

"Don't be silly Jimmy. There's nothing wrong with that, not these days, I was just a little surprised, that's all. Don't make anything of it."

"I'm not the one making something of it. I'm surprised at you."

"Don't try to make it into something it's not, I'm not racialist, I was just surprised after Emma."

"What on earth has Emma got to do with it? You mean because I went out with a white girl you assumed that's my type or something?" James was annoyed but made sure he couldn't be overheard by Rachel.

"Don't make a scene. Let it go, I didn't mean anything by it." She insisted.

They heard Rachel coming down the stairs and let the matter drop. As she walked in James' mother said "That's a lovely skirt Rachel, is it Indian?"

"I'm not sure," said Rachel sitting beside James, "I think the print might be."

"Well it's very nice where ever it came from."

As they sipped their tea James said "I've got some good news. I've got a new job."

"You've only been at this one eight months, why are you changing?" His mother asked.

"It's a better position, I'll be doing similar work, but it's down in London."

"London, that's a long way, how long will that take you to get here?"

"It's only a couple more hours on the motorway mom, I'll still be able to get up."

"And what about Rachel, how will you continue seeing each other living apart?"

"We're not… it's not like that mom. We're friends." He avoided looking at Rachel as he spoke, he didn't want to see her reaction.

"Oh I'm sorry, the pair of you, I thought because you brought her up to meet me it meant you were together."

"I came because we're friends," Rachel's voice was calm and there was no hint of how she was reacting. "I thought it would be nice to see a little of James' background. I hope you don't mind."

"Of course not Rachel, it's lovely to meet you."

They chatted for another hour or so until James declared that it was getting late and they'd have to set off. While he visited the toilet his mother took Rachel's hand, "He obviously likes you love. He was very upset when he broke up with his last girlfriend, I hope you'll be careful with him."

"Don't worry, I think a lot of him. We're not together like that, but I wouldn't hurt him."

James returned to find them still holding hands and he threw his mother a suspicious look. "Right, let's break this up," he said, "we've got to get back. I'm sorry this is a flying visit, I just wanted to catch up before I move."

They both kissed her goodbye and she followed them out and waved them off from the gate. Rachel smiled, "You must have taken after your father in more than just his looks."

"What do you mean?"

"She's nothing like you, she's lovely, don't misunderstand me, but you're like chalk and cheese."

"I'm glad to hear it," laughed James. "She's great, I think the world of her, but she drives me crazy sometimes."

"Why didn't you tell her about India?"

"She wouldn't understand, she'd wonder why we were going together. It would just mix things up for her."

"I don't think she trusts me James."

"What! Why would you say that?"

"While you were out of the room she told me not to hurt you."

"You're kidding, I'm so sorry Rachel; she can't help herself."

She held his arm as he drove, "I told her not to worry, and don't you."

If he hadn't been driving he would have turned to kiss her, but instead he glanced across and caught the warmth in her eyes. "Well, that's the injections taken care of," he said, "we better start packing."

Chapter 19

Birmingham airport was two bus rides from James' house, the second of which was an airport shuttle, and at nine at night there were only four other passengers making the journey. His case sat beside him with the flight details to New Delhi tied to the handle. Not far from the airport a passenger jet came in low over the road, its lights filling the night sky as it drifted too slowly towards the runway. Excitement rolled through his stomach as the realisation that the trip was a reality hit home. The shuttle manoeuvred in front of the glass doors and James followed everyone off the bus and into the airport. It was busy with people dragging cases in every direction. James looked around for his terminal and followed the arrows. He had a couple of hours to check in and meet up with Rachel, and felt relaxed now that he was safely on site. All day he had been plagued with the fear that something would go wrong and prevent him from making it and now he was calm.

She was standing at a counter ordering a coffee and didn't see him approach. She was dressed in the plainest clothes James had ever seen on her, a simple brown cotton skirt and a dark blouse. At her feet was a small canvas rucksack but no case. "Hello Rachel," he said as he came up behind her.

She turned and smiled, he had never seen her look so beautiful, "You made it!" She said.

"What have you done with your bag?"

"This is it," she said looking down at it, "I can buy anything I need in India."

"I've got too much stuff," James said.

"Not at all, you'll be glad of everything I put on the list, trust me. Your first time in India is a strange enough experience without being without all your familiar little things. Don't worry about it."

James paid for their coffees and they found a table where they could watch the travellers go by.

"Excited?" She asked.

"Yea, definitely. But I'm a bit nervous about the flight; nine hours is a long time."

"They keep you occupied. By the time you've eaten and watched their films you won't notice how quickly it passes. Besides, it'll be a chance to get some sleep." She glanced around, "We might be able to spot some of the others before we register."

James was disappointed that he would have to share her company but tried to hide it. "Do you know any of their names?"

She pulled out a sheet of paper from her shoulder bag, "Yes, I've got a list of everybody who'll be there and where they're from. There should be four other pilgrims on our flight. It'd be good to introduce ourselves before we board. They won't be seated near us so it'll be our only chance before we're there. I'd rather make contact here than when we arrive at Gandhi: you'll see what I mean."

"That sounds ominous."

"No, nothing to worry about, in fact I love the chaos, but if you're trying to arrange things it can be hectic."

They couldn't spot the other members of the group before they eventually boarded. As the Air India stewardess pointed them to their seats James was relieved to see the 'plane was as modern looking as any he had ridden and realised he had been carrying some negative

132

assumptions. Rachel took the window seat and the remaining place beside James was unoccupied. He tried to conceal his anxiety about taking off in the dark, something he never enjoyed, and seemed to be the only person who bothered listening to the stewardess as she ran through the emergency procedures. He knew it would make little difference to his chance of survival if he had his head between his knees if the 'plane did come down, but there was a sense of comfort in imagining there were practical things he could do to increase the likelihood of surviving the flight.

As Birmingham fell away beneath them the pilot banked sharply to the left and their window was filled with the city lights that looked too close. James was disorientated and imagined the sensation of the aeroplane losing height. As they levelled off and then began their ascent James relaxed a little, remembering as he always did the statistics that assured him that landings and take offs are the real moments of danger. He took comfort knowing that they were a straight through flight and wouldn't have to repeat the danger at some stop off. The cabin signal told everyone they were free to loosen their belts, but James ignored the instruction. Half an hour into the flight the food trolleys were being pushed down the aisle and James and Rachel talked about nothing important. It was the first time he could remember seeing her so casual in her manner and he enjoyed the opportunity to engage with her this way. Every so often the smell of the oils she wore wafted over him and he would be reminded that there was a part of her that was still alien to him, but this only made her more attractive. This was especially true since they were heading to India where he imagined this part of her belonged. Having her beside him gave him confidence, a reassurance that he wouldn't be totally out of place.

After they had eaten their meals a Hollywood film was shown on the screens over their heads but Rachel had no interest in watching it and so James followed suit. It was the typical action movie which felt utterly out of place in the context of their journey. Rachel was looking through her list of names, and James asked "Have you met any of them before?"

"No, none of them." She folded the paper and pushed it back into her bag. "David has a skill in bringing people together. I don't just mean the groups, but the way he selects characters and personalities that can bring out the best in each other. He's very perceptive, he gets to know people very quickly. I mean know them spiritually."

"When I went to see him to discuss the trip, we meditated together."

"Oh good," Rachel said, "did you make a connection?"

"I'm not sure I'd use the same words, but I felt the energy from him."

"That's important, some people are very resistant to that experience. In that moment he will have learned so much about you. I remember Simon saying he believed David knew more about him than he knew himself. It's such a powerful tool in helping us discover and face where we need to work on ourselves. Without that kind of insight we might waste years."

James needed no convincing that what he had experienced with Munro was profound, but he was reluctant to accept or even admit that he needed Munro's insights to know himself the way she was describing. However, he wasn't about to say anything that could disrupt the closeness they were sharing and kept his reservations to himself. Instead he tried to show interest in what she was saying, "What do you think he's helped you see in yourself?"

"There are so many things James, I hardly know where to begin. Part of it for me has been to accept who I am. I

134

didn't even realise how much I was struggling with being mixed heritage. Mom was always mom, and dad was dad, I thought I was seeing myself as the product of the two of them just like anyone else does their parents. David cut through all of that and helped me realise that there were deeper questions I needed to resolve about myself that I didn't have to be afraid of."

"Why would you be afraid? Do you mean in terms of being upset or shaken with where it led you?"

"No, David helped me see that I could choose who I wanted to be without feeling I was rejecting one of my parents. I hadn't even realised I was carrying that burden until he helped me see it. Allowing myself to follow my Indian heritage doesn't mean I'm rejecting the other half of my family. There's a level of fears we can have that are under the conscious level, an emotional reality to us that can sometimes influence us more than the choices we think we're making. It comes back to that rational mind thing again, letting go of the world we think we've constructed and seeing the deeper reality beyond it."

"I'm so glad it's helped you find peace about yourself." James immediately regretted his inane comment and hoped she wouldn't recognise his insincerity.

She turned her body to him, "What you are about to experience could do more for you than anything you've known so far. But only if you're willing to let go of your old rational world at times. Please, believe me, I know you have a gift, David knows it too, but you won't discover how powerful and how deep within you it runs if you cling to your old terms."

"I want to see beyond it all Rachel, I do. That's why I'm sitting here."

"Alright," she turned back in her seat. "There are going to be demands made of you that might surprise you."

"I know I'm not just going on a holiday, I'm ready for it," he said honestly.

"Without struggle nothing of value can be achieved. I'm not talking about just physical struggle, although there are going to be times when you're exhausted, but inner struggle. I don't want to say too much now, I might say the wrong thing and create obstacles. What will happen will happen, just know that you're not alone in this."

"I don't feel alone, I'm glad you're going to be there."

She nodded and smiled, "I will." As she spoke she closed her eyes and James sensed a wave of energy move between them. It was softer than the contact with Munro, he felt it create a warmth that swelled through his chest. He closed his eyes and allowed himself to move out into his meditative state so that he became only aware of her, the whole world around them faded from him. The sense of being thousands of feet in the air was now no different to him as it would be standing firmly on the ground, all he could feel was her presence as she opened a part of her inner heart to him. Within the energy was something hidden, something held back from him. He knew she wasn't yet willing to completely reveal herself and he accepted this. As the energy moved out from him he tried to surround her, even engulf her in what was within him.

The sensation of intimacy was joyous, he wanted to hold on to it and pursue it, but he felt her withdraw and heard her whisper "I need to sleep." He opened his eyes, hoping for some kind of explanation or shared reflection on what they had experienced, but instead she had pulled back into herself and was now withdrawing even deeper from the world he inhabited.

He said "Good night" and watched her for a little while. Being so close he studied the features of her face, the contours of her skin; it felt almost like a violation to study her without her knowledge. It was like seeing parts of her for the first time and he noticed the particular way her nose curved upwards at the tip and how her eyelashes rested on her cheek. He worried that she might open her eyes and catch him and forced himself to turn away. A few seats ahead of him, up on the TV monitor, a Hollywood hero was chasing a villain down a freeway. To James it looked like a world of insane people, and he became aware of his fellow passengers sitting motionless as they absorbed the images. He was aware once more of the absurdity of sitting in this thin metal tube as it raced through the sky while everyone around him watched Tom Cruise pretending to be a regular guy. He closed his eyes to shut out the distractions and immediately before him he saw the eye.

Chapter 20

After nearly nine hours in the air the aeroplane had jumped fifteen hours into a new day. James had slept very little as the wheels jolted on impact with the ground of New Delhi. The pilot wished everyone a happy trip and warned them that it was a hot day: thirty-eight degrees. James shuffled forwards along the aisle and as he stepped out into the sunshine a wall of hot air hit him in the face. He felt the heat in his lungs and for a moment had to steady himself at the shock. Before him was the flat world of another international airport, but here the intense sunlight reflected back off every surface and wasn't like any place he had seen before. At the bottom of the steps a battered bus waited to carry the passengers into the shade of the low buildings and James looked back at Rachel as they descended. She was too busy taking in the scene to notice him, her face was masked in a serenity that gave the impression she had seen it many times before.

The bus ride was crammed and bumpy and it was a relief to everyone to make it into the air-conditioned space of Gandhi Airport. But the relief was short-lived, the chaos of customs and passport control was a test of everyone's patience. Small Indian men pushed their way forwards, many of them yelling insistence that they be seen first. Armed security guards looked on with indifference, and James felt a surge of prejudice welling within him. At the counter the official barely glanced at

James' passport before stamping it and sliding it back through the gap in the screen. As James waited for Rachel he tried to identify the smell that was filling his nostrils and concluded that it was the sickly mixture of incense and urine. It blew in from the streets outside and reminded him of how much of a stranger he was here.

Rachel finally made it through the throng and finding James said "I'm going to look around for the others while you pick up your case." She slipped away and James headed over to the carousel where suitcases were being assessed by the waiting crowd. Pulling his case from the conveyor belt he looked for the main entrance and held his belongings tight. He spotted an AMT and slid his card into its slot. No Indian currency can be purchased outside the country and James was keen to feel the security that having cash in his pocket would bring. The machine flashed and his card reappeared. A little confused he pulled it free and tried again with the same result. He began to panic a little as he didn't want to head out into the middle of nowhere without any money. He looked around for another machine but doubted it would solve the problem. As he stood staring at the mystery of the Indian AMT he heard an English voice from behind him: "Do you want a hand with that?"

James turned to find a slightly built, fair haired man in his mid-twenties smiling back at him. "Yea, please, it doesn't like my card." As the man stepped closer James wondered if he was about to be ripped off but went along with what was suggested out of desperation.

"It's just a matter of knowing which buttons to press, they work differently to ours." He indicated for James to re-insert his card and punch in his number, and looked away to assure him he wasn't memorising his pin. After a couple of electronic bleeps the options flashed up and James sighed with relief as a wad of money appeared from the machine.

"Thanks, I didn't have a clue."

"No worries, where are you heading?"

"A little place in Rajasthan."

He laughed, "Rajasthan is a big place. Are you with Munro's group?"

"Yea, you too?"

"I've just met Rachel, she asked me to find you. We're meeting up near the entrance. Careful where you put your money. I'm Daniel." They shook hands and he led James through the crowds of travellers to the main doors where Rachel was standing with a group of young westerners. She waved when she saw him and James recognised two of the group from the aeroplane.

It was clear that Rachel had assumed to take charge, "Now that everyone's here," she said, "we need to find our ride." They followed her out of the airport into a sea of brown, smiling faces, and to James' amusement many in the crowd were holding cards with misspelled English names. A middle-aged little man held one to his chest which simply read "Munro" and they waved to him with relief. He offered to carry more bags than the group were comfortable allowing him to take and led them to a white mini bus parked at the side of the road. They climbed in and began introducing themselves. James had forgotten most of their names before everyone had finished but at least he remembered Daniel and a tall red haired woman called Heather.

The mini bus weaved out into the traffic which seemed to come from every direction. James was excited to see a man leading an elephant by the side of the road and the whole world was suddenly filled with colour and movement. Some of the group were keen to talk but James couldn't take his eyes from the window, there was something new at every glance and listening to someone born in Manchester came a poor second. Eventually he reluctantly turned to the inside of the bus where one of the young women was telling them all about the difficulty she had had finding her luggage. James surveyed the group, there were ten of them, mostly younger than himself except for a man who looked to be in his fifties called Dereck and a middle-aged woman who sat quietly listening to everything that was being said. Rachel had a note book open on her lap and was busy writing something until she looked up and saw James watching her. "I'm trying to record my observations," she said, "it's easy to forget things at times like this."

"I think it's all being burned into my brain," said James, "it's like another world."

"Hold on to that feeling," said Rachel, "before long you'll grow used to it all. Don't forget that sense of seeing it for the first time." James didn't need any advice on remembering what he was seeing, though he appreciated the sentiment.

The heat inside the mini bus was unbearable and James thrust his arm out of the window in the hope of reaching some cooler air. But the temperature outside was no different and the bus never made it passed thirty miles an hour and so there was no benefit at all.

"How long until we reach the camp?" Daniel said.

"Once we make Neemrana it'll be about two hours," Rachel said. "But we won't be in Neemrana for another two or three hours," she added, "so you better try and get comfortable."

Despite the heat James didn't mind how long it would take, he was happy to gaze at the sights. He watched the camels trotting by at speed and cattle with painted horns slowly pulling their loaded wagons through the traffic. Daniel tapped his arm and James looked to see him extending a bottle of water to him. "Thank you," James said gratefully.

"How long have you been meditating?" Daniel asked.

"Less than a year," said James, not wanting to admit exactly how few months it really was. "What about you?"

"Yea, about a year and a half, I still feel pretty new to it all."

"Do you know David well?" James said.

"I've only met him about four times, I couldn't believe he invited me on to the pilgrimage. I'm sure there's other people more worthy."

"I don't think it's a matter or worth," said James, "Rachel told me he likes to give the opportunity to new members. Let's hope we can make the most of it."

The lack of sleep finally caught up with him and James accepted how tired he was. He folded his jacket up into a pillow and pressed it against the window. With the noise of traffic outside and the excited conversations around him he quickly fell to sleep.

He woke to the sensation of his arm being squeezed and his name being repeated. As he opened his eyes Daniel was saying "We're in Neemrana." James checked his watch, he was disorientated, his body was telling him it should be the middle of the night but he had to squint against the sunlight. He sat up and looked out at the flat roofed houses that squatted on each side of the road. Ahead of them there were hills on which he could see some kind of monument.

"What is that? He asked.

"Rachel says there are ancient Hindu temples here, we all agreed to take a break before finishing the journey," Daniel explained.

In fact the structures they could see turned out to be an elaborate palace built on the steps of the hillside. As they climbed from the bus they tried to take in the extraordinary building before them. Elaborate arches were built into the sand-coloured walls that gave the impression of a fortress. "We won't go up there," announced Rachel, "it's too touristy and it gets expensive.

142

The driver knows a less expensive place to get something to eat."

James was a little disappointed but followed the group to a road-side restaurant where the customers were a mixture of Indians and tourists. "Only drink the bottled water," the driver said, "or else you will have loose motions." The phrase was greeted with a little laughter, and the driver added "I have potion to add to your drink that will solve it. No problem at all."

The group sat around two large tables and a friendly waiter made no hesitation in tending to them. James ordered an omelette and a beer and was glad he had aired on the side of caution when he saw some of the food that appeared for his companions. Most of it was consumed to save face and everyone commented on how cheap it was.

While most of the group went with the driver to look at some local temples, James and a few others returned to the bus to rest. He got into conversation with a young woman from St. David's called Carol who came across as very innocent, and James took to her immediately. About forty minutes later the rest of the group appeared and Heather was complaining about how sunburned she was. Her forehead and cheeks looked painfully inflamed and a couple of the other women were fussing over her, offering various creams and lotions from their bags. "You need a bigger hat," Dereck advised, and Heather thanked him a little sarcastically for his insight.

From Neemrana they drove down to Behror before turning north-west towards Narnaul. The driver told them there were shorter routes but he didn't want to use the back roads. After another hour of driving the sunshine became muted and without the familiar western twilight the day became evening in a matter of twenty minutes. The speed of the change of light added further to the sense of strangeness that James still felt, and the sudden coolness of the air was very welcome. Driving now by headlights the world disappeared from view into a mysterious darkness that could have been hiding anything. As they left the larger towns the traffic thinned out and the driver hummed contentedly to himself as they bumped along the road.

Everyone's attention moved inside the bus where they began to get a feel for one another's personalities. James had already decided who he wanted to get to know more of and who he had already decided to avoid. Heather in particular was beginning to irritate him, she seemed to have a negative perspective on almost everything that could be said and James knew he would be dodging her as much as possible over the next two weeks.

They pulled off the main road and followed a bumpy dirt track into a small village where few lights seemed to be burning. It was difficult to form much of an impression of the place in the dark except that the people there were poor. The absence of vehicles outside the homes and the number of pot holes that tested the bus's suspension made it clear there wasn't much money around. The bus swerved through the entrance in a high fence and came to a stop between two single-storey buildings. With a grin of pride the driver twisted to look at his passengers, "We have made it safely," he said.

"Do we tip him?" Daniel said to James.

"I'm not sure, is he staying with us the whole trip? So shouldn't we tip him at the end?"

The driver solved their problem, he leapt out of his seat and trotted off to one of the buildings. His passengers pulled their luggage from the bus and felt the cold night air which was such a contrast to the day. "There are two beds per room," Rachel said, "there will be enough space for some of us to have a room to ourselves tonight, but more people will arrive tomorrow. So choose how you want to settle in, and stick to the bottled water. Don't be tempted to drink the tap water or even wash your teeth with it."

The rooms were plain but spacious, metal rails ran along one wall for hanging clothing, each room had two beds, and in the light of the low-powered bulb that hung from the middle of the ceiling everything looked clean and comfortable. Daniel looked at James nervously, "Shall we bunk together?"

"Yea, of course, you don't snore though do you?" James laughed.

"I don't think so," Daniel said, lifting his case onto one of the beds. "Do you fancy having a walk, we could take a quick look at the place?"

"Yea, I'm up for that, shall we leave the rest of them to it?"

Daniel nodded, "It might be easier if there's just the two of us."

The large wooden gates had been closed and James had to force an old iron lock to open them. Once outside the compound they found themselves in narrow streets where no one seemed surprised to bump into them. A few groups of men sat near open doorways and as James and Daniel passed they were greeted with friendly shouts in broken English. The sense of poverty only intensified as they explored, the sanitation system consisted of a small channel that ran alongside the road, and in the end they headed back to their room not wanting to feel like voyeurs.

James took out a few clothes and hung them up, but left most of his possessions in his case. He stripped down to his shorts and lay down on the low wooden bed. He could smell the cheap washing powder in the sheets as he lay listening to the calls of unknown animals in the Indian night. After so many hours of travelling his mind struggled to switch to the sensation of stillness, his body felt like it was still moving, but despite sleeping on the bus he had no trouble drifting away.

Chapter 21

James woke early. The room was already warm and he lay for a moment taking in the sense of being in a new place. Somewhere far off there were Indian voices shouting to one another, and the rhythm of their unfamiliar language confirmed he really was so far from home. He swung his legs over the side of the bed and rubbed his hands over his face. Daniel was already up and about and his bed was left neatly made. James retrieved his toiletries from his case and found a bottle half full of water. He followed the narrow corridor outside their rooms and found the washrooms at the end of the building, One of the women had left some of her things on a sink and James wondered how it would work out sharing mixed bathrooms. He washed and shaved and caught himself looking back from the mirror; it was exciting to see himself in such a foreign place.

Back in their room he returned to find Daniel sitting on his bed putting on sandals. "It's too hot for anything else," he said. "How did you sleep?"

"Like a baby," James said, pulling out his own sandals, "what's first on the agenda?"

"Breakfast is in ten minutes, then the guys who run the place are introducing themselves. Other than that I don't know."

They crossed the yard together and went into the other main building. It consisted of a large hall with windows along every wall that allowed the sun to fill it with light. There were a few tables to one side where most of the group were sitting. Rachel was deep in conversation with a young barefooted Indian man who was dressed in cotton shirt and trousers that reminded James of pyjamas.

From a door to their right an Indian woman appeared with a large tray of plates. "Looks like we timed that well," Daniel said as they sat at one of the tables. The woman placed a tray near them, it was filled with dishes of rice and green leafy vegetables, and in the centre of the food was a bowl of something that looked like curry. Everyone stared at the food for a moment, not sure what the etiquette would be, but when the man who had been talking to Rachel reached out and folded some rice into one of the leaves everyone took it as their cue to start eating. Jugs of water were brought out and though it was slightly warm James swallowed two glasses before trying breakfast. The unknown dish turned out to be very spicy but it gave some much-needed flavour to the rice. Conversation was friendly and it was clear that everyone was pleased to be there.

When they had finished eating the Indian man stood up and everyone fell quiet. "Good morning, and welcome to Rajasthan. My name is Aditya, but please, call me Adi. We are expecting the other pilgrims to arrive around mid-day, so I am saving the full introduction to then. I will explain the pattern of life here and what you can expect over the next two weeks. That is all I really want to say until then, but please, ladies, when you are walking around town please be sensitive to local customs. It is not seen as appropriate for women to walk unaccompanied, so please take one of the gentleman with you." He glanced at his watch, "I propose we meet back here in four hours when we can start things properly. Is there anything anyone wants to ask?" There was a moment's silence and he concluded with "I will see you then." He bent to say something to Rachel and then quickly walked away.

"Do you fancy seeing the place in the daylight?" Daniel asked James.

"Yea, that would be good," and James looked around at the others at the table, "anyone else fancy it?"

"It might be good to go out in small groups," said Dereck.

James was relieved to hear him say it, he didn't really want to traipse round in a big gang. "That sounds sensible," he said.

The Indian woman who had brought out the food collected the plates and nodded indifferently as people thanked her. Daniel and James were the first to leave, at the gate they decided to head in the opposite direction to their first exploration, and walked down the road the mini bus had brought them along. They quickly realised how different parts of the town could be within a short distance. The impression they had formed the previous night of poor mud buildings with tin rooves was replaced as they came out onto a wide road that looked similar to the chaos of New Delhi. The road was bordered by stalls cooking and selling food as well as bags of spices, rice, meats, and everything from rolls of cloth to engine parts. The traffic was loud and busy and James realised they were in a far more exciting place than he had first imagined. As they sauntered through the crowd James saw a group of men carrying towards them what looked like a statue. He couldn't make it out properly and stood studying it as it went by. As it passed within a few feet of him he realised it was a funeral brier and the statue was a corpse. He looked away, embarrassed to have stood staring, wondering what kind of impression his rudeness could have made.

The smells from the stalls was rich with spices and the two men agreed to come back when they were hungry. They tried to signal to the stall holders that they intended to return as they were loudly invited to spend their money there. As they reached a junction James looked across at a half built three story construction surrounded by dangerous looking scaffolding. Along the planks and bars workmen hanging without harnesses juggled with stacks of bricks as the crowds walked beneath them. "Not a lot of health and safety regulation going on there," laughed Daniel.

They turned the corner to meet a cow casually walking towards them. Coloured powders had been sprinkled over its back and they watched as it stopped and began to cough. It wheezed and shook its head until it threw up on the footpath. The smell of food was now replaced with the smell of garbage that was piled up against one of the buildings. No one else seemed to notice but James and Daniel decided to cross the road to get away from it. As they stepped out from between the stalls they realised they couldn't understand the traffic system. Whichever way they looked there were vehicles and motorcycles coming towards them and they had to wait before an opportunity to cross safely presented itself. They dashed between the last of the cars and laughed with relief to still be alive as they made it to the other curb.

All around them brown faces looked back full of curiosity, and beggars approached with outstretched hands in the hope of a few rupees. Women in every conceivable colour of sari looked away as the men admired their beauty, and old men shouted unfathomable instructions to the boys in their charge. Eventually Daniel pointed to a set of tables and stools at the side of the road where a woman was serving drinks. Her English was good and they ordered two teas which she poured out into metal cups. James declined the yellowish milk and sipped at the sweet, hot liquid that cut through the dust and heat of the morning. "This is nothing like anywhere I've ever been before," said Daniel.

"I know, I can't believe this has been going on all my life and I never knew it," James observed.

"Last night I was a bit disappointed when we went out, I thought we were going to have trouble filling our time."

James laughed, "I don't think they're going to leave us to our own devices too much, Rachel was saying it gets full on once the sessions start."

"I don't mind that," Daniel said, "but you know what I mean."

"Yea, I do, this is great. If I wasn't so worried about looking like a tourist I'd be taking a million pictures."

"Does it matter?"

"What?"

"Does it matter what you look like?" Daniel asked. "If you want some photos, just take them. Does taking them make you more of a tourist than we already are? It's just our perception of what tourists do. These people might interpret taking pictures in a completely different way."

"I suppose so, I'm thinking of the cliché of Japanese tourists snapping at everything."

"Yea," Daniel said, "but it's just ideas in your head. It doesn't change or affect anything other than your own feelings."

"Yea, I agree, but I think I'll save the picture taking until nearer the end of the trip."

To prove his point, Daniel took out his 'phone, "Smile," he said, and captured the moment. "See, are we tourists now?" He grinned as he said it and James accepted his point.

Daniel had a pocket full of loose change and paid for their drinks. They continued on along the main road until they realised the stalls were much like each other all through town. Fearful of becoming lost they stuck to the one road and then risked the traffic once more so that they could return to the compound along the opposite side of the street. As they reached the place where the cow had been sick they were disgusted to find a dog now eating the vomit. "I can't believe what a mixture of things this place is," James said, "one minute it's blowing you away and the next it makes you want to throw up."

"That must have been the cow's reaction too," Daniel laughed to himself.

They had only been out of camp for a couple of hours and when they entered the yard they found it silent. "I'm going to find a drink," Daniel said as he walked towards the dining hall. James went back to their room and sat on the floor beside his bed. He did some stretches and then performed a little yoga. It had been two days since he last practiced and it felt strange to have left it so long. As he went through a short routine he felt the energising effect in his body and as he finished he sat back on the floor and crossed his legs. Almost at once he was able to move into a deeply still meditative state and felt a calm wave pass through him. The eye looked into him and he began to see himself as the eye observed. He saw the confusion of feelings he was still harbouring for Rachel, and tried to look deeper into their roots to understand their full meaning. Looking at himself as though from outside he recognised the strength of attraction he felt for her but also a knot of guilt that grew out of his worry that he might be seen to have come on the trip for the wrong reason. His peace was shattered as he remembered what Jacob had said and James opened his eyes in frustration. Without thinking he lightly slapped the side of his head and felt annoyed with himself that he had allowed such concerns to disrupt his meditation. He shook his head as he realised how far he still had to go.

He glanced at his watch and saw that there was only an hour before everyone was meeting. He decided to take a stroll by himself and rubbed some sun cream on his face and pulled on his hat. He wondered where Rachel might be and hoped to find her, but as he approached the gate he had to step aside as a blue mini bus came into the compound. The back doors swung open and a group of about a dozen men and women in their late twenties and early thirties started to climb out. As they called out to each other it was clear they were American, and James hesitated, he wasn't sure whether to go over and greet them, and decided they would want to settle in a little before meeting the English. So he slipped out and sauntered along one of the side streets where children were playing and life looked more familiar to him than in the main part of town.

He walked for about forty-five minutes before coming back to find people already wandering over to the main hall. He went down to the washrooms and quickly freshened up before joining the meeting. Inside the hall the dining tables had been pushed back against the back wall and on the floor were rows of mats. A few people were sitting alone meditating, but most of the groups were standing along the walls introducing themselves. The American voices were louder than everyone else's, and with the noise around them James wondered how anyone could be trying to meditate. He knew he secretly thought they were making a show of meditating to impress everyone but didn't want to acknowledge this to himself. He didn't know them and for all he knew they could be extremely experienced in things he knew nothing about: but still his suspicion persisted.

He looked around for Rachel and saw her talking to two tall American men, one of whom was enthusiastically waving his hands as he explained something. Her hair was tied back which made her look older, and as James looked she glanced across and smiled at him. At the front of the room Aditya gently clapped his hands and the murmur of conversation died away. James noticed that he was still barefooted. "Welcome everyone, please, will you sit." He waved his hand toward the mats and the groups spread out and sat down. James was in the second from back row and could observe Rachel just a few rows in front of him.

"Please note where you are sitting, Aditya said, "and make this your regular place. You have taken your place for a reason, even if you do not yet know what it is. From now on you will not have to think about where you sit, this moment has decided for you. Welcome to our American friends, I am Aditya and I will be leading you through the programme. First let me explain how our time is to be structured. The first five days we will be based here, we will then be making a trip for six days, which I will explain more about later, and then the final full day will be back here." He stood motionless as he spoke, looking out over their heads at the wall behind them so that his gaze fell on no one in particular. "Our days will be divided up between yoga before each meal, twice per day, a lecture will be given each day, and there will be meditation every evening. I will present most of the lectures, but we will also have visitors for some of them. As with your mats, can I ask that the rooms you have taken, you should stay in that place and not swap around. What may seem unimportant or accidental may have a deeper purpose and we cannot know what it is if we deny its resolution. This is part of our learning to observe what the universe is giving us and where it is leading us. But we shall speak more about that in the week." He paused and then the tone of his voice changed, he said "we must ask that you follow certain rules while you are here. Please make sure that mobile 'phones are turned off within the compound. When you enter this hall, can I please ask you to leave your sandals outside. This is not because we are on holy ground, but simply to ensure the floor remains clean so that we can sit here without getting dirty. Alcohol is not permitted in the compound and we ask that no sexual activity takes place here. This is a centre of meditation, we must preserve our focus, but also respect the energy that has been placed here over many years." He smiled and resumed his relaxed tone, "I am sure that if you give yourself completely to what happens here you will learn a great deal and experience many things."

Everyone sat in silence, there was an expectant hush that confirmed how eager the pilgrims were to receive everything the trip had to offer. Aditya finally sat down and crossed his legs. "I will start the week with a short talk about different aspects of meditation. Please understand that I am not claiming any one type is better than another, although I will be leading you in my own chosen form, this does not mean I am critical or reject any other. Our first point is to recognise that every possible option may be embraced for good, and that we must be open to whatever the universe gives us. If we ignore something because we have already rejected it before knowing its truth, then we are closing ourselves off to the infinite possibilities that life brings." He glanced at the audience before him and nodded and smiled as he made eye contact. "I know that many of you are familiar with the idea of the inner self, and I want you to understand that meditation is the means by which we discover our divine self. The deities we focus on become alive to us and enable this discovery to happen. Do not worry if this language is unfamiliar to you, it is natural that some people are more drawn to meditation and others to devotion, I am not proposing one to be higher than the other. Both can involve mental and physical effort, but in devotion it is the heart which is the foundation, while even in spiritual meditation it is the mind which is the foundation. The physical aspects of devotion we often call rituals, and these, like yoga, can serve to immerse the heart in divine love. We will explore both of these this week, so that we taste something of the

155

ecstasy that comes through elevation of the consciousness. This will involve experiencing heightened emotional and spiritual states, but again, do not worry about these, all will be natural to you when we get there. In all of this we will seek to move to Samadhi, this is the condition of overcoming our duality, so that we may know union with our divine self."

As Aditya spoke James tried to remind himself of the advice to look beyond the terminology, to recognise the cultural context from which the teaching came, and so find the reality that was applicable to him. He struggled to conceive of what his divine self might be, but accepted that what was being said contained universal truths that were so much more than the language of Hinduism might suggest.

Aditya said "I must warn you who are beginners that it takes many years of yoga to truly enter a state where true devotion is possible. Please believe me when I say that though you are indeed going to experience realities far beyond those of your ordinary lives, this will be only the first rung on a very tall ladder. Many lifetimes of practising yoga are necessary to achieve the final goal. I am not criticising anyone for being a beginner, we are all on the same path, whatever stage we have reached; these weeks will offer you the chance to climb many rungs in a short time. I am not talking as a scholar, the men of books argue over these things and cannot find common ground. Hindu teachers are divided over the merit of these different paths, but as genuine travellers we come to know the truth of each road and can speak, not as those who study ancient words, but as men who have drunk from the moving waters of reality. We are each living with a delusion, or perhaps I can say an appearance. We live with the belief that we are the centre of the universe because we believe we are supremely individual. We must see beyond this delusion and destroy the idea that we are the seer or the seen: we are not one or the other but all things. This is one way to overcome duality, it enables us to worship the one divine source and simultaneously be that divinity. If you would rather refer to Brahman as supreme consciousness, it does not make any difference, we are not concerned with labels. But for people raised in the west, it is difficult, if not impossible to sustain a clear focus on the formless oneness that is beyond all things. And so we use images, divinities, idols, to help us concentrate and focus. I encourage you to see beyond the outward appearance of these, they are useful, but do not worry if it appears to you like an alien religion. The images are no more than tools, ways to channel our minds down the right paths and escape our mental creations and replace them with finite forms of God."

As Aditya paused, James found his head was swirling with ideas and questions. There was too much for him to understand in a single sitting and he wished he could have time to reflect on what was being taught. It was a relief to him when Aditya said "I have many more things to say, but for now I will answer any questions you have before we finish with a yoga session."

Immediately one of the Americans raised his hand. "Thank you for your instruction so far," he said, "I'm struggling a little with what you've said about overcoming our dualism. My meditation instructor back home has taught me to embrace the separation between my true self and the supreme divinity. He says that we must preserve the distinction in order to see the real opposition in the universe. Please, Aditya, I'm not rejecting what you've said, I just don't know how to relate it to what I've been taught."

Aditya had a broad smile and was nodding enthusiastically. "Please," he said, "what is your name and where are you from?"

"I'm Dave, I'm from Dallas, Texas."

"Please call me Adi, Dave. I understand your question, and there is no contradiction here, so please feel comfortable with what you have been taught and what you are hearing here. It is true that there is a form of meditation that does not seek to transcend the duality I am talking about, but tries to use it as a means of becoming absorbed into the supreme self. Of course there are opposites, there are the highest and the lowest forms of life, there are good and bad actions, there is good and bad karma. All are opposites, If we focus on this then of course, we will say duality is real, it is inevitable. There is a path which attempts to seek truth within these pairs of opposites by understanding the nature of the universe through these bonds. I am not asking you to throw this away, and when you return to Texas you may choose to return to this approach without any problem. But for now I am inviting you to attempt to enter into union without holding on to the perception of distinction by using the different parts of God as a way of dealing with those opposites. The manifestation of the infinite one in distinct forms can enable us to accept these opposites without confusion, whether they be creation and destruction, or birth and death, or good and evil. We will accept that these manifestations are not creations of the mind but actual emanations of the one supreme self. In this way everything we encounter, everything in the universe may become to us a sign of the one God, and so worthy of worship. We may enter a state where our being is in perpetual worship of all things, because we have seen beyond diversity to the oneness within it all." He stopped to gauge Dave's response and said "Does that make sense to you?"

"Thank you Adi, I think so. Are you talking about a form of vishishtadvaita?"

"No, no," Aditya said, "please let me explain to everyone. Vishishtadvaita is a teaching that does indeed

158

maintain that God is one, but permits many names and personal qualities to be attributed to him. I am not limiting the images and idols we will use to this, I am saying we should accept them as forms of parts of God, a reality not just of thought but of existence. We must not struggle with what appears as contradiction to our rational minds. The divine love falls on each of us equally, whatever road we take. Nothing we do can shield us from this love. So we must walk the roads we find our feet placed upon, accept the gifts offered to us and sing to the melody the universe plays for us. We must let go of our pride, which is the root of western man's thinking, always setting himself up as judge of all things. Please, try to humble yourselves, let the universe lead you by the hand. I will speak more on this tomorrow, but now let us calm our minds and bodies and begin to enter the reality that is beyond words." He invited everyone to stand and demonstrated a posture James had never seen before. As he arched his back and stretched out his arms James felt the muscles pulling in completely new ways. Much of the session consisted of a form of yoga many of the pilgrims hadn't encountered and its novelty only added to their sense that Aditya could teach them many things. They practised for no more than thirty minutes and Aditya suggested they take an hour to reflect before dinner. He encouraged them to avoid needless conversation, and before dismissing them he began to chuckle to himself but didn't explain what was amusing him.

James found his sandals and looked to see where Rachel was heading. To his disappointment she had already left and so he walked back to his room. A lot of what he had heard had left him wondering if he was really suited to what was to come. He sat on his bed and tried to understand what it was he was feeling and how he was really responding to what Aditya had said. Daniel caught him deep in thought and hesitated before disrupting him.

James looked up and said "How do you feel about what he said?"

"It sounds positive, I'm not entirely sure what school of thought he's coming from, but the yoga particularly was excellent. How about you?"

"Yea, I found the yoga really useful, I'm just not sure I'm connecting with everything he said," James admitted.

"It's early days, we're in at the deep end now. Even if just one thing stays with you, maybe that's all you need."

James nodded, "Yea, I'm sure you're right." He was impressed by the younger man's thoughts.

"We're going to have to learn a new headspace, it's not gonna happen overnight."

James felt the younger man was right and was glad of his advice. He relaxed a little and stretched out on his bed. Daniel was reading a book and so James closed his eyes and tried not to allow too many thoughts to enter his mind. He felt frustrated at having no opportunity to spend time with Rachel and tried to reassure himself that there were still plenty of days to come. He focussed on the sounds of the birds in the trees outside the compound and rested.

Chapter 22

When James woke he was alone. He checked his watch and realised he was a few minutes late for dinner. He quickly pushed his feet into his sandals and rubbed the sleep from his eyes as he crossed the yard at a trot. Inside the hall he found everyone seated around the tables and no one paid much attention as he found himself a space. To his right was one of the tall American men who was talking very earnestly with an American girl sitting opposite. To James' left was the middle aged English woman who said very little, she was eating with her head down, clearly not wanting to engage in the Americans' conversation. James reached out and lifted some of the curry onto his plate. It looked exactly like the dish that had been served at breakfast except that this time there was more of it with mountains of yellow rice.

The American girl glanced his way and James smiled but couldn't say anything without interrupting her compatriot's monologue. He was explaining a state of mind experienced during a particular form of meditation and delivered his message with all the enthusiasm of a TV evangelist. His American accent only added to the impression and James realised that what he had always mocked about the US Christians he had seen on television wasn't so much to do with their religion as it was their culture and national character. He found it hard to take seriously anything the man was saying, and hoped he wouldn't get drawn into the conversation. To his surprise the English woman turned her head to him and asked "Do you think you'll get much from this trip?"

It struck James that the directness of the question was odd, and he said "I hope so."

"What about today's talk," she continued, "did it put you off?"

"Of course not, what do you mean?" Why would it put me off?"

"Good, I'm glad you're okay with it. I didn't think it should put you off, I just wondered how you coped with it."

James was uncomfortable with the way she was discussing the lecture, he feared it could be overheard and misinterpreted. "Was there a problem for you?" He asked.

"No, nothing. I thought it was everything I wanted to hear. I'm so relieved we're here getting fed meat instead of the milk they fob us off with in England."

"Who?" James said.

"The teachers of yoga and meditation. Unfortunately so few of them know much about what they're teaching. They do a few courses and get their certificate," she emphasised this last word as though it was distasteful to even say, "and then they assume to go out and teach their wisdom. Half of them are still under thirty and don't know what their own lives are about, let alone presume to go advising others on how to find inner peace. It's pride, basic human pride. We all like to be important sometimes, and eastern mysticism is just one way some people feed their ego. I'm tired of it. That's why I was so grateful to get the chance to make another trip out here, this is where the real masters are."

"I'm sure there must be people around you that can help. I mean, back in England, in your group," James said.

"Oh yes, of course, through Munro I've encountered a completely different level of people, that's not what I mean. I'm talking about the ladies who put their advert up in the local sports centre and run a class next door to the aerobics and the slimmers." She seemed to catch herself and recognise how negative she sounded. "I'm sorry," she said, "it sounds awful to put it like that. It's just frustration. I feel for all those people who are seeking the truth and they end up in the hands of some western girl who has moved on from her hippy stage and is now into the deep stuff. They deserve better. We all do. I'm just so glad we're getting the real thing."

"So why did you think I might have been put off?" James said.

"I didn't mean to offend you, it's just that I wondered how someone coming for the first time might react to hearing what Adi was saying. Back home we don't tend to hear our yoga discussed in the context of Hinduism, we pretend it's different. Suddenly being confronted with the truth can be hard for some people."

"No, I took on board what he said about the language. Back home I've been working through some of those ideas for a while."

"Which ones?" She asked.

"You know, about not getting hung up on the images and terminology of Hinduism."

"Do you believe in God, James?"

The question took him by surprise, even Emma had never been so forthright (perhaps out of fear of what the answer might be), and as he stumbled over his answer he realised the American girl was now listening to them. "I'm not a religious person," was his first easy response, and before he could develop his explanation the English woman snapped back at him.

"Religious! What does that mean? I know monks who aren't religious. What does that have to do with God?"

163

James was flustered, he said "I'm not saying they're the same thing. I just meant I don't have any formal ideas or frameworks about God."

She laughed a little, and said "Frameworks! You're losing me a little now. All I'm asking is if you believe in God?"

Having managed to avoid addressing the question with any real honesty James was reluctant to answer. "I'm not sure," he said.

"Well you need to think about it. What do you think Adi was talking about when he used the word divinity? This isn't some kind of metaphor. We're not dealing with fables. You're going to experience something very real over the next two weeks, and unless you're prepared to face up to asking real questions, you'll end up missing a lot of what is offered to you."

The American woman looked concerned, she raised her hand and in a gentle voice said "I don't think we need to brow-beat anyone into anything."

"It's okay," James tried to assure her by lying, "I don't mind the questions." He welcomed her intervention and smiled to show his thanks.

The American man beside him took the opportunity to demonstrate some more of his higher thinking. "Which god? Who god? It's all labels," he said. "We have to move on from the restrictions of language. These words are just sounds we make, but they don't signify any kind of truth beyond which we have experienced. If I say god to a child in Sunday school, it will mean something completely different to what it means to a yogi. And why? Because one of them has experienced the divine."

"I'd be careful about dismissing the experiences of a child," the American woman said. "Wisdom isn't always something gained through time. Maybe children are closer to God in their innocence."

"Well I don't reject that possibility," he said, "but judging from the average American child you meet I doubt very much whether many of them are seeing visions of god before eating their cornflakes."

"That's not their fault," James said, "if you take the typical western adult, or parent, you won't find much evidence for a higher spirituality either. Because they're blinded by the world they've been born into, it's not their fault. You should come to Britain and watch a few hours of the BBC and you'll soon understand what I mean."

"I thought your BBC was meant to be civilised. You'd be amazed if you watched US TV," said the American girl, "utter garbage. I agree, we're training our kids to grow up to be zombies. They get taught empty knowledge that masquerades as wisdom, but when you talk even to the college kids, they mouth slogans. It's like the ability to think has been hammered out of them."

The English woman chipped in "You don't think that's an accident do you? There are dark forces at work in the world, the education system is organised by corrupt people. I don't mean the teachers, they haven't got a clue either; it's the men at the top."

The statement sounded too much like conspiracy theory for any of them to want to respond and they fell into silence as they ate. James glanced across to where Rachel was sitting and she looked back at him. They signalled their hellos and James was relieved that they had made contact. As people began to get up from the table James quickly got to his feet and went over to her. "Hi, how's your day been?" He asked.

"Good, how are you?"

"I'm well, thanks. It's been a good day. Do you fancy a stroll?"

"I'd like that," she said. "The meditation session begins in less than an hour, how about after?"

"Yea, that'll be nice."

"Okay, well, I've got to go and freshen up, I feel like I've got an inch of grime on my face. I'll see you later." She touched his arm as she stood and he walked back across the yard with her. It was already dark and the only sound they could hear was the insects chirping and clicking at each other. As they were about to part Rachel stopped and said "I'm glad you're here." She smiled and he watched her walk away.

In his room James tried to calm his thoughts, he wanted to be in the right frame of mind for the meditation but was struggling to overcome the excitement his infatuation was stirring. He sat on the floor and closed his eyes, he practised his breathing exercises and managed to control himself. He recognised how tired he felt and how much India had impacted on him. He followed his breath and began to feel his consciousness moving with the air. It was now such a familiar sensation that he calmly allowed it to develop until he was moving out from himself and beyond the physical space around him. As he began to move forwards he sensed a presence drawing close to him. He tried to focus on it but it remained just out of sight so that no matter how close he felt it was coming he couldn't hold on to it. Suddenly the shape emerged and before him was the vilest face, its features were deformed and grotesque, and it leered at him with a hateful intent. James was overcome with panic, he pulled back like an animal retreating from fire, and the presence moved with him. The eyes of the thing before him were filled with lust, and James let out a short cry as he slumped forward on the floor of his room. He looked around into the natural shadows and was still afraid. He stood and dashed to the light switch, and only when the dim light of the bulb revealed that he was alone did he begin to come to his senses. He raised his hand before him and watched it tremble and realised he was breathing too quickly. He sat on his bed and gripped his hands together in his lap,

166

forcing them to stop shaking. He looked around the room once more, half-expecting to see something, but all was as it should be. He went down to the washroom and threw water into his face. He felt calmer now and the ordinary objects around him were reassuring. He looked at himself in the mirror but for reasons he didn't understand was afraid to look himself in the eye. He buried his face in his towel and stood like that for a few moments, smelling the familiar chemicals of his washing powder from home. It helped to steady him and once his breathing had returned to normal he went back to his room. He dropped the towel in his case and went out into the yard. A few people were standing around talking outside the hall, and so he walked over near the gate where no one would bother him. He looked up at the stars and didn't recognise the patterns. But the stillness of the night sky looked unshakeable and he was glad of its presence. He began telling himself he had let his imagination run away with him and that he was obviously affected by the unfamiliar environment. After a few minutes he had convinced himself that he was being foolish and that he had just spooked himself in the dark. He noticed people were going into the hall and decided to follow them.

Chapter 23

James found his mat and made himself comfortable. He closed his eyes and ignored the sound of people coming in. No one spoke and Aditya gently clapped his hands to get everyone's attention. James opened his eyes to find Aditya was holding a small statue of a figure he didn't recognise. One of the women who served dinner carried out a wooden stand and Aditya placed the statue on it so that it was about a foot higher than the pilgrims' heads.

"This is Vishnu, please don't be alarmed by his presence. We believe he protects and sustains us, he is the source of our being, and while we are meditating tonight I have brought him here to watch over us. I am not asking that you believe in him, I am not trying to convert you to Hinduism." He chuckled to reassure them, "He is here to protect us, but those of you who do not believe, I suggest you see him as a symbol of goodness, an image of your safety and protection. Our meditation this evening will help us experience this protective power, it will give us the security we need for everything that we will do over the next two weeks. So, if you are not familiar with Vishnu, look on him as a sign that you are safe, and that the energy of the universe is directing its positivity to you as you look upon him."

James studied the statue, he found it hard to imagine it as anything meaningful and dismissed it as nothing that was going to help him. Instead he tried to concentrate on his breathing in his usual manner and as Aditya's spoke tried to use his words as a guide.

"Lord Vishnu has come to each of you to charge you with energy," Aditya said, "open your heart to receive this power. Let the creative energy fill you so that anything negative within you is overcome."

James interpreted the directions as a means to connect with the energies he had already experienced at home and was able to move along the path that Aditya was describing. The session passed quickly and when they were instructed to open their eyes there was a deep peace in the room that was penetrated by a sense of purpose. The silence was more than an absence of sound, and James began to understand the sense of things beyond his usual rational thoughts. He was experienced enough not to allow his mind to try to interpret it, and so he simply accepted the sensations for what they were.

In a soft voice Aditya said "Take this energy with you as you leave. Let this moment shape your coming hours and feel yourself moving on along the road you have chosen."

Rachel turned as she stood, and as she looked at James there was a light in her eyes that reached out to him. He followed her to the many sandals neatly laid out in the yard and as he found his and buckled them to his feet he was aware of the whispered voices as everyone tried to honour the stillness that they had shared. Rachel came over to him and said "Shall we go for that walk?"

"Yea," James said, "I just need to grab a bottle of water."

Three minutes later he was back and offered her a bottle. "Which way do you want to go?" He said.

"I don't want to be around the main street," Rachel said, "I don't want to lose this." She waved her hand from her head to her chest, and he knew what she meant.

"Me and Daniel went up the little streets last night, do you fancy it?"

"Okay," Rachel said, "I know a nice place we can go."

They strolled through the gate and into the shadows of the little backstreets. The dim light from some of the windows was enough to navigate by, and they felt safe in the quiet of the night.

"How have you been today?" Rachel asked.

"It's been a good start, I'm happy to be here."

"Every time I come I wish I didn't have to leave. There's something about India that takes hold of me. Even my own face looks different in the mirror."

"I know what you mean," James agreed, "the light is different, the air is different, it's impossible not to be changed by it all."

"It's more than that, I find myself recharged by the energy, the spiritual energy; it's like plugging into the mains after relying on batteries." She smiled at the image, and started turning her head as she assessed the choice of streets ahead. "I think it's this way," she said pointing.

They walked on for about twenty minutes, and as they progressed the number of houses decreased until the road emerged from the town and snaked ahead of them into the pitch darkness. James began to feel nervous, "Are you sure you know where this is?" He said.

"Yes, don't worry, I know exactly where we are." She led him a little further until she saw a dirt track disappearing to the left. "This is it, not far now." They were surrounded by tall trees which climbed high above them, their upper branches seeming to touch the stars, forming a web of silhouettes.

"What about snakes?" James whispered.

Rachel laughed, "Stop worrying. I'll protect you from the snakes if you guard me from the robbers."

He glanced her way to be sure she was joking and was happy to see her grinning back at him. She slipped her arm through his and guided him into the shadows. They stepped out from the thick bushes and before them was the shining surface of a pond reflecting back the lights of the sky. James came to a stop and looked across the water, the moonlight lit up the trees opposite; their branches seeming to reach down into the pond in a gesture of devotion.

"This is amazing," he said, "beautiful."

"I knew you'd like it."

As they stood in silence for a moment, Rachel still had her arm looped through his and the small physical contact was everything to him. But even now he wasn't sure how to interpret it, and as they stood motionless he had to overcome the urge to embrace her. Being here alone with him seemed such an act of trust, and he knew how disastrous it would be if he had misinterpreted it all. He tried to find some way of bringing her attention to their being together and said "Thank you for bringing me here."

"I am happy to be here," she said. "I wouldn't come alone, you have nothing to thank me for. At night it is one of my favourite places on earth. It's such a humble little pond, but it has all the beauty of the universe captured in its details. It helps me understand how extraordinary human beings are."

He looked at her quizzically, unsure of her point.

"It reminds me of how close to divinity every person truly is. When we see the poorest, simple beggar on the streets, if we look at them in the right way we can glimpse God. Even when people are cruel and unkind, they cannot destroy their capacity for union with the divine, it's an astonishing mystery. And when people strive to fulfil this purpose in themselves, something magnificent happens and the whole universe is changed. When we draw close to divinity we make God more manifest in the universe. What an honour to be granted this privilege, and what a responsibility we have when we come to realise it."

She pulled away from him and knelt close to the water's edge. As she stared into the impenetrable blackness she looked tiny to him, like a little girl. She dropped a stone into the water and the reflection of the stars wobbled as the little waves grew out from the impact. Without looking back at him she said "Look at the ripples, this is divinity pouring out from the seeker into the lives of everyone around them." She stared into the water a little longer and said "Being here now is very special, I will remember this for the rest of my life." She stood and as she looked up at him the moonlight caught her face and her eyes looked as dark as the water. She stepped forwards and slipped her arms around him and pressed the side of her head into his chest. He held her properly for the first time, her small frame felt fragile in his arms. Her hair was filled with the scent of oils, and James finally gave himself completely to the feelings of desire for her. After a few seconds she released him and began walking back towards the trees and without hesitation he caught up with her. Once more she slipped her arm through his and he felt the warmth of her beside him.

"How did you find this place?" He asked.

"A group of us came with Munro last time I was here. He flew in for a few days and introduced us to the area."

They followed the dirt track into town and now there were less lights in the windows. The sounds of muffled Indian voices escaped through open windows and every so often a television was blaring its messages into the little huts. The air was now very cold and Rachel pulled in tighter to James' side and by the time they reached the gate of the compound James had put his arm around her shoulders to keep her warm. Before they entered Rachel pulled away and stopped walking. "What is it?" He said.

She reached out her hand and slipped her fingers through his, and without a word kissed his cheek. "We will spend some time together tomorrow," she said, and

172

then entered the compound. James followed, wanting to speak further, but at the entrance to their sleeping quarters she simply waved and was gone. He stood staring at the door for a moment, elated but unclear about how she had left him. Near the other building a mixed group of Americans and English had brought out some of the dining chairs and were sitting in a circle. From where he stood James could make out a little of what they were saying and decided it sounded like they were repeating their most impressive lines from the various books they'd read. He walked up to the other end of the building and into the washrooms. Someone was taking a shower in the little cubicle and there was nothing on display on the sink to indicate whether it was a man or a woman. Not wanting to be there if a female appeared half-dressed James quickly washed and left.

Daniel was already sleeping as James entered and he quietly undressed and got into bed. He repeatedly played the evening over in his mind, remembering the sensation of her touch and kiss. All thoughts of the lecture and meditation session were now forgotten as his every thought led back to Rachel. He rebuked himself for not having kissed her at the pond, and tried to imagine how she would have reacted. He was confident she would have accepted him, but even now there was doubt and he pictured her angrily telling him he had got it all wrong. He lay in the darkness staring up at the ceiling, listening to the sound of Daniel's breathing.

Chapter 24

Fresh from his shower James stood in the yard, his face tilted to the sun. The morning heat on his skin felt like a lifetime dose and he could immediately feel the slight burning sensation in his cheeks which wasn't unpleasant. As he entered the hall he found sitting alone at one of the tables Aditya who looked and smiled at him. James poured a coffee from the pot kept on a small side table and joined the Indian.

"Good morning to you," Aditya said in a friendly voice.

"Hello, I'm James." He was unsure whether to offer his hand and in the end just took the seat opposite him.

"You are English, I know, I can hear your accent."

"Yes, from Sheffield."

"I did not know there was a meditation group in Sheffield."

"No, I live in Birmingham now, but I'm from Sheffield originally."

"Ah yes, western people move around so much today. Do you still live near your family?"

"No," James admitted, "but it's not a long drive to visit them."

"What is your impression of my country James?"

"It's very beautiful, and hot."

Aditya laughed, "Yes, I expect you are used to more rain in Sheffield."

"Adi, you said in your talk that we are going on a trip. Can you tell me where to?"

"Yes, I am going to explain this to everyone, we are visiting a centre in the hills about eighty miles from here."

"What is there that we're going to see?"

"It's not a what, but a who," Aditya said. "We're going to be taught by Bhakti Charandas, it is worth travelling many more miles than this to hear him. He is my guru, and everything that I teach comes from him. We will stay with him and learn a great deal."

James had read the word guru many times in the books he had been studying, and the thought of meeting one in the flesh was an exciting prospect. "Who is he?" He asked.

"Bhakti Charandas is a great man, people travel from all around the world for just a few minutes with him. We are being given so much time with him because of Mr. Munro. I don't want to say too much about him because you will learn everything you need to know when you meet him. It is better that reality paint its own picture rather than my words which might mislead you. Let me assure you, it will be worth the little bus ride."

A few others were drifting in and bringing their coffees to the table and Aditya began to address what he was saying to the whole group. "I have been a disciple of Bhakti Charandas for nine years. I made a vow of obedience to him two years ago and my life has been full of blessings since then. He is a living saint, when I look at him I see God, I hear God in his voice, I receive God through his teachings. You will understand very shortly. He lives as a renunciant; earthly attachment has no hold of him"

More people began to arrive and breakfast dishes were brought out: once more containing the green leaves and rice with a little curry. The table where James sat quickly filled up as the pilgrims hoped to hear something from

175

Aditya and when Rachel arrived she found a place at the other table. She had her back to James and hadn't appeared to see him as she came in. James noticed the shape of her shoulders through the thin cotton blouse she was wearing and the way her hair hung down her back. As much as he wanted to learn from Aditya he was already looking forward to the time when he could be alone with her again.

As they ate breakfast an American woman in her early thirties who James hadn't spoken to before introduced herself as Jemima. She was keen to tell him all about the part of Texas she came from and before he had said anything about himself James felt he knew most of her life story. Being more a natural listener than a speaker he didn't mind, it took the pressure off him, and besides, he enjoyed the sound of her accent which was still novel to him.

When the meal was over people started moving to their mats without being asked and Aditya gave instructions to one of the Indian women. She appeared a few moments later with another statue which was placed on the little table with the first one. Its blue face was contorted to stretch out its tongue and its eyes were wild and bulging. Aditya said nothing to explain it, but simply gave two light claps and everyone fell silent. "Good morning to you, I hope you slept well. If you ate too much breakfast you may find sitting in one position becomes difficult, so please stay relaxed and adjust yourself so you can stay focussed. This morning I am going to talk to you about good and evil." He looked around to see if there was any response in anyone's face, and seemed satisfied that no one was troubled by the topic. "If I use the words good and evil, it will be so easy for you to misunderstand what I mean, so we must be careful about what the words bring to our minds. You have travelled here from lands where good and evil are portrayed as battling forces, your whole interpretation of life and people and history has been coloured by what you think good and evil are. It is important that we throw off these shackles and free our minds. This kind of dualism is so destructive and prevents us from discovering the fullness of who we are. Since we are seeking the divine within ourselves, we must accept that what we may once have seen as good and evil are in fact part of the same divine being. We have spoken about how God is reflected in every human being, well we must move our thinking on to understand that God is reflected in a worldly, materialistic man just as he is in a saint. There is nothing we can do to destroy the reflection of God in us, even the gross, selfish man reflects part of God's nature. You may ask yourself then, why should we struggle? If God is reflected in me whatever I do, why don't I live to satisfy my every desire, a life of pleasure? The answer is that from the holy man the whole world may come to learn the purest vision of God, our essential nature can be satisfied because God makes himself known to each of us and through each of us according the degree of our purity. Therefore, a holy man may see God in the worst criminal, but the criminal may not see God even in a saint."

Aditya paused to take a sip of water from a small cup at his side, his movements were controlled and deliberate. He placed the cup back on the floor and without a word studied each of the people before him. His eyes moved slowly from person to person, and as his eyes rested on him James felt a wave of energy pressing against his chest. As Aditya moved his attention to the next person James felt the sensation end, and as he looked at others in the room he realised from their smiles that a few of them had experienced the same phenomenon.

Eventually Aditya said "I have not judged any of you, but amongst us there are different levels of capacity to function in the realm of divine energies. We are going to divide into smaller groups for the meditation in the evenings, please do not fall into turmoil by trying to figure out which group is which, this is ego. Please will you close your eyes, I will walk amongst you." Everyone did as he instructed, a few bowed their heads, and Aditya walked to the back of the room. He then began passing between the lines, and as he walked behind him James felt him lightly touch the top of his head. Once he reached the front of the group he said "Please, open your eyes again. Those of you who felt me touch your head will meet in the room through there." He pointed towards one of the doors. "The other group will meet here in this room. This is so that we can all move at the pace best suited to us."

Realising they were to be divided James began worrying that he and Rachel would be separated, especially as she was so much more experienced than he was. He feared that when they visited the guru the two groups might be engaged with different activities and immediately his mood began to darken. James paid little attention to most of what Aditya went on to say, his emotions were absorbing his attention and he gained nothing from the session.

After the talk James stood in the sun waiting for Rachel. She was clearly looking for him as she emerged from the doorway and their eyes locked on each other. She found her sandals and as she came up to him said "Did he touch your head?"

"Yea, what about you?"

"Yes," she smiled, "I'm glad he saw in you what I see."

Pride was stirred in him and he tried to conceal it by saying "I'm lucky to be in your group."

"Do you want to go into town with me? I want to buy a sari."

"Yea, I'd love to," James said, "let me grab my sunglasses." He went back to his room and took out some money and as he was about to leave Daniel entered.

"It's a shame they're dividing us up," Daniel said in a low voice so as not to be overheard.

"Why do you say that?" James was keen to join Rachel but could see he couldn't just walk away.

"I think there's something special about the whole group being together, it creates divisions treating us like this."

"Which group are you in?" James asked.

"I'm in the hall, who knows who'll be leading our meditation while Adi focusses on the others. What about you?"

A little sheepishly James admitted "I'm in the other group. But I wouldn't read too much into it, I think he knows what he's doing, we're not the first group he's had here."

"I know, I'm just disappointed, I suppose I thought I was getting somewhere. You must have made real progress to have been selected after only practicing for such a short time."

James could sense Daniel's resentment and said "We have to trust him. It's easy for us to make judgements that are based on our own feelings, but Adi isn't thinking about egos. It'll work out for the best, I'm sure."

Daniel pulled a face, "I suppose so. Do you fancy coming for a walk?"

"I can't Dan, I've promised to do something. I'll have to go, I'll see you later." As he returned to Rachel he felt guilty at not having invited Daniel along but didn't want to share her company.

"I know a little stall, if it's still there we can get some bargains," Rachel said.

The main street was as busy as ever and Rachel held his hand as they pushed through the crowd. Once more

James was bombarded with sensations, noise, colours, smells, everything became vivid and alien. As they walked they came across a man lying on the floor in a bundle of filthy rags. His leg was bare and they could see a huge open gash that ran along his thigh. A swarm of flies covered the injury as the man lay with his eyes closed as though oblivious to his predicament. A number of people had to step over him as they walked by and no one paid him any attention as he held out his hand for a little change. James found a few coins and dropped them into his palm and the man quickly hid them in his shirt. As he moved his blanket rolled off him and a thick cloud of flies took to the air. As they moved away James said "He'll be dead before the end of the week."

The stall wasn't far and Rachel began lifting lengths of silk and cotton and holding them to the light. The woman stall holder immediately began trying to convince her that every sari in sight was perfect for her but Rachel ignored her sales pitch. She selected a deep blue sari and held it up for James' approval. "What do you think?" She said.

She held it across her chest and James said "Yea, it suits you."

Rachel turned and without any hesitation began bartering with the woman. The woman's voice became agitated and James couldn't tell how genuine their mock aggression really was. In the end a price was agreed and both women looked happy with the deal. The sari was wrapped in a sheet of brown paper and James offered to carry it for her.

They walked on a little further and Rachel persuaded him to taste a sugary treat from one of the stalls. It was far too sweet and he struggled to finish it. She could see his discomfort and laughed, "My mother used to make them when I was little, they always remind me of her."

"Aren't you going to have one?" he asked.

"Oh no, they'll rot your teeth."

"Thanks very much," James pretended to be annoyed and she laughed. She looked completely relaxed and at ease and all he wanted was to be alone with her. "Where shall we head now?"

"There's a little park not far from here, we can sit in the shade for a while if you like."

It was further than Rachel had remembered and when they got there she began to apologise. The grass was dead and the few trees dotted around the little enclosure looked to be heading the same way.

"I think park was a little generous," he said. They found a bench with a little shade and sat watching the wild peacocks strutting along the path.

"That poor man lying on the path," James said.

"The uneducated Hindus believe they have no responsibility for him because they think it must be his karma to suffer that way"

"It's a cruel philosophy."

"No, it's an ignorant interpretation of the teaching. They use karma as an excuse to look away, there are countless Hindu saints who taught that we must show compassion and mercy. Human nature will use anything as a way of being selfish," Rachel explained.

"I don't understand karma at all."

"There are different attitudes, the Buddhists see it as reminding us that every action has a consequence. Hindus believe it is a form of spiritual medicine, a way that the soul learns and grows. Seeing someone suffer like that should be taken as an opportunity to practise kindness, and so earn good karma."

"It sounds a selfish way of looking at things," James said.

"Only when it's described in this way, it is far more complicated and meaningful than I have said. You should ask the guru about it if you get the chance."

"Have you met Charandas?"

"Oh yes, very briefly. David took us to a temple about a hundred miles west of here, Bhakti Charandas was performing a ritual which we attended."

"What did you make of him?"

"He's an astonishing man, you won't be disappointed."

"What sort of things is he going to teach us?"

"I don't know, it depends what he thinks we need. He's very perceptive, David said he can say something which sounds quite ordinary but will meet someone's spiritual needs so completely that it's almost like you've told him your deepest secrets. David couldn't speak highly enough of him."

They fell silent and James said "Last night was special."

Rachel turned to him and in her eyes he could see everything he wanted to know. She slid her hand over his and leaned closer to him and he kissed her gently on the lips. As she opened her eyes he could see the flecks of browns and blacks surrounding her pupils as she looked at him. "We must be careful," she said. "We mustn't break the rules of the pilgrimage."

"We've done nothing wrong, Rachel."

"No, but we must try to hold onto our feelings until we go back to England. This isn't the place for romance. We're here for something else, we have to keep our focus."

At that moment he couldn't have cared less about the rules but was encouraged by her suggestion about what would happen back home and said "I know, I think you're right."

She squeezed his hand, "We will talk about it another time."

Chapter 25

Still feeling invigorated from the afternoon's yoga James walked across to the main hall eager to begin the meditation class. He was one of the first to arrive and was glad not to have to pass anyone who hadn't been selected for the other group. The door had no lock and as he entered the side room he found it small and dimly lit by two candles. A few mats had been arranged in a tight circle and he sat down on the one furthest from the door so that he could see people entering without having to turn around.

From the mat his attention was drawn to a low table on which sat the small statue of Vishnu. Being alone with it felt odd, there was a presence about it that he hadn't detected before. He couldn't be sure what it was he was feeling and was relieved when the door opened and one of the American women from breakfast came in. She smiled, "Hi," she said, "I'm glad I'm not the first."

"No, I got here a few minutes ago, I'm James."

"Carrie," she said as she chose a mat. "There aren't many places set out, I guess this is a select group we're in."

"It looks that way, it'll be interesting to see what he has in mind."

As they were talking Rachel and two of the American men entered. They greeted each other in hushed voices and the two men sat and immediately closed their eyes.

Rachel glanced at James and he read into her look nothing but good things. It was a few minutes more before Aditya appeared, he crossed to the statue and touched his head to the floor before it. James watched as he lit incense sticks which he waved back and forth a few times before placing them into small holes drilled into a stone that sat at the feet of the statue. He turned and sat on the remaining mat in front of the table and looked around at the group. "Welcome to you," he said, "we are going to move at a different pace to the other group and there are some exercises I want us to try which are not for everyone." He spoke in barely more than a whisper which added to the sense of purpose in the room. The scent of the incense quickly filled the space as light clouds drifted in the still air. Around the candle flames James could see the movement of warm currents as they gently lifted the smoke up above them and even before entering the meditation he began to feel himself drifting into an altered state of mind.

"We are going to start by using our imagination," Aditya said. "The power of visualisation can open the door to powers of healing and light." He moved from in front of the statue so that everyone could see it, "Look into the face of Vishnu. Accept the power that he gives, the protective power of the universe. See the energy coming forth and surrounding you, accept it, allow it to enter you."

As James followed the directions he began to imagine the light moving towards him, in his mind he could see it clearly as it reached out and held him. He closed his eyes and the vision continued, he felt the comfort of its touch and as he began to trust its intention he accepted it into his body. His chest was warmed and the ends of his fingers began to tingle as though with pins and needles. Aditya continued to guide them, and as he led them deeper into the experience James felt a tugging sensation,

184

as though he was being encouraged to move out from his body. Initially he resisted but the warmth that now spread out into his whole body was so assuring that he gave himself to the movement and felt himself lifting out from the physical weight of his chest. For the briefest moment he was in the room but not held by it and as he continued to rise he looked down and could see himself sitting on the mat. It struck him how strange he looked from this angle and as he looked around he felt Aditya's attention on him. The sight of the room was too startling and he snapped back into himself and opened his eyes. Aditya was still staring at him and grinning. "Welcome back," he said.

"What happened, how did you know?" James asked.

"Don't worry, you are safe, we will talk about that another time. You are back now."

The others looked at James, unsure what was happening, but Aditya didn't allow them to ask anything. He began the next part of his instruction and they focussed once more on his words. Even James was able to move on, he resumed his meditation and followed the guidance they were given.

After forty minutes Aditya brought the session to an end and they silently sat listening to the group leaving the hall. Once it was completely quiet Aditya stood and left and the group followed him out. As they found their sandals Carrie asked him "What happened?"

James was reluctant to talk too much about it and said "I'm not completely sure. But whatever it was Adi could see it. If he hadn't have said what he did I might have thought I was imagining it."

"Imagining what?"

"I left my body, just for a little while, I was out of my body."

"That's amazing," she said. "What did it feel like?"

185

"I'm not sure, I need to reflect on it." He looked at her thoughtfully.

"I understand, I'm real happy for you James, it makes me think we're getting somewhere."

Rachel was already walking back to her room and James decided to take some time to think it through. A few people from the other group were standing around talking in the yard and amongst them was Daniel who made a small gesture of a wave to him as he went past. In the room James kicked off his sandals and stretched out on the bed. His experience left him excited, he wanted to talk to Rachel about it; he had an endless stream of questions to ask, and had to force himself to be patient. He tried to remember exactly what he had felt as it happened, he didn't want a single detail to be forgotten. Everything that he had been through up to this point had brought strong feelings, but this was different, this was something objective and real that was the kind of proof he needed that it wasn't all imaginary. He felt a tremendous gratitude for what he had been given, and he decided that if nothing else came from the trip, this would be enough.

He was lying in this state when Daniel returned. James considered pretending to be asleep to avoid conversation but instead turned his head and said "How was your evening?"

Daniel looked serious, "It was good. I wished I hadn't allowed myself to get envious of you in the other group. It was stupid, just my ego getting away with me. Tonight's session was excellent, more than I could have hoped for."

"I'm really glad to hear that," James said. He admired Daniel's honesty and sensed he could trust him but he was still reluctant to say too much about what had happened.

"How was your group?" Daniel said.

"Yea, really good," was all he would say.

"A few of us are heading out for a walk, do you want to come?"

"No, thanks Dan, I'm tired. I think I'm gonna get an early night."

"No worries," Daniel said. He changed his shirt and took out a bottle of water from his bag. "I'll be as quiet as I can when I get back."

Once he was alone James began thinking through the events of the day. Rachel was the first thing he remembered but then he quickly focussed once more on the meditation and what had happened. He was still lying on top of his blanket and wearing his shirt when he drifted into sleep.

The room was pitch black when James woke. He looked up into the ceiling and realised he couldn't move. His entire body was paralysed, and he began to panic. As he struggled to move he became aware of a presence at the foot of his bed. He couldn't lift his head to see properly but could sense something utterly evil moving toward him. It came to the very edge of his bed and suddenly grabbed him by the ankles. Unable to scream James was overcome with terror, fearing what would happen next. And then he was released, the grip on his ankles and the presence itself was gone and he had control of his body. He sat up and peered into the shadows, still shaking in fear. He could hear Daniel sleeping and not wanting to wake him ran to the door. He emerged into the moonlight and looked around at the buildings to check that he was alone. Every shape and shadow was now threatening, the whole world around him looked menacing, and there was no where he could run. Then he remembered Rachel and knew he couldn't find the comfort he needed from anyone but her. He went back into the building and jogged to her room. He didn't want to alert anyone else to himself and so instead of knocking he opened the door slightly and called into the gloom "Rachel! Rachel!"

Instead of the response he hoped for Heather called out "What is it? What are you doing?"

"I need to speak to Rachel, I'm sorry."

"It's nearly half three, what are you doing?" Heather's voice was loud and irritated.

From inside the room James heard movement and then Rachel's face appeared from the shadows. "What is it James? What's wrong?"

"Rachel, please, I need to talk to you, please."

"Okay, let me get my jacket." She disappeared for a moment and James stepped away from her door and leaned back against the wall. She reappeared pushing her fingers through her hair. "What's wrong?"

"Come outside Rachel, I don't want anyone hearing me." She followed him into the yard and he threw his arms around her. "Rachel, I'm so scared, please, hold me, I don't know what to do."

"You're shaking, what's happened?"

"There was something in my room, I couldn't move, I didn't know what it was doing to do to me. I felt it hold my legs, it was evil."

"Okay, calm down, let's get a drink. You need to sit down."

He let go of her and she led him to the dining hall. The door was unlocked and Rachel found him a cup and poured some water from one of the jugs there. "Sit down, it's okay now, whatever happened has passed."

"Nothing has frightened me as much in my life, I can't put it into words. My body was rigid, completely paralysed. It could have done anything to me."

"But it didn't, so don't let your fear take over. If grabbing your legs is the worst it could do then there's nothing to worry about."

James began to gather himself, "I'm sorry for getting you up. I couldn't be alone and I didn't know who else to turn to."

She smiled and gripped his hand, "I'm glad you could come to me. You're looking a little calmer now."

"Yea, I feel it, thank you."

"Are you sure it wasn't just a bad dream?"

"No, I was awake, whatever was in the room was real. It wasn't a dream."

She squeezed his hand, "Okay, I believe you. Maybe you should speak to Adi tomorrow, he might know what it means."

As he sipped the water James could feel the fear subsiding and he managed to smile. "I hope Heather isn't too angry about being woken up."

Rachel shook her head, "What does it matter? She'll be asleep by now and tomorrow it won't matter at all to her. Are you sure you're okay?"

"Yes, thank you. I knew you'd help."

She got up from her chair and came over to him and put her arms around him. She pulled his head into her stomach and said "You'll be okay, come on, let's get some sleep."

He walked her back to her room and they silently waved goodnight. Alone in the corridor James forced himself to return to his room and there found Daniel still sleeping. He undressed and slipped under the blanket, trying hard to convince himself that everything was back to normal. But the fear of it happening again persisted and as he looked around from his bed it was all he could do to control his panic.

Chapter 26

Aditya showed neither surprise nor alarm as James described his experience the night before. He let James finish what he had to say as they sat on the mats in the small meditation room. Finally, when he was sure the story was finished he said "Do not worry James. This is nothing new, and no harm will come to you."

"You know what it means then?"

"Oh yes, it is known. Let me first explain that there are certain times when we are on the threshold of sleep, and at that these moments we are on the threshold of far greater things too. We call it Viśvarūpa, this means sacred terror. I can hear in your voice there is still fear, but it is not always so. Sometimes there is a great joy in this experience. There are gurus who deliberately enter this state through techniques used before they sleep, Bhakti Charandas teaches this as a way of entering spiritual ecstasy. You should rejoice James, it is the first sign of your soul coming into union with God."

"But the presence I felt wasn't good Adi, it was terrifying."

"Stop, stop, you are allowing your old head to jump ahead and tell you how things are. Try to separate awareness and interpretation in your mind. Awareness is simply allowing the experience to occur, so that you truly experience whatever is happening. Interpretation is entirely different, and in some ways unnecessary. Bhakti Charandas told me he once entered this condition for three days without waking. When he woke his face was said to shine with a beautiful light that slowly dimmed after a few hours. There is a guru who achieved cosmic consciousness and remained in Viśvarūpa for eight years." Aditya grinned at James, "Yes, I can see your surprise, imagine that, eight years."

"I couldn't stand it for a minute longer than I did Adi, I thought I was going to die."

"You westerners are so worried about death. If only you would do what is possible you need never fear it. You should fear birth more than death."

"Why would anyone deliberately choose to enter into this state? I still don't understand."

"When we enter Viśvarūpa there are many things that can be achieved that are not possible in normal sleep or when we are awake. For example, it is possible for the life energy to become so removed from the limitations of time and space that it may see future events and present them to the unconscious mind. This is how some gurus may see the future, they have learned to read what is written in the hidden parts of the mind, read it as visions of future events."

It was all too much for James to take in. Connecting what Aditya was saying to the experience he had had was difficult, and however much he tried to believe what he was hearing the emotional memory persisted and he knew he never wanted it again. He hid his concerns and nodded, "Thank you Adi, I appreciate your advice."

"There is still a little time before the others come. We must meditate a little." He pulled his legs under him and closed his eyes, and James could see he was quickly entering a meditative state. James relaxed and allowed his attention to follow his breathing and almost immediately he could feel his anxieties lifting from him. He became aware of Aditya's mind, not just the sense of him being in the room, but a closeness of his thoughts and feelings. As his breath led him forwards he began to feel the warm

191

energy from Aditya's chest and he projected his own forward to meet him. The sharing of themselves brought their conscious minds into one another and James imagined he was experiencing the emotions flowing through the other man. There was a calm stillness that seemed to caress him and as he drew deeper into its presence he felt Aditya probing his own hidden thoughts and feelings. The profound intimacy of the experience broke down any reserves James had and he knew the secrets within him were laid bare. He felt utterly exposed but the calm sensation that continued to emanate from Aditya assured him that he was safe. As waves of energy flowed through him James heard Aditya's voice speaking from within himself. "Open, open," the word was soft but insistent, and only when he questioned how this could be happening did he pull back from the experience and find himself sitting once more in front of the little Indian. He opened his eyes and found Aditya looking at him with an expression it was impossible to interpret. Neither man moved, their eyes were locked on each other, and the realisation that he was once more completely alone within himself made the short physical distance between them seem like a chasm.

As though reading his thoughts Aditya said "We are created for union, all life will be reunited in God."

The door opened and Carrie entered. She hesitated before sitting, as though she could tell she was interrupting something, but Aditya smiled at her and said "Welcome little American, we are making progress." She glanced at James who gave her a reassuring smile and as she sat she quickly closed her eyes to escape the need for further interaction. Rachel came in soon after and James was impatient to speak to her. Once the whole group was present Aditya led them through a series of exercises that were similar to those of the previous night, except that this time all but one of the American men failed to experience the sense of rising above his physical body as James had done. The atmosphere in the little room was highly charged, and Aditya's voice continuously pushed them further as he recognised their responses. By the end of the session they were all sharing a feeling of excitement and expectation, a sense that something more was about to happen.

Outside in the yard James approached Rachel and asked "Do you want to go for a walk?"

"No, I can't, I said I'd talk to Carrie. She's having a few problems."

"I'm sorry to hear that, is there anything I can do?"

"No, thank you James, I think she just needs to talk one to one. She'll be alright."

James headed back to his room to read, he was still feeling the effects of a night's broken sleep and didn't really feel up to much. He found Daniel sitting on his bed in thought, "Are you okay?" James asked.

"Oh hi Jim, yea, I've just got a few things on my mind."

"You okay?"

"Yea, thanks." He pressed his face into his hands and leaned forward, resting on his elbows, and with a sigh stood up. "I'm gonna take a walk, I'll catch you later."

"Okay Dan, look after yourself." James watched him leave, he wondered if he should have made more of an effort to give Daniel the chance to speak, but was too tired to play agony aunt. He undressed and pulled his blanket over himself. He reached over for the book of Indian philosophy he was reading but looking at the cover decided he wasn't up to it. He tried to order his thoughts about what Aditya had said and their meditation together. He could feel things building, events were assuming a momentum that left him wondering where it was leading, and it added to his excitement. It wasn't long before his body gave in and he fell to sleep.

Just after three in the morning James woke to see the dark shape at the end of his bed. He tried to scream but his throat was shut and he couldn't make a sound. He tried to move but his body wouldn't respond and in horror he saw the figure climb onto his bed. It moved up his body and James felt its legs either side of his chest as it sat on him. He struggled to breath as the weight of the shape pressed down on him and his lungs were unable to draw in air. The reality of its presence was overwhelming, again he tried and failed to scream as he felt the hatred for him over his face. He struggled to squirm free and still his limbs were frozen and he feared he was going to be smothered to death.

Suddenly it was gone and his body jerked free. James let out an animal groan of terror as he jumped from his bed. "What's happening," Daniel said from the other side of the room, "are you okay?"

"There was something in here Daniel, it attacked me."

"What!" There was a hint of panic in Daniel's voice. "Was it a snake?"

"No, I can't... I can't explain." James rushed from the room and gasped at the night air as he ran out into the yard. The night was cold but all he could feel was relief not to be in the room. His eyes darted from corner to corner of the yard, needing to be sure that he was alone. He knew he couldn't wake Rachel for a second night and dropped to a crouch with his chin pressed against his chest. He held his arms around his head wondering what he should do. The fear still hadn't left him but he began to feel the cold and so went back for his blanket. The room was unwelcoming, the walls seemed to bristle with hostility and as quietly as he could he pulled the door shut behind him as he left. He wrapped the blanket around his shoulders and walked over to the dining hall. Bare footed he went in and pulled a chair out from under one of the tables. He pulled the blanket tight around himself and sat looking towards the door, half-expecting something to charge in. As he began to regain his ability to think properly he tried to convince himself that what had happened was a dream. But no matter how many times he told himself it couldn't have been real, the vivid sense of the thing on his chest returned and he became confused.

He was startled by the sound of an animal in the yard and his eyes fixed on the door. He stared from the shadows for nearly an hour listening for further movements, and only when he was convinced that there was nothing there did he lean forward and rest his head on the table. He pulled some of the blanket to form a make-shift pillow, and with his eyes still open, tried to rest. Above all he wanted the night hours to pass so that he could feel safe in the day. He didn't care how it might look when the others found him like this, his only concern was to make it through the night.

The transition from night to day was as brief as the Indian dusk, and as the sunlight began to pour through the window behind him James felt the temperature of the room rising. Relief flooded through him and he went over to the water jugs and filled a glass. It was still cold from the night and he swallowed it quickly. As he was refilling the glass one of the Indian women who prepared their food came in through the main door. She was surprised to see him and James felt the need to explain himself. "I couldn't sleep, I thought I'd get some air."

"Please put the blanket back on the bed," was all she said before disappearing into the kitchen. James was glad of her indifference, he couldn't face going over what had happened, at least not with anyone who couldn't help him. He considered seeing Aditya again but decided it wouldn't do any good. He couldn't accept that the presence in his room was anything but evil, and the idea that someone might deliberately put themselves through that experience was madness to him. He checked his

195

watch, there were still more than three hours before breakfast, he could hear the Indian woman chopping vegetables and there was some reassurance in the ordinariness of it, a sign that the world was getting on with life as normal. He had to speak to Rachel, and guessed she wouldn't be up for a couple more hours. So he decided to swap the blanket for his jacket and went back to his room. Daniel was still snoring as James found his jacket and left. The gate to the courtyard was unlocked and he followed the road towards the main street. A few stall holders were preparing their goods and James found a woman selling cups of tea. It was strong and bitter and as it cut through to the back of his throat James looked at the cup in his hand as it shook with the tremors in his muscles. He knew it wasn't the cold, his nerves were still responding to the event; he looked up and the little Indian woman said "You not well."

"You might be right," James said before swallowing what was left and giving back the empty cup.

Chapter 27

James skipped both breakfast and the morning lecture. He walked up to the patch of scrub land that Rachel had called a park and sat watching the sights. Even in his condition the reality of India was enough to distract him from his thoughts and the time passed quickly. He needed time to gather himself and decided to avoid the others for a while. He had enough cash on him to take care of food and if he was being honest with himself, it felt good to have time alone without the time table of the pilgrimage. As his plan began to form he realised Rachel would become concerned over his absence and he had to let her know he was okay. He checked his watch and decided to go back and speak to her before the next session started.

When he reached the gate he could see there was no one in the yard and he walked in the shade of the building to the end where her room was. As he passed the bedroom windows he caught snatches of conversations in English and American accents and everything sounded as it should. In the corridor outside Rachel's room he stopped to listen and couldn't hear anything. He tapped a few times but there was no response. He turned the handle and opened the door enough to call through and in a hushed voice said "Rachel! Rachel!" Still there was no response and he leaned his head through the gap to check the room was empty, which it was. He thought for a moment and decided to leave her a note. He went down to his own room and again listened for anyone present. Daniel wasn't around either and so he quickly pulled a sheet of paper from a notepad and scribbled a quick message to reassure her he was alright. He asked her to let Aditya know too, and promised he would explain more that evening. He folded the note and wrote her name in large letters across it and went back to her room. He listened once more and knocked before entering and as quickly as he could left it on the wooden chair next to her bed.

As he was about to leave the door opened and Heather walked in. "What are you doing?" She barked.

"I'm just leaving a note for Rachel." He pointed to the sheet of paper. "There wasn't anyone around so I just popped in to leave it. I'm sorry."

"You shouldn't be in here, this is too much."

"I'm sorry Heather, I didn't want anyone to worry about me, so I thought I'd pop back to leave a note."

"Please leave, I'm not happy about this at all."

"I understand, I'm sorry, I only came in for a minute to leave the note. Do you know where Rachel is?"

"A few people have gone with Adi to visit a temple not far from here."

"Oh I see, I'll go. I really am sorry."

As he walked by her she seemed to be surveying the room to check that nothing had been disturbed and she made a great show of shaking her head. James resented her reaction, however much he knew he was in the wrong, and as he stepped back out into the sunshine he was relieved to be away from her. Without anyone else seeing him he left through the gate and went back to the main street. He stopped at one of the stalls and bought a plate or rice and beans and eagerly filled his stomach despite the flies which competed for every mouth full. Then he found a bench next to a small patch of waste ground from where he could observe the busy street. As he sat he began to remember the fear he had felt in the night and as the memory intensified he began to grow uneasy. He could feel his heartbeat in his chest and took a deep breath to calm himself. Before long it would be evening and he couldn't bear to think of being alone in the dark again. His mind raced looking for a way to prevent it happening, he considered sitting up all night but this was unsustainable. In the end he decided a different room might help, and began figuring out who to speak to about moving. Having a plan gave him a little confidence and he began to feel a little better, even to the point of trying to feel like a tourist. He remembered his conversation with Daniel earlier in the week and couldn't believe how little time had passed since then.

James kept an eye on his watch so that he could catch Rachel before dinner. He decided the best thing would be to wait in the yard so that he didn't have to approach her room again and walked back through the crowded streets. Once at the compound he could see everyone's shoes beside the wall of the hall and within ten minutes people began to emerge. Rachel saw him immediately and with her sandals still in her hand trotted over to him.

"I got your message, what's happened, James?"

"I need to speak to you, can we go somewhere?"

She looked back at everyone coming from the hall and said "Yes, of course, when?"

"Can we go now?"

She frowned and said "Okay, let me put these on." She fiddled with the clasps on her sandals and followed him out into the street. "What's happened? Where have you been?"

"I just took some time to think, I couldn't face anyone."

"Why? Is it connected with what happened the other night?"

"It is, it happened again last night. I need to talk about it."

"Okay," she said, "we can sit on the other side of the compound, there are some stones to sit on, it'll be shady."

They followed the compound wall to an area where a low wall had crumbled leaving rocks and masonry lying around. With the high compound wall behind them it felt secluded enough to talk.

"It was worse last night, something was there again; it was on me."

Rachel shook her head, "What did it do to you?"

"It was on my chest, I couldn't move again. I sat in the hall most of the night, it was terrifying."

"You must speak to Adi, he'll know what to do."

"I don't want to Rachel, I don't think he can help. He told me it wasn't a bad thing, I don't think he really knows what it is."

"What did he say?"

"He thinks it's a positive experience, but I promise, it was evil. It was the most frightening thing I've ever experienced, there was nothing good about it. If he's going to keep telling me otherwise I don't want to hear it. I know what I experienced, do you believe me?"

She looked at her feet, "I believe this is your interpretation of it. But I don't know if it's right to dismiss what Adi is saying. He's had a lot of experience of this kind of thing, I think you should listen to him."

"Please, Rachel, you're not hearing what I'm saying. Whatever was there was full of hate. I could feel it."

She looked at him and her eyes softened, "You can't run away from this. Come back with me and talk to Adi. Whatever you're going through, don't try to deal with it by yourself. You're new to this, you could make mistakes; you need guidance."

He looked back at her, it wasn't what he wanted to hear. "I need to change rooms, who do you think I should speak to?"

"That's not a problem, we can tell everyone you're not well and will be up all night. We can pretend it's to avoid keeping your roommate up. I'll tell everyone you've missed the sessions because you're feeling sick, there'll be nothing but sympathy for you."

He appreciated her help and put his hand on hers. "I'm so glad you're here," he said.

"So will you come back with me now?"

"Okay, if I can get a different room I'll be happier. I think if I try and sleep in the same room tonight it'll happen again. Do you think it's haunted?"

Rachel laughed, "Haunted? Are you serious? Do you think a ghost sat on you?"

Hearing her put it that way made it sound ridiculous and he managed to smile. "I know, I'm being silly. I don't know what to think."

"That's right, which is why you must speak to Adi. Please James, I can't help if you won't listen to my advice."

He nodded, "Okay, I'll see him after the meal. But I'll stay away from everyone else for now."

With relief she said "Good, thank you. I'll speak to a few of the American boys and see what I can do about a room. Craig has the small room next to the showers to himself, he won't mind moving in with Daniel for a couple of nights. I'll see him at dinner. It's going to be fine, don't feel embarrassed about any of this. This won't be the first time someone's felt overwhelmed by what's happening."

Her comment left him fearing she didn't really understand what he'd gone through but he was glad to have spoken with her and let it go. As they stood he embraced her and she squeezed him lightly before stepping back. "We mustn't be seen doing this, it's not appropriate here. If the locals think the visitors are hooking up the centre will get a bad reputation."

"I'm sorry Rachel, I just needed to hold you for a moment."

"Don't worry, I understand. Come on, let's sort a room out for you."

In the yard James hung around in the sunshine while Rachel went off to make arrangements. A few minutes later she returned smiling, "You see, no problem at all. Craig has swapped with you. I told him you've got the belly and need to be close to the toilets. He's getting his things together now."

"Thank you, I'll go and get my stuff."

Daniel was reading and lowered his book as James entered. "Where have you been? I was getting worried about you."

"I've eaten something I shouldn't. I can't keep off the toilet."

"You poor soul, one of the American girls has come down with it too."

"I'm going to swap rooms with Craig until it settles down, so I don't have far to run in the night."

"Don't blame you, do you want a hand with your things?"

"No, don't worry, most of it's still in the case."

As James was stuffing a few clothes into a bag Craig appeared at the door and said "I'm sorry to hear you've been stricken."

"Thank you for swapping, hopefully I'll be over it pretty quick." The American had brought his bedding and so James stripped his bed. "Probably wise if I've got something contagious."

"I doubt it is, but you can't be too careful," Craig said.

James took his things down to other end of the corridor and was relieved to shut the door behind him in the little room. It had a small window at the foot of the bed and was just large enough for a small desk and chair. James dumped his case beside the bed and threw the bedding down before lying back across the bed. The new environment was reassuring and he felt happier being there. It was also more comfortable not having a roommate and the space around him immediately felt private and personal to him.

He heard people chatting as they made their way to dinner and he checked his watch. He would wait forty minutes before trying to find Aditya which would give them enough time before the evening session. The mattress was firmer than the one in the other room and he relaxed properly for the first time that day. It was all he could do to stop himself sleeping as he periodically checked the time.

When he was sure dinner would be over he hung around outside the hall as everyone began to leave. He spotted Aditya talking to one of the American girls at their table and stood a little way off waiting for them to finish. Eventually Aditya looked across at him and brought the conversation to an end. He rose and signalled for James to approach. "We've been worried about you James, come through, we must talk." He led him into the side room and waved his hand indicating he should sit. "What's been happening?" He asked.

"I don't know where to start," James said, "I suppose it's more of the same as before. I had the night terrors again, but this time it was more intense."

"How? What exactly happened?"

James described the events in as much detail as he could remember, and all the time he spoke Aditya studied him carefully, observing every change in his voice and the slightest movement of muscles in his face. When James finished his story Aditya said "This is all good. We have begun to give your conscious mind over to the subconscious."

"I'm sorry Adi, I don't understand how this can be a good thing. It was horrible."

"Your unconscious mind is a source of great power, in order for you to release it you must allow your subconscious mind to dominate your conscious thinking. What is inside you will become your waking experience."

"Please, I'm sorry, I still don't see how experiencing such terror can be good."

"No, no James, please let me explain. You are only feeling such fear because you have not yet disassociated from your emotions. They are continuing to rule you and you are giving them the power over you. Your experience of what happened was determined by your interpretation of it, and this was dominated by your negative emotions."

"But Adi, the presence in that room was evil, I could feel it. That wasn't my interpretation."

"You see, you yourself used the word feel, this is your mistake. Why should you feel anything at that moment, since it was something you didn't understand, why place your feelings as a veil between you and the experience? We can tear sown that barrier and welcome what is on the other side."

James wasn't convinced but wanted to assure Aditya that he was willing to listen. He said "Can you tell me who or what it was that was there?"

"I cannot say for sure who visited you, or even if anything at all outside of yourself was there. This is not my experience, we each find our own path and who knows where we choose to walk? When we begin to spirit walk we may meet different energies and beings, some of them are so far in advance of us that we can hardly see them for what they are." He watched James' reactions and said "Did you come to any harm? Did the things you feared happen? No, of course not, no harm of any kind was done to you except how your fear made you feel. Do you see, James? The only truly negative part of your experience was your emotions."

"What do you mean by spirit walking? Is that when I saw the room from up there?" He lifted his eyes to indicate the space above them.

"There are different forms of this happening. Sometimes our spirit may leave our body, sometimes the power within us may enable us to see other places or from other views. When you began to rise I was with you James, like a mother guiding her new-born child I wasn't going to let any harm come to you."

He smiled and James sensed his care for him. "Thank you Adi, that helps."

"Bhakti Charandas travels in a third way, he is able to move to other places in his body."

"You mean make himself materialise or appear somewhere else?" James said incredulously.

"Oh yes," Aditya chuckled, "why would it be so much more difficult to send the body somewhere than it is to send the spirit? Except of course, unless you do not really believe either is happening."

"I don't know," admitted James, "you might be right. So much of this is new to me, I'm taking some time to adjust."

"Time is running out James, we have one full day here tomorrow and then we will travel to meet him. We must make every preparation for this journey, we must all be as prepared as we can be if we are to receive from him everything that is possible. These sessions are really only to make you ready, everything that we are doing and even your night terrors may make sense once we let Bhakti Charandas prescribe what is needed." He smiled again and there was genuine kindness in his expression, "You are to receive a great blessing, James."

Chapter 28

The rest of the group began to arrive and one of the American men began asking Aditya questions about using images as a focus in meditation. The questions sounded dry and academic and James suspected they were an attempt to impress their teacher more than any genuine desire to learn something. Aditya patiently listened and explained his answers as the American nodded enthusiastically. James had no time for such intellectual games, his whole world was now consumed with understanding what was happening to him and the philosophical niceties of ancient teaching mattered nothing to him.

Rachel smiled as she entered and James tried to convey to her that all was well. She looked relieved and he was glad of her concern. As everyone grew silent Aditya lit incense sticks and waved them before the statues as he always did. This evening he invited a few of the group to join him and together they offered their clouds of sweet smoke to whoever was waiting to receive it. James remained on his mat, he couldn't connect these ceremonial acts with his experiences and stared into empty space lost in his thoughts.

Once Aditya was satisfied that they had made a sufficient offering he took his mat and gave his familiar smile to each of them in turn. "Tonight," he said, "we are going to delve deeper into ourselves and release our spirit to guide us to where we each need to go. None of us will find the same thing happening because we all have different needs. So do not be alarmed if someone experiences something completely different to yourself, this is natural and to be expected. One of the ways we can overcome the resistance of the conscious mind is to focus on a mantra. It does not have to be long, or complicated, or even particularly spiritual, but it must be something that our mind will take and keep as its own. I am going to give each of you a different mantra, it will be personal to you, something you must keep hidden from the world." He got to his feet and knelt beside the American who had asked all the questions, he brought his lips close to his ear and cupping his mouth with his hands he whispered something. The American nodded and Aditya asked him to whisper it back to him in the same way to confirm he had heard it right. Satisfied that he had, Aditya moved on to the next person, once more whispering in his ear. He moved round the group until he came to James. As he came close James could smell a mixture of food spices and incense, Aditya's clothes, hair, everything about him was full of scent. His breath was warm in James' ear as he whispered something in an unknown language. James tried to repeat it back to him but Aditya shook his head and corrected his pronunciation.

"What does it mean?" James asked.

"It is a mantra for positive light," Aditya said, "It will bring you positive energy."

Aditya completed his circuit of the room and paused for a minute while everyone rolled their mantra around in their head trying to get a feel for its rhythm. "We will use these mantras to take us deeper into our journey," his voice was soft and assuring, and the group allowed him to lead them into their session. They each quietly repeated to themselves the words he had given them, trying to ignore the murmurs around them. James quickly fell into a pattern of repetitions that began to follow itself without effort so that soon it was as though the words took on a form beyond sound, he could feel them lifting and pushing him far beyond his conscious thoughts. It was an experience filled with joy and he longed for more. The sensation of pleasure grew and he felt a longing to be consumed by it, to give every part of himself over to it. Time lost all meaning and he found himself entering a state of detachment from all thought and even any sense of himself.

As he went deeper into the experience the whole group were suddenly pulled out of their meditation as the American woman beside Rachel began to laugh uncontrollably. Aditya waved his hands to prevent anyone interfering as the noise grew into a hysterical pitch before slowly subsiding. She opened her eyes and stared back at everyone, still making a slurred sound that came from deep within her. Her face looked manic and disturbed, and James was unsettled as she looked at him. And then, just as suddenly, she said "I'm sorry, I don't know what happened. I just felt so happy, I couldn't stop myself."

"Holy laughter is most welcome," Aditya said, "do not be ashamed of your happiness. What did you all feel? Where did your mantra take you?"

There was hesitation before the other American man said "I felt angry, Adi. It just welled up in me. I was sitting here trying not to let it out."

"This is common," Aditya assured him, "we live lives that so often hurt us. Anger dwells in many people. Do not deny it, even your Jesus got angry in the gospels, it can be a force for great change in the world. What else? Who felt something?"

"I felt jealous of Rachel," the first American man said. "I wasn't angry, but I envied her being able to be here as one of the people, and it grew into jealousy." He turned to her and said "I'm sorry, Rachel."

"I thought it was just the British who always apologise," laughed Aditya, "and here you Americans cannot stop yourselves. Listen to me, there is no reason to say sorry, truth is truth, we must not hide it, whatever form it comes to us."

Rachel threw him a smile to show she wasn't offended and the American raised his palms as a sign that he accepted it. Aditya looked pleased, "Who knows what will bubble up from within? Now that we have lifted the lid we can pour out the contents and refill with whatever we choose. We are not bound by what has gone before, what has been forced on us by circumstance, we can become free as we choose our own paths. We will use our final session tomorrow to push this further, but this is enough for tonight. Go to your beds and let your spirit rest." He stood and made a deep bow to the statues before leaving. The group looked at each other and began to get to their feet, and once they were out in the main hall they began to talk about their experiences. James waited for Rachel and as she came close said "What did you feel?"

"My experience wasn't emotions, I saw something far away."

"What was it?"

"I can't say at the moment, it was a fleeting vision of something. I have seen it before, but never so clearly as tonight." She squeezed his arm, "It was something good, but I can't describe it in words. It will make sense in time."

Outside the building members of the other group were still standing around in the evening light as James' group came out and found their sandals. Rachel turned to James and said "I need to get back, Heather has sunstroke and I think she needs someone to nurse her."

James was disappointed but said "I hope she's on the mend. I'll see you tomorrow."

He went back to his room and as soon as he sat on his bed began repeating his mantra. It soothed him and helped relax his mind. The pleasant sensations began to return and he chased the feelings as far as he could. As he closed his eyes he began to see a swirling spiral and as it turned he felt himself drawn through it. He could still feel the weight of his body pressing on the bed but now he sensed himself simultaneously moving through the spiral. The light around him was almost fluorescent in its brightness and as he felt himself slowing down, the eye appeared before him. He gazed into it as it seemed to look into him. It was now so familiar to him that he barely responded to seeing it, he opened his eyes and brought himself back into the little room. The fears of the previous nights had now left him and he felt secure in this new space. He checked his watch and was surprised how late it was and after visiting the washroom he stripped down to his shorts and climbed into bed. He tried to keep saying his mantra but within a few minutes had fallen asleep.

Around three in the morning he woke to a strange sound above his head. It was like an electrical charge in the air that crackled and popped. He knew immediately that there was something there with him and he tried to take control of his reactions. He wasn't paralysed like before and so started to repeat the mantra to stay calm. As his lips moved he found the pace at which he was reciting the words began to increase, almost as though he were gathering speed as he rolled down a hill. The words began to tumble over one another until they became a jumbled nonsense. But still his lips kept moving and he began to feel his arms and legs shake. Though the presence above him came no nearer it assumed a sense of threat that James tried to resist by forcing his mind to focus on the mantra. Suddenly he stopped and the presence was gone, James sat up and tightly gripped the mattress. There was something moving across the floor from the shadows towards his bed and James instantly realised it was a snake. He went rigid with fear and tried not to make a sound in the hope it would leave him but it continued to crawl towards his bed. As it reached his side of the room it vanished from view and James strained to hear where it went. There was silence and he wondered if it had curled up beneath him. He listened for a little longer and then leapt as far from the bed as he could toward the light switch. As the room erupted into light he pulled open the door and jumped out onto the corridor. He looked back and could see nothing was following him. He waited a moment and then crouched to look into the shadows beneath his bed. There was enough light to see the snake wasn't there and he peered round the door to see where it had gone. There was still no sign of it and slowly he eased back into the room to check his bedding. In one move he grabbed and pulled the blanket to the floor and stamped his foot on every lump he could see. There was no movement and so he lifted the blanket in the air and shook it but still there was no snake. He pulled the bed into the middle of the room and walked round it, checking every possible hiding place. He held his sandal above his head ready to strike at anything that moved. His heart was still beating quickly but as he became convinced that there was nowhere left for the snake to hide he began to relax. He shut the door and sat in the chair, trying to figure out how it could have escaped from the room without being seen. He hadn't seen it clearly enough to try and identify it but the thought of any kind of snake in the room unnerved him.

Lack of sleep was now blurring his vision and he knew he had to rest. Without pushing the bed back into position and with the light still on he climbed in and began to take long, controlled breaths. He could feel the effect on his heart rate and as his body began to relax his mind started to find some peace. He chose not to persist with the mantra and with images of snakes still flashing through his brain he managed to get back to sleep.

Chapter 29

As soon as he woke James felt an odd sensation running through his body. A tingling ran down his arms and legs and there was a soft fluttering in his stomach. He wondered if he was coming down with something and worried that the trip tomorrow might be spoilt. Bright light was already streaming through the window and as he lifted his hand he could feel the warmth of the sun's rays. As he slowly gathered his thoughts he remembered the snake. He looked around for signs of its presence and quickly jumped away from the bed in case it was waiting to strike from beneath him. But he was alone and he felt foolish at allowing his fear to get such a grip on him. He sat back on the bed and closed his eyes and even before he started to recite his mantra the bright spiral appeared in his mind and he felt himself moving into it. He pulled back and opened his eyes. It worried him that he had no control over the experience, and he tried to explain to himself what it could mean. He tried to recall Aditya's advice and as he remembered what he'd said about not allowing his conscious mind to over-interpret what was happening he was able to relax a little and accept whatever might occur.

He washed and dressed and out in the yard met Dereck who looked troubled as he saw him. "Is everything okay?" James asked.

"I don't know, I had a terrible night's sleep. I kept thinking someone was calling my name outside the room.

I went out a few times but there was no one there of course. I haven't had a dream that kept coming back like that before, it was very odd."

"What was the voice like?"

"Hard to say, it was almost a whisper, it just kept calling me by name. I was getting a bit pissed off after a few hours, I shouted for it to shut up and I heard it laugh. I wasn't asleep at that point, it wasn't a dream, James. I heard it as clear as day."

"Do you think someone was messing around?"

"I don't know. It wasn't very funny if they were. But no, not really, it didn't feel like that, it felt strange. The whole thing left me feeling strange."

"Maybe you should speak to Aditya about it," James suggested.

"No, I don't think I will. Now that he's just leading your little group in the evenings I don't feel the same connection with him. And that woman they've got leading our group is a bit crackers." He looked around as he said it, to be sure no one had overheard his comment.

"Why do you say that?" James asked.

"Some of the things she's had us doing are a bit nutty. I came to develop my yoga and meditation, but she's got us doing stuff that's borderline voodoo." Though he was serious, he grinned as he said it.

James laughed at his comment, "Voodoo? What's she been doing?"

"Last night she had us passing different objects around and we had to describe the thoughts or images that came to mind as we handled them. I said I was thinking of a bus and she got all excited and said the watch belonged to her father who's a bus driver. I mean, really James, are they serious? I don't believe in ESP or any of that stuff, what am I supposed to think?"

James was sympathetic but didn't agree. "I've found it really useful being here, my whole way of thinking is

213

changing. I think the yoga was just a stepping stone, there's another world to all this that we're only just discovering."

"I'm pleased for you James, I'm glad it's what you want. Maybe I'm a bit long in the tooth for all this. I feel guilty, Munro has been so generous and I'm not really making the most of it as I should."

"Don't get down on yourself, who knows what you're going to take back with you. We don't always have to second-guess everything. Give it time."

They went into the dining hall where Aditya was holding court with some of the Americans. They hung on his every word and Dereck turned to James and rolled his eyes. It was just what James needed and he laughed at the down to earth attitude Dereck was maintaining even while all of this was going on around them. After breakfast Aditya used the morning lecture time to prepare them for the coming trip, advising them to take anything of value and stock up on bottled water. There were to be no yoga or meditation sessions that day as Aditya had what he called preparations to take care of. A whole free day was welcomed by the group and when Aditya left them people began discussing where they would go and started organising themselves into groups. James approached Rachel, "Would you like to go somewhere today?"

"I'm sorry James, I've promised to take some of the ladies to a temple in town. There is a festival of water and we're going to bathe together."

James had no interest in such pursuits but managed to fake a little enthusiasm. "That'll be amazing," he said, "what time do you think you'll be back?"

"We don't know, it could go on for hours. It depends on how much of a crowd they get."

James hid his disappointment and said he looked forward to hearing about it when they got back. He went

214

to his room and used the absence of a roommate to avoid getting invited on anyone's adventures for the day. He hid away until the building was completely silent and only then emerged into the sunshine. He took a book and pulled a wooden bench into the shade of the dining hall. For the next few hours he sat quietly reading, enjoying the solitude and occasionally looking up from the pages to watch birds swoop down into the courtyard to catch flies. Eventually he lay the book beside him and closed his eyes, and immediately the spiral turned before him and at its centre was the eye. The words of his mantra began to shape his breath and he entered a state of peace that seemed to still the whole universe. As he opened his eyes he sensed himself riding the planet through the darkness of space, his unimportance was a relief from all anxiety, nothing was able to pull him from the calm assurance that beyond existence there was no meaning or unnecessary explanation, the reality of the moment was greater than anything future or past could claim.

As the first groups began to return to the compound James was still sitting on the bench. He waved and smiled as people called out their hellos, but made no effort to join them. His thoughts were now turning to Bhakti Charandas and a deep expectation was growing in him as he understood that all they had done so far was to prepare them for their meeting. Even as he sat there, he knew this man was thinking about them and through his thoughts he somehow was already connecting with them.

Chapter 30

James slid his bag into the back of the minibus and climbed into the claustrophobic heat. He made eye contact with Daniel and felt obliged to sit next to him. The driver swung the doors shut behind them and they sat looking through the windows at the Americans who were arguing as politely as they could about who was getting the front seats. Eventually an agreement was reached and the second minibus driver climbed in and started up the engine. The compound had been their base for just one week but as they drove away it felt as though they were setting out from home on a new adventure.

"I will point out all places of interest," the driver announced as they pulled out into the mayhem of morning traffic. James smiled to himself and watched the people on the street as they continued with their everyday lives. It seemed impossible that long after the group had returned to England these same Indian scenes would continue. The driver cursed at someone pulling a cart down the road and around them motorcycles swerved from every direction as though their riders had never heard of death.

As they left the outskirts of town they spotted hill forts, fields of crops and marigolds growing everywhere. The road was pitted with every size of pot hole and Daniel said "The driver doesn't need a map, he can navigate using the bumps in the road as a system of brail."

"It'll rattle your teeth loose," James agreed.

Even after a week in the country James was transfixed by the colours and strangeness of it all. Now that they were travelling together as a large group they felt like tourists again and they were aware of the locals studying them as they passed. After a couple of hours the driver pulled over behind the other bus and invited everyone to stretch their legs. It struck a few of them as an unnecessary stop but no one complained. Rachel was standing at the back of the bus waiting for James and said "No matter how long or short the journey is in India, you better allow for more time than you think."

As they strolled along the road James asked "How much longer do you think it will be?"

"I think they were a little ambitious, it'll be at least another three hours," she said.

They reached a low bridge and leaned over to watch a small stream trickling along a very dry river bed. As they watched the birds flitting from tree to tree a battered old Fiat pulled up behind them. Two young men jumped out and shouted to them as they approached. James stiffened nervously but then saw the big smiles and relaxed. "What's this?" He said.

"You are American?" One of the little men asked.

"No, British. From England."

"Ah yes, please, a photograph?" One of the Indian men offered Rachel his 'phone and pointed to the right button to press. They stood either side of James and smiled for their picture. As they took back the 'phone they said "Thank you so much," and jumped back into their vehicle. They waved and smiled as they drove away.

James began to laugh, "Can you believe that?"

"Your light skin makes you a celebrity out here, they probably thought you were Tom Cruise."

"I'm too tall to be mistaken for him," James said, "that was not what I expected when they got out."

They walked back to the bus where people were already climbing back in. Rachel returned to her seat near the front and Daniel was there as James sat beside him. "The driver says we're about half way," Daniel said.

"I wouldn't bet on it," James said, "Rachel thinks it's much further than that."

Daniel didn't want to hear it and shrugged. Their seats began to vibrate as the engine rumbled into life once more and the driver allowed a large truck to pass before pulling out.

The driver's estimation was ambitious, and by the time they began to climb the hills to where Bhakti Charandas was waiting most of the conversations on the bus had fizzled out. A few people were dozing as the driver loudly called out "There, there, do you see? There it is." He was pointing to a small collection of flat topped buildings that nestled ahead of them. Everyone leaned to get a view and James felt excited to know how close they were. The last stretch of road was little more than a dirt track and the bus bobbled along at little more than twenty miles an hour. As they drew closer they could see a single green flag hanging limply from a high pole on top of one of the buildings. The bus stopped in front of a wire gate where a young man sat in the shade of what reminded James of a Sheffield bus shelter. He exchanged a few comments with the driver before lifting the gate and waving the buses through. He gave the thumbs up sign to them as they passed and a few of them returned the gesture. The buildings disappeared from view as the path dropped behind a low hill until the bus turned a corner and there was their destination just ten metres away. The walls were painted a brilliant white that perfectly reflected the sun, making the whole place shimmer in light. As they drove around the first building they found themselves in a horse shoe shaped settlement of five buildings, the largest of which sat in the middle. All of the other buildings were simple structures with little to note but the main building drew everyone's focus. Beside a set of steps that climbed to a huge ornate wooden door were rows of thick pillars that looked unnecessarily sturdy for the light roof. Across the walls were painted slogans in Sanskrit that reinforced any feelings of being aliens the western visitors might have already had. To James they were a reminder of all the books he had been reading before the trip and confirmed his hope that he was finally where he should be.

The buses pulled up alongside each other and the drivers helped people out with their luggage. As they gathered in front of the large building there was still no sign of life and a few expectant glances were exchanged. Aditya had ridden in the bus with the Americans and he gave a little clap of his hands to which everyone went silent. "Welcome to you all, it is a joy to be here, I will show you to your rooms and then we will meet Bhakti Charandas for our first time. Please remember to remove your shoes before entering the hall." He pointed at the building behind him and then paused for a moment before instructing them "Take what you can from this experience."

He led them to one of the smaller buildings where they found a long corridor to which a series of small rooms were attached. Each room contained a low bed and a water bowl, and none of them had doors. As the group followed Aditya individuals peeled off into their chosen room so that by the time he reached the end of the corridor he was alone. James dropped his bag by his bed and noticed that there was no window in the room. Even at the height of the day he was standing in shadows, and there was no artificial light source. On the bed was a thin pillow and a single blanket and he wondered what the night time temperature was likely to be in these hills. He bent down and splashed some of the water from the bowl into his face. It felt good to wash away the grime of the journey and he let the moisture dry from his face in the heat. He pressed the bed to test the mattress and was unimpressed with the support it offered. But he reminded himself that he needed to strip away these selfish concerns and tried to convince himself that the bare little room was perfect for the task.

He sat on the bed and realised how tired he was, the journey had worn him out. He closed his eyes and tried to meditate and the appearance of the turning spiral confirmed why he had made the trip. He allowed himself to drift into its centre and was quickly absorbed in the sensation of moving forward beyond his physical body. There was no resistance in him, he had neither positive or negative feelings about what was happening, he felt like a neutral observer on the whole experience. As the sense of movement increased in pace he became aware of a presence. It wasn't close but it demanded his attention and as he focussed on it he became certain it was Bhakti Charandas. The urge to connect with him was strong and so James tried to direct the energy within him towards the presence. As he opened himself he felt the flow of energy back into him, an insistent force that was too strong to resist. James was about to begin chanting his mantra when the experience suddenly came to an end and he was alone in his room. A split second later a bell was struck a single time and he heard the other pilgrims leaving their rooms. As they passed his open doorway no one so much as glanced in and as he joined them he adopted the same etiquette as he passed other rooms.

Outside the mini buses had been removed and were now parked out of view behind one of the buildings. The group climbed the steps and began removing their sandals as the large wooden doors were slowly pulled open from within. James peered into the open doorway but his eyes couldn't adjust to the low light and so he followed the others in. They immediately felt the wall of cool air and James heard one of the Americans whisper "air conditioning at last." Two young Indian women dressed in white saris appeared from behind them and waved them forwards. James could now see they were in a wide hallway and before them was a second set of doors. The bell they had heard hung from a wooden stand and as they passed it James estimated it to weigh more than any man could lift. The doors opened and before them was a huge room at the end of which was what looked like an ornate throne surrounded by long white silks that hung from the ceiling. The room was painted entirely in light blue, walls, ceiling and floor, and as they entered they could see two more women dressed the same as the others standing to the sides of the throne. But these were westerners, and they both looked like they had stepped off a catwalk; their hair was long and blonde and both were tall and beautiful. James was not alone amongst the men in finding himself so distracted by them that he failed to see Bhakti Charandas make his entrance. As James spotted him he became transfixed. Of average height with long black hair and a thick beard that extended to his chest the guru was dressed in white robes which left his arms and one side of his abdomen exposed, and around his neck hung a garland of orange flowers. James couldn't help noticing the layer of fat that covered his body and tried to focus his mind on something more appropriate.

Bhakti Charandas smiled and as he walked he made small waving gestures with his hands. When he reached the throne the two female attendants draped a white silk over the seat for him and he gently lowered himself onto it. Everyone would later remark on the sense of charisma that surrounded him, it was impossible to look away. When he finally spoke his voice was almost childlike in its pitch but his English was good. "I am happy to welcome

221

you," he said, "you have come a long way to hear me. I have many students from all around the world, I was on Indian television last year; my message is universal. But for each of you there will be a time this week to meet with me by yourself, we will talk and understand what it is you need. I know you come with many questions, this is understandable, but for now we must leave them to one side. They may or may not be answered here, but the things you really need you may find. The questions you have carried with you are the product of another life, a place far away, part of our goal is to help you cut the ties with that old life. Therefore your questions may actually be a barrier if we let them dominate our time."

As the smile fell from his face his tone grew more serious, "You must be prepared to lose everything if you are to gain what is eternal. Many of you come with western educations, I know people from England and America take great pride in their learning. But your pride in your intelligence can hold you back. Here you must learn a new kind of intelligence, this is a university of the spirit. Yes," he nodded at his own comments, "a place for you to acquire a new learning. There are nameless ecstasies awaiting you, but only if you can free yourself from the chains that bind you to your old life. To do this we must be strict, for the first half of the day we will remain in total silence, we will eat just one meal each day, but do not worry, you will feel no hunger. I once fasted for five weeks and never once thought of food, this is the power of true freedom. Your fears and worries are no more than hunger, they can be overcome too, but your old self clings to everything that brings you pain." He stood up and began walking back and forth before them, "You have been practicing yoga, this is good, your minds would not be ready without it. With Aditya you have been to nursery school, and now it is time to move on to become seniors. True yoga is union with all things, it is

222

obliteration of the self, we will practice yoga every day, we will meditate, and then I will meet with each of you to identify your sickness." He began to chuckle to himself and said "I will be your doctor, I will prescribe to each of you a different medicine." He walked back to his large chair and seemed to consider sitting again but instead turned to the group and said "Food will be served in an hour. I will see you all tomorrow." His hands met in front of his chest and he bowed before quickly walking out through a door behind him with the two blonde attendants following him.

Aditya trotted to the door and disappeared after them and the pilgrims began to look around at each other, unsure of what they should do. One of the Indian women opened the large door behind them and gestured with a wave of her hand that they should leave. As they put on their sandals Daniel came over to James and said "Wow! He's incredible."

"This is an amazing place," James said, "I'm glad we're here."

Aditya came out to join them and clapped his hands. "Would you all return to your cells until the bell rings for the meal. Enter through that door there," he pointed to one of the other buildings, "this is an opportunity for everyone to meditate. Bhakti Charandas has spoken with me and I have the order in which you will meet with him. After the meal tonight it will be Rachel and then Carrie. I will announce who is next tomorrow."

James looked across at Rachel who was clearly happy to be meeting with him so soon. They began walking back to their rooms and as they entered the building Dereck signalled to James by pointing to the washroom. James nodded and after waiting for a few minutes in his room went up to meet him.

"What's wrong?" James asked.

Dereck was frowning and he kept looking towards the door as though he was afraid someone would catch them. "I've got real doubts about this, something doesn't feel right."

"What is it? What's wrong?" James asked.

"Don't tell me Charandas is only eating one meal a day, and what's with the super-models?"

"He doesn't make any attempt to hide his body," James said, "I don't think he's pulling a fast one. Couldn't you feel anything from him?"

"Oh I felt something alright. I smell a fish James, I think this bloke's a fraud."

"I don't know what to say, I'm not feeling it Dereck. Give it time, see how you feel when you've had a chance to speak to him. You might be surprised."

"Don't tell anyone I've said this will ya? I don't think it would go down too well. I just needed to get it off my chest."

"So what are you going to do?"

"There's nothing I can do out here, I'm uneasy about it though. This isn't what I thought the trip was going to be." Dereck grew pensive.

"Give it a couple of days, see how you feel when you've acclimatised yourself to the place. I think you'll be surprised."

Dereck patted his arm, "We'll see. Just don't say anything, I don't want to spoil the mood for everyone else."

"I don't think anyone would react badly if they knew how you're feeling. We're here to find the truth, not play games. If this is how you're feeling then that's the truth. You don't have to pretend, what would be the point? Why don't you tell him exactly what you're thinking, see how he reacts."

"We'll see James, I don't know what I'm going to do yet. Just don't say anything."

"I promise, not a word. Are you going to be okay?"

"Oh yea, I'm not about to get all upset. I just needed to say it."

"We better get back to our rooms, it might look odd being up here like this."

"Oh yea, I see what you mean," Dereck managed to smile, "thanks for listening."

James waited while Dereck returned to his room and then quietly made his way down the corridor. As he passed the open doorways he caught glimpses of people in different yoga positions, some on the floor, some in mid-stretch, and back in his own room he lay down on the bed. As he closed his eyes he sensed the presence of their teacher and the power of the feeling convinced him that Dereck was wrong.

Chapter 31

At the sound of the bell James swung his feet over the side of the bed and rubbed his eyes. He had been dozing and it took a moment to reorientate himself to his surroundings. The shadows of people passing his doorway fell across his room and he slipped his feet into his sandals. In the corridor he met Carrie and they exchanged smiles. "How are you feeling about speaking with him tonight?" James asked.

"I'm excited," she said, "but I wish I had more time to prepare. I've been going through a few things in my room, but when I come to say it out loud it all sounds silly. I don't know what I'm going to say to him."

"Don't worry, he'll have plenty to say I'm sure. And it's good to meet him early in the week, it'll give you the chance to put into practice whatever he suggests."

"I know, I'm still overthinking everything, I need to let go."

As they walked out between the buildings everyone looked up into the evening sky which had turned a deep purple. A few stopped and gazed at it, and no one felt the need to say anything. James looked around for Rachel but couldn't see her and so he went on into the dining hall. Inside there was a long table with benches running along either side. A number of people were already seated and James squeezed in between Carrie and one of the tall American men. Large pans were laid out in front of them and Aditya encouraged everyone to lift the lids and help themselves. Carrie took a large spoon and began serving generous portions of a thick vegetable curry onto the plates offered to her. There was no sign of steam rising from it and it turned out to be lukewarm but very spicy. "If this is what we're eating all week we'll be dropping a few pounds," the American man said to anyone interested, and a few polite smiles were thrown his way.

Rachel was seated at the far end of the table and was in deep conversation with Heather who looked like she was still suffering from sunburn. There was a contented level of conversation amongst the group and the American next to James began explaining the history of yoga in the United States to those sitting across from him. James glanced up towards Dereck who was deep in thought staring down into his plate as he ate. James felt concerned for him but still believed his worries would be resolved with time.

At the end of the meal Aditya climbed out from the bench and went over to Rachel. He bent down and quietly began explaining something to her. Rachel nodded her understanding and stood up to follow him. As they passed where James was sitting she widened her eyes to let him know how excited she was and James gave her the thumbs up as encouragement.

"Does anyone want to take a walk in the field?" Carrie asked.

"Do you think you should wander too far if you're due to meet with Bhakti Charandas?" James said.

"Maybe not," she admitted, "but I want to take in the view before it gets too cold. Adi can find me when it's time."

Some of the others agreed to go with her and James remained at the table as they left. Dereck walked off alone and a couple of small groups sat at the table talking. James eventually left the dining room and sat on the steps in front of the pillars. He could see the silhouettes of the others as they walked through the field and the sounds of dogs barking somewhere off in the night reminded him that the rest of the world still existed.

Eventually the wooden doors opened and Rachel stepped out and looked surprised to see him. "What are you doing out here?" She asked.

"I wanted to hear how it went. You don't mind do you?"

Rachel pulled the door shut behind her, she hesitated and then came down the steps to where he sat. "I don't think we should be alone tonight, this isn't the place."

"I'm sorry, I didn't mean to do anything wrong, I just wanted to know how it went."

"I need time alone to reflect, I have things to do, I don't want to start trying to explain things before I've even had time to absorb it myself."

"I am sorry, I just thought…" James was flustered.

His voice trailed off and Rachel stood silently looking at him. In the end she said "I have to go and tell Carrie it's her turn to go in, I'll speak to you tomorrow."

"She's out in the field."

"What? Where?" Rachel began to look out into the shadows but there was no sign of them.

"A few of them went for a walk. You stay here, I'll go and find her. I saw which way they were going."

"Okay, thank you." There was little warmth in her voice and James left her wishing he'd joined the others on the walk. As soon as he emerged from the buildings he spotted the group and jogged down to them. Carrie was pleased to receive the news and he walked back with her while the others continued on down the field.

Rachel was still waiting at the steps when they returned and she managed a half smile when she saw them. "I need to say a few things to Carrie before she goes in, do you mind giving us a minute?"

"Of course," he turned to Carrie, "I hope it all goes well."

James went back to his room and sat on the rickety little chair beside his bed. He tried to meditate but was too affected by Rachel's demeanour towards him. He tried to rationalise the situation and was able to convince himself that he'd been in the wrong. He decided to apologise to her in the morning and this gave him a little peace. He stood and did a few stretches before performing a short yoga session. It helped calm him and distance him from his emotions. He sat back on the chair and closed his eyes. As he began to recite the mantra the spiral turned and the eye stared at him. He made a conscious effort to send positive energy to the other pilgrims and as he moved from room to room in his mind he came to Dereck. As much as he wanted to send healing energy his efforts came to nothing and he found it impossible to even sense his presence there. As he struggled to give what he could to those around him the clear sense of Bhakti Charandas came into his mind.

As he tried to strengthen the sense of connection he was snatched from his meditation by the sound of growling in the corridor outside his room. The depth of the sound came from a large animal, and James slowly stood and picked up the chair. He heard the shuffle of paws on the concrete and tried to detect any sound that might indicate which way it was moving. The growl came again and lifting the chair high above his head he rushed the doorway shouting with all his might. There was no sound of paws scampering away and James shouted even louder, trying to make as deep and guttural sound as he could.

There was movement along the corridor and he could hear people coming his way. "Look out," he shouted, "there's an animal loose."

One of the American men looked round the doorway into James' room, "Are you okay?"

"Can you see it?" James lowered the chair at the sight of him.

"No man, there's nothing here. Were you dreaming? The only thing I heard was you."

"I wasn't sleeping, there was an animal growling, it sounded like a dog or something."

"Take it easy James, there's nothing here. I promise. Come out and see for yourself."

As others arrived to find out what was happening James became embarrassed. "I'm sorry everyone, I heard an animal. It must have been outside."

"Like your dreams before?" Daniel said.

"I wasn't dreaming, I was wide awake. I heard it. We need to be careful," James insisted.

As people began to drift away James saw Rachel watching him. She was frowning and as James moved towards her she went back to her room. He sat back on the chair in his room and shook his head. He bent down and cupped some of the water from the bowl in his hands. It was warm and smelt stale but it brought him a little relief. He had no doubt that he had heard the animal and couldn't understand how it could have escaped so quickly without anyone seeing it. He questioned whether it could have been outside the building and dismissed the idea. He thought about moving his bed to the wall furthest from the doorway but decided not to risk making any more noise.

He lay down and watched the doorway. He felt vulnerable without anyway to close himself in and, more importantly, close out anything that wanted to get to him. He could hear someone snoring along the corridor and it comforted him to hear the sound of other people so close. Eventually his tiredness became stronger than his anxiety and he drifted off, still wearing his jeans and shirt. His sleep was fitful and shallow and gave little rest. Early in the morning he woke feeling very cold and realised he hadn't climbed under the blanket. He pulled it over himself but the damage was done and the cold had taken hold of him. He shivered in the dark, he pulled his knees up against himself and tried to protect what little body warmth he had. It was then that he heard the same shuffling he had heard before. He went rigid with fear and like every wild animal listening for hunters his ears strained for every hint of danger. He couldn't risk shouting like before, and lay still in his bed. This time there was no growl, instead he could hear the heavy breathing of something that was close. The panting was so clear he could almost feel its warmth in his face. There was nothing within reach to grab as a weapon, and he held his breath in absolute silence hoping it would pass his room by. He even longed for the snoring down the corridor to start again and lead whatever was out there to seek other prey.

James' eyes bulged as he stared at the doorway, and though there was no further sound he became convinced it was standing motionless waiting for him to give himself away. As the seconds passed he began to hope it had left again and as the seconds became minutes his hope increased. It took a long time for him to be satisfied he was alone and with the blanket still wrapped around him he went out into the corridor. There was nothing there, and as he stood looking down the corridor he expected it to come bounding round the corner. He knew that if someone found him like this it would only add to their concern about his behaviour and seeing nothing he persuaded himself to go back to bed. He pulled the blanket tighter around himself and not knowing if he was shaking because of the cold or fear he managed to get a few hours of broken sleep.

Chapter 32

The following morning the bell was rung just before seven. The sound of feet slapping their way to the washrooms was enough to get James out of bed. He tried to overcome the sense of exhaustion with a few stretches and though it improved his mood he knew he was facing a day sapped of energy.

Forty minutes after the first bell another called everyone to the meditation hall and they reverently entered through the imposing doorway and found places on the floor around the room.

Bhakti Charandas made his entrance after a few minutes and today he was dressed in bright yellow robes. The four attendees followed him in and stood either side of his throne. "Last night," he began, "I have learned that there was disruption in your rooms. It is important to maintain silence in the night. I must impose a new rule: that we do not speak after the meal. There is time for chit chat in the afternoon, we are not here for distraction."

James felt his face redden knowing they all knew who was responsible for the noise. He felt sweat running down his back despite the air conditioning, and kept his focus straight ahead for fear of catching someone's eye. It was a relief to him when the guru invited them to stand and demonstrated to them a series of postures he wanted them to try. They weren't particularly demanding and everyone performed them without difficulty. The physical movements helped James to feel less self-conscious and by the end of the session everyone was relaxed.

Bhakti Charandas began to clap, "Well done, good, you are excellent students." He giggled a little, "These postures will help to prepare you for our meditation this afternoon. Nothing we do here is unrelated, even to the whole of your lives, your childhood, your old age, everything is one. You must trust me if you want to go further." He turned and said something over his shoulder to one of the Indian women who went out through the door behind his throne. She returned with a painting, a mixture of shapes and colours that at first glance was completely abstract. However, Bhakti Charandas took the painting and walked towards the group holding it aloft. "Look carefully at this image, it will be the focus of our meditation today. I wanted you to see it now so that your minds will be ready later. Don't try to interpret it, this is not western art. Look and let your spirit accept the truth it finds here." He returned to his throne and the Indian woman placed the painting on a stand she had brought out.

Bhakti Charandas grew silent, his head was bowed and his hands cupped in his lap. His head lifted and he looked straight at James. As their eyes locked he remained expressionless and his blank stare made James uneasy. After a moment he looked away and began to smile once more, "That is it for this session. Don't try to question how much you have learned, allow your spirit to take what it can. There is more here than meets the eye." He giggled to himself again and some of the group laughed in response. The guru stood and without another word left the room.

Everyone got to their feet and James saw Rachel to his right. He followed her out and caught up with her in the yard. "Can we take a walk, Rachel?"

"Yes, okay, let me have a wash first. I'll meet you by the field in a few minutes."

As Rachel walked away Aditya approached James and said "Bhakti Charandas will speak with you tonight after dinner. Go through to the hall and wait before his seat, he will join you there."

James was excited at the news, and as he strolled out from the buildings he began to run through the kinds of things he wanted to ask about. He sat at the edge of the dry, yellow grass and looked across the hills. The only other building in sight was a small hut about a mile away, and he watched the crows dancing around each other as they looked for seeds.

Rachel came up behind him and said "It's a beautiful place isn't it?"

"It's so still, I love it here," James said.

"Do you want to sit here or walk a little?"

"Let's wander down there," James pointed to a small clump of trees near the side of the road. As they walked he said "Adi told me I'm meeting Charandas tonight."

"Bhakti Charandas," she corrected him.

"I'm not sure what to expect, do you feel like talking about your meeting now?"

Rachel pouted a little, "I don't want to say anything about what he told me. It's not the kind of thing you can explain to someone else. It's so specific and personal to me, if I tried to share it I wouldn't be able to explain it properly." She looked at him and said "I'm sorry I was sharp with you last night. I didn't mean to be. I was just surprised to see you and my head was still trying to deal with what he said to me."

"There's nothing to be sorry for, let's forget it."

She looked back at the buildings and then slipped her arm through his. As they reached the trees they stepped into the shade and James gently pulled her in front of him. "I've missed you," he said. He bent down and kissed her and then slipped his arms around her to pull her closer.

234

She held him tight but whispered "We shouldn't do this, not here."

"It's okay, no one can see us."

"I'm not bothered about what anyone else thinks James." She pulled free and looked up at him, "this isn't why we came. I told you, we mustn't give in to these feelings on the pilgrimage. This is too important, it's too much of an opportunity to let slip by because we're distracted by our emotions. You understand don't you?"

"Of course, I'm sorry, I didn't mean to spoil anything," James said honestly.

Rachel stepped away and sat on the root of one of the trees that protruded from the soil. She looked down at the ground and James wanted nothing more than to embrace her again. But instead he sat on the ground with his back against one of the trees. "What can you tell me about your meeting that you think will help prepare me?" The question was intended to show he was focussed on the right things and it seemed to work.

"It will be just you and him when you meet. He'll invite you to sit on the floor in front of him. Carrie says he meditated with her before talking but he didn't do that with me. It all depends what he sees you need. I think the best thing is not to go in expecting anything particular, just see what happens."

"Did you get to ask many questions?"

"Only in response to what he told me. I didn't go in with a list, don't prepare anything like that. Just listen and if you need to ask about anything he says that's fine. But he'll know what to talk about." She paused and looked at him, "He's amazing James. I can't tell you how incredible he is."

He could see how affected she was by the experience and it filled him with anticipation for what was to come. He considered telling her about the animal in the night but didn't want to risk sounding foolish, especially after what the guru had said to them. He glanced towards the buildings and saw a small group of people walking their way. "We've got company," he said.

Rachel got to her feet and waved to the other pilgrims. James hid his annoyance that they had interrupted his time with her and managed to join in with the waving. As the others approached Daniel called out "Are you hiding from us?" Clearly no one was following the instruction to remain in silence.

"No, just getting some shade. But it's still hot in here, I might get some water," James said.

Daniel offered him a drink from his bottle but James refused, "No, that's okay. It served me right for forgetting to bring any. I'm gonna walk back up and get some. I'll see you all later."

"I'll take a walk with them," Rachel said, and she stepped out into the sunshine and began chatting with one of the American women who was wearing the widest brimmed straw hat James had ever seen. He strode back to the buildings, waving flies away from his face, feeling the sweat soaking through his shirt. There was no one about when he reached the yard and he headed for the washrooms. He inspected his burned skin in a little mirror fixed to the wall above the sink and tried to reduce the heat by splashing water in his face.

From behind him he heard Dereck say "Can I speak to you?"

"Yea," he said, reaching for his towel. "Are you feeling any better?"

"I'm leaving, James, I'm going back tonight."

"What? Where are you going?"

"I'm going back to the centre and I'll wait for everyone there. I can't be here anymore."

"Are you sure Dereck? We've only been here a little while. Don't rush your decision."

"It's already sorted. I've arranged it with one of the drivers. There's a railway station about forty miles north of here, I can get a train straight through. I don't want to cause any fuss, so I'm not going to announce it. Will you wait until after dinner and tell everyone I've gone?"

"Yea, of course I will. I'm really sorry to hear it didn't work out for you."

"Don't worry about me, just watch out for yourself. I mean it James, you need to be careful here."

"What about? I don't know what you mean."

Dereck's voice grew quieter and his frown more intense, "There are forces here that we don't understand. You aren't the only one getting visits in the night."

"What? That was nothing to worry about. Don't let me be the cause of you going."

"You're not listening to me James, I've said all I'm going to say." He extended his arm and they shook hands, "I'll see you in a few days. Just be careful."

Dereck left him in the washroom and James leaned over the wash basin trying to make sense of what he'd heard. He looked in the mirror and felt afraid to look himself in the eye. He couldn't account for it but he just knew he couldn't meet his own gaze. He felt his hands trembling and tightened his fingers into fists. He grabbed his towel and went back to the shade of his room. The lack of direct sunlight made little difference to the temperature and he swallowed half a bottle of water. He began to run through what Rachel had said about her meeting and he struggled to understand why she couldn't speak openly about what had been said to her. He wondered if it revealed her lack of trust in him or if she thought him incapable of being advanced enough to understand the message. He reminded himself that he had been one of those chosen by Aditya for the more advanced meditation sessions and this had to show her that he was capable of grasping what she had to say. He felt belittled by her refusal to tell him and when he realised it he was shocked at himself. He tried to look at his emotions and understand if it was simple jealousy or something else, but his own feelings were a mystery to him. He couldn't account for what he felt, he only knew it was making him resentful and angry. He reminded himself not to allow his emotions to dominate him and sat on the floor to meditate. He used the mantra and began to feel a soothing sensation rising through his body. By the time the others were returning from their walk he was at peace, and as they passed by his open doorway he enjoyed the knowledge that they would see him so deeply immersed in his meditation.

Chapter 33

The day turned very hot and as they entered the hall for the meditation session the air conditioning came as an enormous relief. A young Indian man was gently palming tabla drums in the corner, he didn't seem to notice the pilgrims entering and maintained his intricate rhythms as they passed him. James sat on the floor and felt the drum beat affect his internal rhythms so that he had to deliberately stop himself from swaying with them.

Bhakti Charandas was back in his white robes and his entrance brought everyone to attention. The usual grin was locked across his face and he waved to a few individuals as he walked to his seat. The strange abstract painting looked down on them from its stand suggesting something none of the pilgrims understood. One of the western attendees began lighting incense placed around the room and the air quickly filled with its smoke. James was sure he detected a hint of cannabis mixed in with the other scents, a smell he hadn't encountered since his days at university. As he inhaled he couldn't be sure if he was feeling the effect of a drug or still struggling with a lack of sleep, but whatever the cause he became light-headed and a little woozy.

"Today we are going to practise an ancient form of mediation that uses sounds to help us go beyond what we might normally achieve." Charandas looked over to his attendants who moved over to the drummer and began to sing softly in time with his hands. "They are repeating verses from ancient texts, we do not need to understand the exact meaning of the words to be affected by them," Charandas explained. "The sounds themselves carry spiritual truths that can lead the spirit. Let the chants inhabit you, let the rhythm become your heart's rhythm, feel the flow of your breathing in time with their voices."

The combination of sounds and scents was intoxicating and James quickly found himself entering a deep meditative state where the reality of his own individuality began to merge with the greater presence of all things. Charandas gave instructions about how they should breathe and how they should focus on the pulse of energy they could now feel coming up from the earth into their bodies. As Charandas described it James felt its movement through him, and as they moved deeper into the experience an extraordinary delight filled him so that he could neither think nor feel anything negative. James found his thoughts becoming blurred, he gave up trying to reason, and now only the feelings of pleasure mattered.

The women's voices began to increase in volume and speed, and the drum beat became more insistent and complex. James felt the energy within him swirling with power, and when one of the American women cried out behind him he completely ignored her. The woman shouted again and one of the English women joined her so that their voices followed the singing but with meaningless howls and shrieks. Somewhere near the drums a man's voice blended into the women's and the cry spread around the room until a cacophony of voices rose to keep time with the drummer who steered the whole sound forward.

Charandas gave a signal and the attendees fell silent and the drummer began to slow his playing. The pilgrims responded by falling silent one by one until only the slowing drums could be heard. Charandas clapped his hands and the drums stopped, and all around the room people swayed and bobbed in response to the charged atmosphere that they had contributed to. Charandas said "Feel your breathing slowing down, your body relaxing, and when you are ready open your eyes."

James looked ahead and was surprised at how dense the smoke had become. It billowed in clouds around them, and as Charandas moved his hands the smoke parted for them. "This is unnameable ecstasy," Charandas said. "Remember this feeling always. You may go and nourish your bodies now, but hold on to what you have been given. Share your experiences over dinner, but remain silent through the night." He stood up and with the four women close behind him he left the room. The pilgrims remained seated for a while, there was no desire in anyone to leave the hall. But then the air conditioning was turned off and the temperature started to quickly climb.

James got to his feet and walked through the few people still seated that were scattered around the room. The sky was beginning to darken but the heat was still intense and he was sweating before he reached the bottom of the steps outside the hall. Some of the group were talking excitedly about what had just happened, relating specific experiences they had gone through, and there was a shared sense of having found something different to anything they had known before. James overheard one of the Americans describe a strange language that he had found himself speaking, that had poured out from him even though he didn't understand it.

The doors to the dining hall opened and the pilgrims took the signal that dinner was ready. James was not the only one who felt very hungry and there was little hesitation in filling the benches around the table of food. The same curry as the previous night was sitting in the pans but no one complained. It was tasty and everyone helped themselves to generous portions. The level of excitement had not dropped and noisy conversations came from along the whole table.

James was interested in the American man's experience of feeling like he was speaking a new language and as he was seated opposite him he asked "Do you think it was an actual language you were speaking, or simply sounds?"

"It felt like a language, I felt like I was speaking. There seemed meaning in it."

"They do that back home in the Baptist churches," an American woman sitting next to him said. "But I doubt they realise what they're doing."

"Speaking in tongues?" James said.

"Yea, sure, but that's just their name for it," she said. "It's a phenomenon found amongst many cultures and religions, I don't doubt that something real is taking place, but I wouldn't agree with the Baptists' interpretation of it." She laughed to herself and it was clear what she thought of her fellow countrymen.

As people began to finish their food Aditya stood up and called everyone to silence with his customary clap. He said "Dereck wasn't present at the meditation and he has missed the meal. Does anyone know if he is ill or where he might be?"

James raised his hand, and all eyes turned his way. "He asked me to pass on a message. He's decided to go back to the centre, he left earlier."

"What?" Aditya's reaction was almost a scream. "You knew he wanted to leave and you didn't tell anyone?"

"He told me not to. He'd made up his mind and didn't want to cause any fuss. He didn't want anyone to know."

"We could have spoken to him, given him some help. You should have said something James, this is terrible." Aditya looked around at the others at the table as if to confirm they understood what had happened. A few shook their heads.

"I'm sorry," James pleaded, "he spoke to me in confidence. He trusted me, I couldn't say anything."

"That's not good enough," Aditya insisted, "you must know how important this trip is. Bhakti Charandas could have helped him overcome whatever was concerning him. But now there is no chance of anyone helping him. Can you see what you've done, James?"

James glanced around in the hope of finding sympathy but was met with blank stares and even some hostility from a few people. He looked up the table to where Rachel was sitting and saw her staring straight ahead at the wall. He threw his hands in the air, "I'm sorry, I thought I was doing the right thing."

Aditya went out and a few low conversations started up again. But James was alone and after a few minutes stood up and left. Outside he remembered he was to meet Bhakti Charandas and wondered if he would still be welcome. He climbed the steps and knocked on one of the doors. There was no response and he knocked again. Still hearing nothing he turned the handle and let himself in. The hall was dark and around the edge of the second set of doors he could see light. He walked up to them and rapped his knuckles against them. He was still feeling shaken by everyone's response at the meal and he lacked the confidence to just walk on in.

After a brief delay he heard the voice of Bhakti Charandas, "Come through, James, you are welcome."

James pushed open the door and saw the guru sitting on the floor in front of his throne. Next to him was a tray on which was a metal jug, two glasses and a small bowl of something that James couldn't make out. The guru's hair was brushed forwards over his shoulders and his eyes reflected back the light of candles placed near him. His smile was reassuring and James closed the door behind him and walked over to Charandas. "Please," the guru gestured for him to sit.

Being alone with Bhakti Charandas felt very different to meeting him as part of the group. The aura of his personal presence was intensified as he focussed on one person. James realised Charandas was much older than he looked from a distance, up close James could see the wrinkles around his eyes and the edge of his beard on his cheek showed signs of grey which he had attempted to hide with dye. His eyes were brown and large and gave the impression of great compassion. He studied James for a little while until he finally spoke in a gentle voice. "You have made surprising progress, I can see that you are ready to make a leap forward. Do you want to go further?"

"Yes," James said, "as far as I can."

"Do you trust me, James?"

Without any hesitation he said "Of course."

"No, not of course, there is nothing taken for granted. You may have come a long way but if you are to truly break through you must trust me with your soul. Can you do that?"

"I don't understand what that means," James admitted, "but I don't doubt you can help me."

"Good, good. We must have trust if we are to travel together. So far you have relied on the fragments or glimpses of another world, but if you are to truly walk there you must be guided by those already there."

"I trust you."

"Not just me James, I am talking about those who do not inhabit this world, but are ready to greet us in the spirit. We all need to be guided, both in this world and in the unseen realm. Are you willing to meet them and follow their guidance?"

James was nervous but wanted everything the guru could do for him. "I will do whatever it takes," he said.

"Good, we must meditate together and I will show you how to meet them." He crossed his legs and straightened his back. "Close your eyes and allow your focus to follow your breathing." James did as he was instructed, and as if Charandas could see what was in his mind said "Move beyond the spiral. You are hesitating, this is only the beginning. You have paused where you should have flown. Go through the spiral, fly, fly."

James felt himself drawn through the turning light and the sensation of movement was as strong as if his body were travelling somewhere. Charandas continued to lead him, "Now move out from yourself, break free from the bond with your body. Break free and fly, fly."

James was lifted up and a small point of light appeared above him. He began racing towards it, climbing high above everything, until the light opened up above him and he was enveloped by it so that everything became a glowing white. Within the light he became aware of two figures, their shape was indistinct and like shadows their form and detail was hidden. At first James felt himself retreat from them, but Charandas said "Do not be afraid, they are here to help you. Let them guide you, trust, trust, you are safe, all is well, do not lose trust." Unlike before James now felt his thoughts take on a clarity, the emotions became secondary to his rational mind, and he began to question what was happening to him. As he tried to look at the figures he felt a surge of anger pass through them and they vanished. James' eyes flashed open and he found himself seated before the guru once more.

"What happened? What was that?" James gasped.

"You have made contact," Charandas said. His grin widened and James felt uneasy, "You have broken through, and now you are not alone. When you meditate you will have guides to lead you. This is a wonderful moment for you, James, it is my gift to you."

"I could sense them here, but I couldn't see them properly," James said.

245

"You will, I promise, you will." Charandas poured them each a glass of water and as James took one from him he felt his hand shaking. "Don't worry," Charandas said, "It is normal for the body to shake when the spirit has been flying. You are a new pilot, don't be surprised if new things start happening."

The water was ice cold and tasted better than anything James had drunk since he'd been in India. He considered bringing up the subject of Dereck but decided against it. Instead he said "Someone told me you may see future events. Is that true?"

"Sometimes I am given knowledge of things yet to happen. Like you for instance, I knew you before you arrived. I saw your face and I knew you were going to make this journey tonight." His eyes glinted and he said "But don't treat me like a fortune teller at the circus. This is not a place for magic tricks."

"No, I didn't mean to suggest that. I'm sorry, I just wondered about something, about a relationship. I thought you might be able to help me."

"Young men are so concerned with their love lives. You mustn't concern yourself with that here. This is the time for other things. When you get back to England I am sure you can pursue those concerns." He winked at James and the two men smiled at each other. James was pleased to see him appear so down to earth after what they had done together. "I have one last thing to say to you, James. You must meditate every day for at least an hour. If you do not work hard the advances you have made may be lost. Will you do that?"

"I will, I don't want to lose what you've helped me find," James promised him.

Bhakti Charandas got to his feet and grabbed James' arms to help him stand. "Go in silence and peace, Aditya will find my next guest. Go and let your guides make your path clear."

"Thank you," James said, "I am grateful for your time."

"What is time? The whole universe is here and then it's gone. Go now, James."

Chapter 34

James went straight out from speaking with Charandas to look for Rachel. Despite the instruction to remain in silence he needed to speak with her. He went to her room and finding it empty decided to search for her near the field. As he walked passed the open doorways he could see that most of the pilgrims were occupying themselves quietly with yoga or meditation and he felt self-conscious walking back and forth along the corridor. Outside the night air was cooling and he did up the last buttons of his shirt in the hope of staying warm. The world was still and the half-moon cast an icy light across everything.

As he reached the field he could see individual figures moving around in the darkness and struggled to identify which one might be Rachel. He decided against walking down to them and instead sat on a rock near one of the buildings to wait for them to return. He thought about what the guru had said and closed his eyes to meditate. This time there was no spiral, no eye, instead the image of a dog appeared in his mind, its teeth bared and its throat trembled with a savage growl. James was startled and opened his eyes, he felt unsettled and realised he was suffering from a lack of sleep. He gave up on trying to do anything meaningful and stared at the stars in the cloudless sky. Without any light pollution the whole universe seemed to be on display and he tried to identify patterns that might be familiar. He was still looking up when he heard the sound of someone coming through the grass and to his relief it was Rachel.

"Hello, I've seen Bhakti Charandas, I wanted to talk to you about it," James said.

Rachel looked around and sternly rebuked him, "We were instructed not to speak, why can't you follow a few simple rules?"

Her response caught him off guard, "It went really well with him, I just wanted to tell you about it."

"It can wait until the morning, I'll speak with you before the first session. I don't want to break the silence now, please let's respect this."

"I'm sorry, it's been a strange evening. I'm being impatient, forgive me."

She seemed to soften a little, but said "Why didn't you tell anyone about Dereck?"

"What? Like I said, he trusted me, he asked me not to say anything; I thought I was doing the right thing."

"You speak when you shouldn't and remain silent when you should speak up." Though she was still critical James was relieved when she smiled. She looked around again and said "Do you want to come down near the trees, we can talk there if you like."

"Thank you, yea, come on." There was no one near so he took her hand and they walked in silence along the edge of the field. When they reached the trees he slipped his arms around her and pulled her to him. As they kissed James felt his anxiety disappear. In a whisper he said "I feel so much for you."

Her dark eyes creased as she smiled and she kissed him again. She held him for a minute and said "What happened with Bhakti Charandas?"

Still holding her James said "I think I've taken a big step forward tonight. He showed me how to meditate in a new way. I sensed something I've not known before. It's really affected me Rachel."

"That's good," she whispered, "I knew you would find something important here."

She lifted her head to him and he kissed her again. As they stood like this a loud voice from behind them said "What are you doing?"

James spun round to find Daniel staring in disbelief at them. "Dan, what are you doing here?"

"I'm taking a walk James. This is ridiculous. I'm going to have to speak to Aditya."

"Don't over react," James said as he pulled away from Rachel. "There's nothing wrong going on here, don't make a big thing of it."

"You're breaking the rules, you shouldn't even be talking, let alone carrying on like this." There was genuine disgust in Daniel's voice.

"Don't cause any trouble Dan, what good can it do?"

"We are here for spiritual reasons, we were told specifically not to get involved with anything like this. It's one thing after another with you, James."

"What's that supposed to mean?" James said sternly.

"First you wake half the group up in the night, then you cover up the fact that Dereck was leaving, now you're chasing Rachel."

"It's not like that," Rachel said, "I'm as much a part of this as he is."

"Oh come on, Rachel, he's been leering after you since he got here, his whole attitude has been messed up. He's having a bad effect on the whole pilgrimage."

"What are you talking about?" James was becoming angry. "Aditya chose me for the first meditation group, he knew why I came. I'm here for the right reasons."

"The first mediation group!" Daniel repeated his words back at him with utter disdain. "I knew you thought you were better than us in the main group. Your ego is out of control."

250

"Come off it, Daniel, you were jealous of us in the other group from the word go. And now you're lashing out because you can't deal with not being special."

"Is that what you are, special? I suppose that must be why Rachel has fallen for you."

James rushed forwards and slapped him across the face with the back of his hand. Daniel staggered back in shock. Rachel cried out "Stop it, what are you doing?"

James looked at her, his jaw was clenched tight and every muscle in his face was taut with rage. Daniel shook his head and spat "I don't believe you. Do you even know why we're here? And you behave like that. You're a disgrace, you're a waste of Munro's kindness. You don't belong here."

"No, that's too much Daniel," Rachel said calmly, "You don't know everything. You're jumping to conclusions."

"I'm speaking to Aditya, I've got no choice, Rachel. Believe me, I don't blame you." Daniel turned and walked off into the darkness and James tried to take hold of Rachel again but she stepped back from him.

"No James, we shouldn't have done anything in the first place, he's right, we're bringing the wrong energy into the trip."

"You mean I am," he said. "Don't listen to him, I know what happened with the guru, Daniel can't deny any of that. He's just jealous."

"What, of not being in the small group?" Rachel said.

"Yea, and the rest,"

"What else, what are you talking about?" Rachel was confused.

"I've seen him looking at you, Rachel, if there was any leering going on it wasn't me doing it."

"That's not true James, you're letting your emotions run away with you. This is why we shouldn't have allowed anything to happen, we can't bring these feelings into the mix. We need to be clear headed. I think it's best if we keep our distance for the rest of the pilgrimage."

"What do you mean? James said. "Is that it? Hasn't any of it meant something to you?"

"Stop being juvenile James, it can wait until we go home. I'm not saying I don't feel anything, we just can't allow any of this to continue until we're in England. Please, have some sense."

It wasn't what he wanted, not least because he didn't want Daniel to think he had got his way, but he nodded and said "Okay. But every time I see you I'm going to feel something."

"No, that's what I mean." Rachel became insistent, "you must put these emotions to rest. Don't burden me with this while we're here, you'll prevent me from achieving what I came for. Try to see the bigger picture, whatever we do here we'll take home with us. We have to focus."

He could see there was no talking her out of it and he wanted no more confrontation. "Okay, I promise, I'll do it," he said.

She visibly relaxed and they headed back to the settlement. They could both now feel the cold and Rachel hid herself as deeply as she could in her sari, pulling it over her head and pulling it tight at the neck. As they reached the buildings Aditya was standing near the pillars and Daniel was a few paces away from him. Aditya came to meet them, his face was stern and even his walk looked serious. James had had enough from Daniel and could feel his anger starting to rise again. Aditya began wagging his finger at him "Daniel has told me what you have been up to. This is a betrayal of the guru. I must insist that you remain completely separate for the rest of our time."

"We've already decided what we'll do Adi, don't wave your finger at me."

Daniel stepped forward and said "You see! He won't listen."

James threw him an angry look and Aditya said "Daniel tells me you struck him."

There was nothing James could say to excuse his actions and he nodded. Aditya looked back at Daniel and then at Rachel. He said "You should know better. Munro puts great trust in you Rachel, how could you let yourself be lead astray like this?"

"She wasn't led astray," James snapped, "don't start telling us what we have or haven't been doing. We've agreed to stay apart for the rest of the pilgrimage, don't stick your nose in beyond that."

Rachel looked at James with surprise, she had never seen him this way and she was concerned he would lose his temper again. She said "It's okay James, let's leave it until the morning. I'll speak with Bhakti Charandas, everything is going to be fine."

"I have already spoken with the guru," Aditya said. "He wants me to report back to him later. He is saddened by all of this, really saddened."

"Let's not make more of it than we need to," James said. "I accept that we've broken the rules, but let's not let it ruin anything."

"You are so short-sighted," Aditya said calmly. "It is not a matter of rules. You have introduced unwanted energies, we are all affected by what you have done. We are here together, everything we do has an effect on everyone else. Just because you are not yet sensitive enough to perceive this doesn't mean you can ignore what is asked of you. Please go to your rooms and remain silent as the guru instructed. I will speak to you tomorrow with news of what he says."

Daniel was the first to walk away and as Rachel started to turn she could see James staring in anger at Aditya. She patted his arm and as he looked at her he caught himself acting this way. He was alarmed at how strong his feelings were and without another word walked back to his room. At the doorway he looked along the corridor but Rachel had already gone into her room. He sat on the bed and felt the adrenalin in his chest. He slowed his breathing and tried to calm himself. He regretted everything he had said and done to Daniel and Aditya and wished he could have the opportunity to apologise. Despite the turmoil he was feeling he recalled his experience with the guru and knew he had to focus on the greater reality that had been revealed to him. He closed his eyes and began to recite his mantra, and immediately obscene fantasies about Rachel began to flash before him. Though he found her beautiful, he had never before given himself to these kinds of feelings about her, but no matter how he tried his head swirled with carnal images.

He got up and threw the little water that was left in the bowl into his face. He felt ashamed and his base feelings seemed to confirm everything of which Daniel had accused him. This was not who he wanted to be and he instinctively stretched himself into a yoga posture to direct his mind into something more positive. For a few minutes he performed some of the movements that Aditya had shown them but he was too tired and soon abandoned them. He pulled off his trousers and quickly jumped beneath the blanket before the cold could take hold. Still shivering he lay on his side, desperately trying to regain control of himself. He knew it wasn't appropriate, but lying there he began to say his mantra in a low voice. He had not yet fallen asleep when he felt the paralysis grip his limbs, and as he began to panic his whole body became unresponsive. His mouth could no longer recite, and only his eyes responded to his will. A fear of death filled him, he imagined he would die like this and it threw him into a state of terror.

In the corridor he heard the shuffle of an animal's paws on the concrete coming closer to his room. On his side he could see the doorway and he watched as a huge dog walked in to his room. Its fur was matted and filthy and now James could hear its breathing, a mixture of gurgling spittle and growling. Though his mouth was silent, James heard a scream in his head as clear as if he had physically cried out, and now he could see its eyes. They were set on him, they met his gaze with a hungry intent and James knew there was nothing he could do to prevent it from tearing him apart.

The dog came to the side of the bed and lifted itself up over the unmoving figure in the blanket. It straddled his chest and James could feel the moist breath in his face and smell the stench of rotten meat. The growling grew louder and he could see its lips snarl to reveal yellowing teeth that dripped with saliva. In uncontrollable fear James shut his eyes, unable to look any longer at the creature. And as he anticipated the first bite he felt his body released and he threw his arms forward to strike the animal. The blanket flew from him and he jumped sideways to escape the bed. There was no pain, no bite, and as he spun to defend himself he could see no intruder. He got up from his hands and knees and a deep groan escaped from him. In confusion he looked around but he was alone in the room. James looked down the corridor to confirm it was gone and then pressed his back against the wall as he panted for breath. He began to sob to himself and buried his face in his hands. For a moment he thought he heard something and froze as he stared at the doorway, but there was nothing there, and his reaction only made him more fearful for his sanity.

He wrapped the blanket around his shoulders and went down to the washroom. There was only cold water but still he threw handfuls of it over his head and into his face. He looked up into the mirror and was horrified to see the face reflected back at him; the confusion and terror was there in his eyes, and through his tired and blurred vision he saw the shadows behind him moving.

Chapter 35

As people passed his room James lay huddled in his bed wrapped in his blanket. He had slept very little and he was physically and mentally exhausted. He imagined their hostility towards him and allowed his own anger to rise in response. As he came to he began to think more clearly and told himself word wouldn't have yet got around about his behaviour and he tried to suppress what he knew to be paranoia.

He waited until he was sure everyone had gone to the morning session and went down to the washroom to clean himself up. In the daylight he could see bags forming beneath his eyes and his skin looked grey despite his tan. He couldn't be bothered to shave and quickly headed out to the field where he hoped he wouldn't be seen. His head ached and the shake in his hands had grown worse. He felt weak from hunger and began to question why it was necessary to treat the pilgrims this way. Whatever attempts he made to think positively turned to resentment or annoyance and he realised he was further away from the peace he desired than at any time since Emma had left him. None of it made sense to him and though he wanted to talk to someone the events of the previous night left him feeling isolated. He took out his 'phone and scrolled through his address book, but there was no one he felt would understand what was happening. He flicked through a few photographs and stopped at one of him and Emma from the year before. Tears welled up as he stared at her, he cursed himself for the choices he'd made that had led him to feeling this way.

He tried to adopt a more detached perspective and told himself he had to re-join the pilgrimage and go through whatever uncomfortable conversations were ahead of him. It was the right thing to do, he was convinced of it, and the possibility of putting the situation behind him gave him a little hope. He checked the time and decided to wait in his room until the second session, that way Bhakti Charandas or Aditya could publicly address any issues they wanted to raise and he could clear the air by acknowledging what he had done.

After a short wait in his room he heard some of the others returning and sat on his bed looking at the doorway. As they passed him in the corridor no one turned to greet or even look at him and he considered going out to find Rachel. But his promise to keep his distance couldn't be broken so quickly and he didn't want her to think any less of him than she already did. He chose to wait where he was and lay back on his bed. This time he slept deeply and only the sound of the bell calling them to the session woke him. Despite the sleep he was still a little groggy and he quickly drank some water before walking over to the hall.

On the steps he met Carrie who gave him a half-hearted smile and it was enough to encourage him. They went in together through the first doors and found the second doors held open by the two Indian attendants. The air conditioning hummed as they found their places amongst the silent pilgrims, many of whom were already meditating. James avoided eye contact with anyone and stared ahead at the throne which was decorated with fresh flowers. Next to it sat the painting which now appeared threatening to James, as though the jagged colours were meant to communicate something harsh and brutal. The guru was smiling as he and the western attendants entered, he stood before his seat and looked around at the pilgrims. His eyes radiated warmth to each person as he came to them and as his head turned to where James was sitting his expression morphed into one of hatred and anger. James rocked back in alarm, but no one else seemed to notice, they continued to smile back at him to demonstrate their appreciation.

"We are not going to practise yoga today, I want to talk to you about the divine presence in each of us and how we can become alive to the god consciousness that we all desire." As Charandas spoke his gaze moved around the room and each time it came to James the same vile expression contorted his face. James couldn't understand how no one else was seeing it, he began to suspect them all of conspiring with the guru, and he realised that even Rachel must be in on it. He twisted round to look at her but she ignored him, maintaining her focus on the guru as he spoke. James realised he had no place in the group, and he stood up and walked out. Heads turned to follow him but Charandas continued his lecture as though nothing was happening. Soon everyone's attention returned to him and James slipped away without causing any real disruption.

He stood at the top of the steps and wondered what he could do next. He couldn't spend any more time alone in his room and no one followed him out to ask what was wrong. He remembered Dereck and the idea came to him that he too should leave. If he went back to the centre the two of them could spend a few days together. The more he thought about it the more attractive the idea became to him and he convinced himself that at least Dereck was someone who might understand his grievances.

James walked round behind the main building to where the mini buses were parked. One of the drivers was leaning into the open bonnet of his vehicle, tinkering with the engine. He looked up and smiled as James approached him. "Hello," he said, "how are you?"

"Not too good, I think I need to leave."

The driver frowned and shook his head. "No, no, your friend left and I was in lots of trouble for giving him a lift. I cannot help you, I will lose my job."

"I'll pay you," James said, "whatever you need."

"You cannot pay me enough to make up for my job. I am sorry, I can't."

"What about the other driver, where is he?" James looked around but couldn't see him.

"He is working inside, we have many jobs to do. We are very busy."

"Please, will you ask him to come out so I can speak to him?"

The driver sensed the desperation in his voice and nodded. "Alright, wait here."

Within a couple of minutes the two men came out, the other driver was wearing an apron and his hands were wet. "What is it?" He asked.

"I need a lift, please, can you drive me to the station so I can catch a train?"

The drivers exchanged thoughtful glances and began talking in what James assumed was Hindi. The second driver then looked at James and said "How much will you pay me?"

"I've got four and a half thousand rupees, and I can get more if you take me to a machine for my card."

The driver didn't hesitate, "Yes, I will do it. But you will have to pay for the diesel as well."

"Fine, when can we leave?" James had more cash on him than he admitted.

The driver looked at his watch and again they spoke in Hindi before he said "In two hours. I have to pick up supplies for the kitchen, you can come with me. They might not notice that you are in the van."

"Thank you," James was flushed with relief, "I'll see you then."

He went back to his room and packed his belongings back into his case. He folded the blanket and lay it neatly at the foot of the bed, wanting to leave as little reason to be criticised as he could. The first hour dragged as James kept checking the time on his 'phone. He wondered how he was going to explain things to Rachel, but despite this he was happy to be escaping. As he heard people moving around he knew he had to speak to her before it was too late. He left his things and walked down to her room. She was sitting on the chair next to her bed writing something in her note book. She showed no surprise at seeing him and he said "Can I speak to you for a moment?"

In a monotone voice she said "What is it?"

"I've been giving it some thought, I don't want to cause any more disruption, so I'm going back to the centre for the rest of the week. I think it's for the best."

She remained impassive and said "I think you're doing the right thing."

He had hoped for as little fuss as possible but her complete lack of concern was the last thing he wanted. She said "You can take some time to sort yourself out before we get back, I don't think it's helping anyone you being here."

"I'm sorry, Rachel, I didn't want to spoil it for anyone."

"I know that," there was finally a tone of empathy in her voice, "it's a real shame things have happened the way they have."

"What about us?" He asked.

"What do you mean?"

"Has all this changed the way you feel about me?"

"I'm not a child, James, give me some credit. I don't really blame you for any of it, but if we continue along this course things could get messy. I'm as much responsible as you are."

He smiled and said "I'm glad to hear you say it."

"Do you know how you're getting back?"

"The driver is giving me a lift to a railway station, I can catch a train through from there. I can see how Dereck is doing, he might need some company."

"Just be careful," she stood up, "I don't just mean the journey. I'm worried about you, I hope you're not leaving before you're ready to deal with what you've learned. And I don't know how good it is for you and Dereck to be alone too long. Don't let his negativity influence you too much. Hold on to the progress you've made, it doesn't have to be the end."

James reached out and held her hand and felt her soft fingers curl around his. He was happy to see concern in her eyes and leaned in to kiss her. "No, don't," she said, "we mustn't. I still want to complete the pilgrimage properly, you understand don't you?"

"Yes, of course, I'm sorry."

"I'll speak to Aditya; it's best if you slip away without anyone seeing you."

"I hope you don't get the same reaction I had about Dereck leaving."

"Don't worry, this is different, it won't be a problem. Daniel is still angry about you hitting him and I think it'll calm him down not having to bump into you every day."

"I'll see you when you get back," he said, and she squeezed his hand to signal him to leave. As he walked along the corridor he knew he had made the right decision and Rachel's assurances were everything he needed. In his room he checked the time once more and decided to wait another twenty minutes before going out to the mini bus. Sitting on the bed his thoughts turned to the dog he had seen the previous night and he began to doubt his memories. Even so soon after the event he wondered how much had actually happened and began to look for rational reasons to explain it away. Hunger and tiredness were certainly factors, but he admitted to himself that his emotions had been in turmoil. He imagined how it would sound if he described it all to someone and he could hear the kinds of sensible responses they would make.

Eventually he slipped the strap of his case over his shoulder and left the room. Even stepping out from beyond this physical space brought him relief and as he stepped into the sunshine he felt exhilarated to be getting away. There was no one around to see him and he walked to the back of the buildings to find the driver. He couldn't see him but found the bus unlocked and climbed in beside the driver's seat. After a few minutes of waiting he saw the driver coming out from the kitchens and they waved to each other as he approached. As he opened the door to get in he said "Do you have the money on you?"

"Yes, right here," James patted his chest pocket. "I'll give it to you at the station."

"And money for the fuel?"

"Yes, no problem," James was irritated by the questions, "let's go, please."

The driver seemed satisfied and started up the engine. James clicked his seatbelt into place and as they followed the dirt path alongside the field James looked at the trees where he and Rachel had stood the night before. As the buildings behind them went out of view James relaxed, knowing that it was too late now for anyone to prevent him leaving. The driver began to hum to himself as he steered them through the potholes, and James stared out at the countryside, trying to distract himself from the memories of the last few days with the beauty of the Indian countryside.

Chapter 36

The station at Bikaner was a mix of old colonial designs and a rail system that was surprisingly modern. As the minibus pulled up in front of a series of arches the driver looked at James with an expression that communicated all his suspicions. The smile on James' face was as much a mixture of relief to arrive as it was seeing the driver's fear that he was going to try and avoid paying him. He reached into his pocket and with his fingers still gripping the money asked "How much for the diesel?"

"A thousand rupees," the driver told him.

James did a quick calculation in his head and decided he was getting a good deal. He counted out the notes as the driver studied every move. Once the cash was in his hand the driver's demeanour changed and the familiar smile returned. "Thank you," he said, "I hope you have a good journey."

James ignored the fake friendliness and reached behind him for his bag. "Thanks, bye," was all he could muster as he stepped down onto the pavement. As soon as he swung the door shut the bus pulled away and James knew he was alone. He briefly imagined the scene as the driver explained where James had gone but knew it would evoke a different response to Dereck's disappearance. The sense of escape was still strong but the realisation that he had no one to rely on sharpened his senses and he became vigilant to the people around him.

The interior of the station was clean and spacious and the signs all had English translations. He joined the queue at the ticket office which slowly moved towards a small grill where a middle aged Indian man looked to be taking his job very seriously. When James reached the counter the ticket seller looked at him with a disinterest that was reassuring: it convinced James that there had been enough western travellers through here that he didn't need to worry about drawing attention. He told him where he wanted to go but the man said "Which class?"

"I don't know, what are the choices?" James said.

"First class which is air-conditioned, second or third?"

Considering how long he was going to be on the train James said "First class please."

"I am sorry, first class must be booked in advance."

James was about to ask why he would tell him about it if it wasn't available but realised the official was simply repeating a script which was no doubt designed to impress travellers that the company's trains had air conditioning. "I'll take second then. How much?"

"No, second class is not available."

James was becoming irritable, "Just give me whatever you've got then."

"Three chair class," the official said as he printed off the ticket. As he slid it under the grill he pointed to James' right and said "Platform three." James forced himself to thank him and lifted his bag onto his shoulder. Faces of every shade of brown moved in all directions and for a moment James felt homesick. He came to a shop selling foods and remembered how hungry he was. Cooking on a hot pan behind the counter were strips of meat and without enquiring as to what animal they came from James ordered a portion. The woman serving him brushed three pieces of the meat with a thick sauce and presented them on a paper plate. The strips had a thick edge of fat which had cooked to a satisfying crispness and as he bit into them James cursed the vegetarian curries they had been forced to endure. He left the shop with a satisfied stomach, the first he'd had since entering the country, and spotting the platform he went out to wait for his train. An electronic board showed he only had forty-five minutes before it was due and he found a space on a bench next to a young couple and their three children.

He sat watching the crowds and the time passed quickly. A voice announced over the tannoy that his train was approaching and everyone around him began pushing forward towards the edge of the platform. James stood where he was, not wanting to risk being pushed under the oncoming train, and as it drew alongside them the pushing turned into shoving and even before it had come to a stop the doors were pulled open and passengers began forcing their way on board. James watched in amazement as young men began climbing into the carriages through the open windows and he realised he had better find a seat before they were all taken.

James walked down to where he could see empty seats and pressed forwards into the mass of bodies and managed to squeeze into one of the carriages. Inside the heat was unbearable and he immediately spotted bars outside the windows which gave the carriage the feel of a prison cell; clearly third class travellers were not trusted. He found a vacant seat and slumped into it as a stream of people continued to force their way down the aisle looking for a place to sit. Two seats down a man and a woman began arguing furiously about who had rightful claim to the space and in the end the young man wandered off as she continued to yell after him.

The train had only been in the station a few minutes when it jolted forwards and began the next leg of its journey. The doors to the carriage had been left open and as the train began to pick up speed young men hung as far out as they could to cool themselves in the breeze. It looked ridiculously dangerous to James who was content to suffer the stale carriage air. He pulled his bag between his feet and tried to make himself comfortable on the torn upholstery. Opposite him an old man was eating something from a paper bag and James seemed to be the only one who noticed the overpowering smell. A woman and two young children occupied the other seats near him and the sound of their perpetual talking eventually became absorbed into the background as James closed his eyes and tried to rest.

Any hope of sleeping quickly faded as James felt his sleeve being tugged. He found himself looking into the face of a man whose concave eye sockets showed a complete absence of eyeballs. He held out a cloth sack into which the woman with the children leaned over and dropped a coin. James fumbled for some change and contributed a few coins and the blind man shuffled on to the next row of seats. James realised that this was how the beggar spent his time, dragging himself up and down the length of the train as it crossed the Indian landscape. Other beggars followed after him but after the blind man their plight evoked less sympathy and few people gave them anything.

After an hour the train arrived at the next station and the woman left her children and dashed out onto the platform. One of the stalls there was selling tea and in the few minutes that the train was standing still twenty or thirty people risked losing their transport for a drink. As the train began pulling away there were still people waiting for their tea and with cup in hand they dashed to climb back in through the gaping doorways. The woman returned and passed the cup around to her children who took sips before she reclaimed it. James made the decision to risk it himself at the next station but for now once more tried to sleep.

The rocking of the carriage relaxed him and he quickly began dreaming. As his mind sifted through recent events he returned to images of Rachel and the thought of her woke him. His eyes opened briefly before he tried to shut out the world once more and began reciting his mantra. There was no eye or spiral before him, just a blank darkness that was impossible to penetrate. As he meditated he recalled the image of the dog and began to fear its return and he became agitated.

The old man opposite him tapped his knee and James looked into his face with surprise. In a strong accent he asked James "Why are you saying that?"

For a moment James was confused, and then realising what he meant he said with some embarrassment "It's my mantra."

The old man shook his head, "No, you mustn't say that, it's not good."

James was in no mood to listen but he gave up on seeking something inward and stared out of the window at the hills and fields. Only a few days ago it had all struck him as beautiful but now he saw only poverty and human suffering. The sense of excitement and mystery had gone, and he felt the perpetual threat of hunger and need that looked back at him from the eyes of all those around him. The world looked brutal and savage to him and he wondered how these people could survive such lives. He felt pampered and spoiled coming from the affluence of Britain, and now all he wanted was to return to it.

His destination was the ninth stop, and by the time they arrived his clothes were soaked through with sweat. Even the ordinary heat of the day was welcome after being enclosed for so long and as he strode along the platform he reminded himself that he had a few days without any pressure in which to reunite with Dereck and try to piece things together in his mind. As he emerged into the street outside the station he saw a line of little taxis and told the driver the address of the centre. He wasn't entirely sure the driver knew where he was going but it felt good to be back in the little town and as he began to recognise a few sites he knew they were heading in the right direction. The taxi turned down the side road and James felt relief as the centre came into view. He paid the driver and walked over to the main gates, but came to a stop when he found them chained shut. He stood for a moment, unsure of what to do, and then walked around the outside of the perimeter wall hoping to find another entrance. There was no other way in, and James wondered if he should hang around and see if anyone showed up. Back at the gates he peered through a small gap but couldn't see anyone inside. He regretted not exchanging numbers with Dereck and felt a surge of panic as he realised he had nowhere to go. He took out his 'phone and began searching for local hotels. There were rooms available for a decent price less than a mile away and he decided to at least have somewhere for the night until he could sort things out. He wasn't sure of the route and took another taxi ride, and as they pulled up outside a two storey hotel James saw a young white couple going into the main entrance. It was a reassuring sight and after paying the driver he followed them in.

The foyer was rundown but clean and the little Indian man at reception looked happy to see him. James signed in and took his key up to the send floor. The room was unlocked and James' immediate response was that it was the most luxurious place he had stayed in since he had arrived in India. The bed was wide, there was a sink and a small balcony outside the window. He dropped his bag and went out and leaned on the railing. He looked down at the busy street beneath him and from his vantage point felt safe. He went back into the room and turned on the large ceiling fan and stretched out on the bed. The mattress was too soft and he enjoyed the sensation of sinking into it as the old springs offered no resistance to his body weight. He stared up at the ceiling and watched the blades turning above him. It reminded him of a scene from Apocalypse Now and as he closed his eyes he smiled at the thought of Daniel back in his little room without a door.

Chapter 37

After a few hours' sleep James went down into the foyer to find the bar. The man at reception apologetically explained that they didn't have one and James began to give up on the hope of a beer. As he was walking away the young man he had seen entering the hotel earlier was standing next to him and said "You need the grog shop."

"The what?" James said.

"The grog shop, it's a little shed with a counter, they sell you anything you need." His accent was Australian and he had the relaxed bearing of someone at home wherever he might find himself. "Take a right as you leave the hotel, follow the street down about half a mile, you can't miss it."

James thanked him and set out for his drink. Just as the Australian had described it, a queue had formed outside a large wooden structure and through the service window could be seen shelves of bottles and cans. Pinned near the window was a sign explaining the limits each person could purchase and when he was close enough to read it James discovered that whisky and wine were completely overpriced, but the local beer was a bargain. He bought four large bottles of lager handed over to him in a brown paper bag and carried them back to his room. He filled the sink with water and hoped it would at least prevent the beer from reaching room temperature, and using the door key popped the cap from the first green bottle. It was the greatest thing he had ever tasted, and he pulled one of the seats on the balcony to a position where he

271

could rest his feet on the railing. The first beer went down quickly and he fetched the second which he sipped more slowly. Drinking beer felt like he had regained control over how he lived, and he promised himself he'd later find more meat for dinner.

As he watched the crowds beneath him he wondered how many of them really cared about the kinds of things Aditya and the guru had been teaching, and as suspicions began to mount he struggled to know how he was feeling about it all. As he weighed the evidence he thought about Rachel and decided that if her convictions were so strong he should see beyond the nonsense that had gone on with Daniel and the others. He knew he had experienced something powerful, something he was sure he could not have reached by himself, and yet he knew he was uncomfortable with so many of the trappings of how it was all being presented. He desperately wanted to talk about it with someone, and he thought about Dereck again. He scrolled through the contacts on his 'phone and realised that Rachel might have Dereck's number, or at least could ask someone for it. He checked the time and decided the evening session would be finished and so tried to contact her. But her 'phone was switched off and he ended the call before leaving any message. At some point she would see his missed call and his imagination began to conjure up a range of different ways she might react.

He opened his third beer and returned to the balcony. The Australian couple were heading into town and he considered calling down to them but in the end watched quietly as they made their way through the crowd, the contrast of their blonde hair making them stand out from the locals even from above. Cradling his beer James closed his eyes and began to control his breathing. He felt the energy moving back and forth within his chest and he focussed his attention on Rachel so far away. He willed everything good he could feel towards her, and as the image of her face filled his mind he became aware of the strength of his feelings for her. As he enjoyed the sensation his thoughts jumped from him, as though they were leaving his control. The thought of her face was replaced with an explicit image of her body and he was filled with lust. He shook his head and said "No!" He opened his eyes but the feelings continued, and as he banged his beer bottle onto the glass table next to him he began to hear the snuffling of a dog in his room. The night sky was streaked red as the sun set, and there was little light falling back through the doorway. The sounds continued and he tried to tell himself that there was nothing there. His efforts achieved nothing and his terror grew, and as he twisted to look down over the balcony he considered jumping to safety. The concrete street threatened to break his bones if he tried and he gave up on the idea, and stepped closer to the entrance to peer inside. There was a low growl that seemed to come from behind his bed, and James grabbed the beer bottle and held it as a short club. He stepped slowly into the room and the grunts continued. He glanced at the door and saw where the light switch was, and jumping forwards he hit it with the palm of his hand while at the same time spinning round to strike anything that was coming for him.

In the yellow light of the bulb he saw that he was alone and the sounds had stopped. He stood rigid at the door, unable to make sense of what had happened. His body shook in fear and he staggered round to the other side of the bed to be certain there was nothing hiding there. He dropped to his knees and looked under the bed and as he saw only empty shadows he heard laughter above him. He bolted upright and knew it was coming from the ceiling near the fan. The voice sniggered again before the room fell silent. James couldn't rise from his knees, he was too afraid to move in any way. His hand curled around the fist of blanket that he held tight, his knuckles turning white as the blood was refused entry. Tears began to well up in his eyes as James realised he must have gone insane. He could no longer trust his eyes and ears or the thoughts in his own head. Eventually he rose to his feet and without releasing his grip on the blanket walked out onto the balcony. There was a small comfort in no longer being in the room and he slid the glass door shut to separate himself further from the space within. He wrapped the blanket around himself and pushed the chair as far as he could from the door.

The sky was darkening and the air was turning cold. He turned on his 'phone and found some music to shut out his thoughts. The familiarity of the songs comforted him and he sat motionless, watching the door to the room, half expecting it to slide open. The music reminded him of people from home and seeing himself like this he began to cry.

It was early in the morning before James felt able to re-enter the room. He found his jacket and without locking the door made his way down to the reception desk. A young Indian man was watching television and looked surprised to see him.

"Where can I get some food?" James asked bluntly.

"There are plenty of places still open, just head into town," the young man said.

Without thanking him James headed towards the door but before he was out stopped dead as the young man called out to him "Where do you think you're going at this time of night, Jamie?"

James spun round and called back "What did you say?"

The Indian looked confused, "Nothing, I said nothing."

James felt anger surge through him and his impulse was to go back and confront him. As the anger began to take hold of him he caught sight of the fear in the young man's eyes and instead walked out into the street. There were very few people around and James walked quickly towards where he could see a few stalls still lit up and dealing with customers. A woman had a huge flat pan sitting over an open fire and behind her hung strips of meat and various vegetables. James pointed to the meat and held three fingers up. She nodded and dropped the meat into the pan. As the hot oil hit the fat it sizzled and spat and James stared at it, unable to look away. He realised the woman was speaking to him and he said "What?"

"Do you want flavouring?" She repeated.

"Yea, why not, chuck it all on," James said, still gazing at the meat.

The woman looked nervous as she asked for payment and James realised he needed to take control of himself. He took his food and sat on a low wall next to the road, and unaware of anyone around him began greedily tearing into the meat. Sauce and fat surrounded his mouth but he did nothing to wipe it away, and when he had finished eating he dropped the paper bag to the floor in front of him. He lifted his head and for the first time looked at the passers-by, still feeling no real interest in anyone. As he noticed their faces he began to be convinced that they were scowling at him, he saw nothing but frowns and sneers. As a pair of old Indian men passed by he strained to hear them as he detected English words, only to recoil as he caught one of them saying "Jamie's a mess, look at him."

James knew he had to be hallucinating, and as he tried to control his panic he decided he shouldn't be out on the street. He began to run back towards the hotel, the cold night air cut into his lungs as he finally staggered back into the foyer. The young receptionist looked at him now with obvious alarm and James forced himself to walk as slowly as he could past him towards the stairs. Once out of view he trotted up two steps at a time and found himself outside his room. He stood staring at the door, he read and reread the number, and as his hand took hold of the door knob he slowly turned it and felt the latch click free. The door slowly swung open before him and he looked into the shadows for signs of movement. From the stairs James heard the voices of other guests approaching and forced himself to step inside. The fan was still turning above him as he stood motionless with his back pressed against the door, listening to the other guests pass his room on the corridor. One of them was laughing happily and he felt a wave of resentment pass through him.

He moved to the bed and sat down, aware of the sound of his breathing and the pulse that beat in his head. His hands shook as he wiped them on the legs of his trousers, the grease from the food left long stains where his hands moved, and he became aware of how dirty they were. He went to the sink and saw the mess of his face reflected back at him, his wild eyes looked out from above dirty streaks that made him look insane. He washed it away in the warm water from the bowl and rubbed himself dry in a towel. From the street outside he heard a voice call his name and he ignored it. He lay down on the bed, and as the voice continued to call out he heard it break into laughter. With the light and ceiling fan still turned on he curled his body into a tight ball and pulled the blanket over his head. He wanted to shut out everything around him, but he knew that what was taunting him was inside the blanket and inside his head. He let out a moan that was ancient and inhuman, and even as he pressed his face into the pillow he could hear the voices from the street still laughing.

Chapter 38

Over the next few days James' condition deteriorated. For most of the time he stayed in his room and ate very little. He slept during the day and spent the nights watching for whatever might be near him. He felt his capacity to reason with himself diminishing and he no longer tried to understand what was happening. What once had been strange and unreal now became normality, and a number of times he considered bringing it to an end by taking his life. The thought of throwing himself off the hotel roof was slowly becoming a sensible option and the worse he felt the stronger the urge became. As he counted the mornings and nights the one hope he clung to was that Rachel would be able to help him. He frequently checked to see if she had responded to his message but there was nothing. He told himself she was exhibiting self-discipline in following the pilgrimage rules but each time he checked and saw no reply his heart sank further and the sense of having been abandoned intensified.

On the day everyone was due to return James worked out the likely time of arrival and decided to show up a couple of hours after that. He packed his passport and a few belongings but left most of his clothes hanging in the room. At reception another young Indian greeted him and began asking how he had enjoyed his stay but when James failed to answer his enquiries he fell silent. When James looked at him the young man avoided his gaze and pretended to check the details on his computer screen.

James longed to tell him how he felt, he needed human contact, but was unable to share even a smile.

On the street James walked down to the stalls where he could buy some food, he had half the day to kill and already the case strap was cutting into his shoulder. In the end he found a bench near a busy road junction and sat staring aimlessly at the passers-by, thinking now only of seeing Rachel again. He began to play through their reunion and each imagined scenario always concluded with her holding him. Despite his hunger he forgot about eating and grew steadily more light-headed as the hours passed.

As the daylight gave hints of approaching evening James walked down to where the taxis were lined up and when he leaned into the window of the first in the queue the driver shook his head and insisted he couldn't speak English. The look on his face suggested more than a language barrier but James accepted his refusal and wandered on to the next vehicle. The second driver nodded when he heard the destination and James climbed in beside him. The driver's dashboard carried images of various Hindu gods and as James studied them he felt something jolt within him. The driver noticed him jerk in the seat but said nothing. As they reached the street of the compound it was with relief that James saw the unlocked gates and he carelessly handed over a few notes to the driver.

As he entered the yard he saw the two minibuses parked over near the dormitories and one of the drivers was sitting with his cab door open smoking a cigarette. It was the one who had refused to give James a lift back at the guru's centre, but still they exchanged waves as he drew near.

"You are well?" The driver asked.

"Yea, okay, where is everyone?"

"They are in the hall," the driver pointed in the direction of the main building, "Aditya is giving them a final talk. You have missed dinner."

James walked off without saying anything further and went into the dormitory to find a place to dump his things. As he walked past the rooms he could see the pilgrims' possessions and decided to head up to the little room he had slept in before they had left. It was unclaimed and with relief he dropped his bag and closed the door behind him. He remembered the events of his last night there and inwardly shrugged at how insignificant it now seemed compared with how he felt. There was no water in the bowl and he felt the dry thirst in his throat that he had been oblivious to up until now. He decided against going out to find something to drink; he didn't want to have to explain himself to anyone. Instead he sat on the bed and waited.

After about forty minutes James heard people returning to their rooms. Their voices sounded happy and there was a lot of laughter. He knew Rachel was somewhere amongst them, and it was all he could do not to rush out and find her. He listened intently in the hope of picking her voice out from the crowd. He reasoned that if this room had been left empty then perhaps everyone had gone back to their original rooms, and he would visit her when it sounded like everyone had settled down. But his plan was unnecessary, after a few more minutes there was tapping at his door and he finally heard Rachel's voice saying "James? James? Are you there?"

He hurried to the door and swung it open, "Rachel!"

She was startled to see him, "What's happened to you? My god, you look terrible."

"Come in, I'm so glad to see you," he blurted.

She continued to gaze at his face. Her eyes full of concern. "I've been so worried about you, are you okay?"

James paused, "No, I…" his voice trailed off and he threw his arms around her. As she held him he began to sob.

"What is it? What's wrong, James?"

"I don't know where to begin," he whispered, "I can't explain it."

"Explain what? What's happened?" Her voice shook with emotion and he was grateful for it.

"I don't want to talk here, can we go somewhere? I don't feel safe here."

"What? I don't understand James, why aren't you safe? Please, tell me what's happened."

"Not here, come with me, let's go to the pool, I need to talk to you."

She stepped back from him, "I can't, James. Bhakti Charandas told me I wasn't to spend time alone with you until the end of the pilgrimage, I don't want to be any more disobedient than we already have. I'm sorry, I shouldn't even be here now, but I wanted to make sure you were back safely."

James felt frustration turning to anger and his voice rose as he said "To hell with their rules, what good are they if they keep us apart. I need to speak to you, Rachel."

"Okay, calm down, we can speak now, I just can't leave the compound with you. I'm sorry. It means too much to me, I don't want to spoil it."

James turned away and slapped the side of his leg in temper. As he turned back to her she recoiled slightly at the look of anger in his face, "James, you need to speak to Aditya, he can help you."

"What good have they done me? They've messed me up Rachel, things are happening and I can't control them. I want it to stop but I can't."

"You've opened a part of yourself that is very powerful," Rachel was calm and spoke softly, "cutting your teaching short has left you vulnerable to forces you were only just encountering. You need to use this last bit of time here to focus the energies into positive, healing effects. Aditya can help you do this."

"You sound like you're just repeating words from the guru," James said, "I don't think he can help me."

"It is what Bhakti Charandas said to me, you're right. He was so concerned for you James, he gave me an extra personal session to understand what is happening with you. Please, trust me, I know something wonderful has happened to you, but you must complete it. It can be harmful to leave it unfinished."

As she spoke James knew she was his only hope and whatever advice she gave he had to take it. He reached out and held her hand, "I'm so sorry for spoiling the trip for you," he said honestly.

"You haven't spoilt anything, the guru made me understand how far you went; it's amazing James, but it's too powerful to handle without a guide. You must put yourself in the hands of someone who knows what they're doing. You could be in real danger if you don't."

"I know I'm in danger, Rachel, I believe you. What about all the others?"

"What do you mean? They're all doing well," she said.

"No, I mean how do they feel towards me? I'm nervous about facing them."

Rachel smiled, "Everything is fine, don't worry. There was real concern when you left."

"Even Daniel?"

"Yes, don't worry, they're not children. They understand what we're dealing with here. We were told that dark energies might try to divide us but that we mustn't judge one another for anything that happened. No one's harbouring any bad feelings, James, trust me."

Her words were reassuring and he continued to be grateful for her kindness. "I've missed you so much," he said. "I've only got through the last few days knowing I'd see you again."

She stepped closer to him and kissed his cheek, and as he felt her lips on his skin a surge of desire passed through him. He stepped back from her and tried to conceal his feelings. "I'll go and find Aditya, thank you."

"He's in the main hall," she said. "He's answering questions about his talk." She smiled, "and get some sleep. You look exhausted. Why don't you have a shower first?"

"Okay, I will. Thank you."

She squeezed his hand and went back to her room. James took a dirty towel and quickly showered. It helped him regain something of himself and as he walked over to the hall he felt a fragment of optimism for the first time since he had last seen them all. In the hall everyone had gone except for a young American woman who was deep in conversation with Aditya. As soon as James appeared the Indian kept looking his way and drew his conversation with the woman to a premature conclusion. Seeing James she understood the situation and left them alone.

"Hello James, I am glad to see you."

"Hello Aditya, thank you, I wasn't sure how welcome I'd be."

"Nonsense, you are most welcome. Our teacher explained to me what is happening, any bad feelings towards you were the consequence of confusion and ignorance." He stood up from the table and as he met James he patted his arm. "We must go into the little room and address some things, are you up to it?"

"Yes, I'm tired, but I need to talk."

"We must do more than talk, James, this is far more than a matter of words. Come in." Aditya led him into the small meditation room where candles still burned either side of a small brass statue. He waved his hand to invite

James to sit and then lit a stick of incense which he wafted before the statue. He placed it in front of the image before joining James on the mats on the floor.

"Bhakti Charandas told me that you have encountered guides beyond this world, I must first tell you something more about them. They are wise and offer help, but they can also be mischievous. We must develop discernment in knowing when they have come to guide us and when they are playing."

"Playing!" James exclaimed. "What's been happening to me isn't help or play. Something has been attacking me."

"You don't look injured," Aditya retorted. "You say attacked, where are your wounds? Have you been bleeding?"

"I don't mean that kind of attack, not physical. There was the sound of a dog, and then I saw it, it was on me, it was going to bite me."

"And did it bite you?" Aditya remained calm in the face of James' agitation.

"No, it didn't, but it threatened me. I was terrified, it was in the room with me, growling."

"Ha!" Aditya grinned, "You see. The danger was in your mind, no real harm came to you except what your own fear did to you."

"No Adi, it was more than that. I couldn't sleep, I've been hearing things, seeing things; this wasn't my imagination."

"No, I don't suggest you imagined any of it, but how you allowed yourself to react is the crucial element here. Can you not see that if you had been dispassionate, removed yourself from your concerns, you could have met this experience with a calm understanding?"

James was tired and though he disagreed with what he was hearing he had no strength to argue and said "Alright, how do I do that?"

283

"Instead of rejecting the experience you must welcome it. Instead of trying to keep your visitors away you must open yourself to them. You are creating conflict through your fear, and it is this conflict that is bringing you turmoil. We can do this together, now, shall we try?" Aditya paused and looked at him expectantly.

James wanted an answer, and no matter how much he wanted to maintain his guard against the experience, he knew he didn't have any way to escape what was happening. He nodded his agreement and they closed their eyes. Aditya began by leading him through a series of breathing exercises but James was faced with the dull wall once more that prevented any sense of movement or energy. Aditya continued to lead their meditation but in the end James said "I can't Adi, it's no good, nothing is happening. It doesn't come now when I try, only when I'm alone or tired. I've lost it. I can't control anything."

"No, James, listen to me, you have stepped beyond the illusion of choice, the illusion of self. It doesn't matter what you choose any more, this is good, you have moved beyond yourself so that the guides themselves select their moments to engage with you. Do not lose heart, this is good."

James tried to believe what he was hearing, "I feel empty, Adi. All my enthusiasm and interest has drained away."

"Then we must respond with a ritual that does not require mental engagement. We can do things with the body that perform worship even if the mind is ignorant. You know the benefits of yoga, what do you think you have been doing all this time except giving honour to the divine ones. We must take that experience and press on. The guides can be evoked through other actions, I will show you."

Aditya took more incense and lit it from one of the candles. As he waved it back and forth he began to repeat something unintelligible. James watched as the Indian began to recite more quickly, sensing something different around them. As the sensation grew Aditya stopped and turned to look at him, "You feel it yes?"

James nodded.

"Then do the same," Aditya instructed him, "take the incense and recite with me."

"I don't know the words," James said, "what are you saying?"

"You don't know the words but you know the sounds. Listen and copy me, say it with me."

Aditya resumed his chanting and James tried to imitate him. After a few minutes he found the rhythm of the sounds and their voices began to blend and harmonise. James felt his lips forming the shapes of these new words and as they escaped from his mouth he knew there was a meaning within them. Aditya began to increase the speed once more and James kept pace with him, and as they waved the incense back and forth they felt their bodies swaying so that soon they were rocking in time with the chant, their voices growing louder and the air filling with thick smoke.

Just as when Aditya had been chanting alone, James could now feel something in the room around them, the physical space was becoming charged with a presence that willed them on. As they became utterly intoxicated in the moment James heard another voice chanting with them, and then a fourth and fifth. More voices began to join them until James could no longer hear Aditya at all. Suddenly James could see the eye before him, and now it was withdrawing from him. As it moved away James saw a second eye beside it, and then the details of a face began to appear around them. James found himself looking at a savage and brutal presence, it stared at him with hatred and James knew it wanted him dead. But he couldn't look away, he couldn't open his eyes, and his mouth continued

285

to chant as his body moved. Finally the face rushed him and James felt the back of his head strike the wall as he was thrown backwards with the impact of whatever it was.

The chanting stopped and James opened his eyes. Sitting across from him Aditya was giggling as he stared at him, giggling through a hateful sneer. James didn't move for a few moments, he lay looking in revulsion at the man before him. Eventually he got to his feet but Aditya continued to snigger manically and James walked out without saying anything. The hall was dark and he left without picking up his shoes. He strode to Rachel's room and banged on her door. It opened quickly and James could see a small group gathered in her room. "We've been chanting for you," Rachel said.

James stared at her in bewilderment, her words didn't register in any way, and he turned and went to his room. A few minutes later she came after him and without knocking let herself in. "James, what happened? How did it go?"

"I want to go home, I want to go back to England." His voice was flat and monotone.

"We will, we're nearly done, what's wrong? Did Aditya help you?"

He looked at her without tears, without desire, with the blank, empty expression that belongs to the face of the dead.

Chapter 39

For the remaining time at the compound James attended no lectures or yoga sessions and ate alone the food that Rachel brought to his room. When it came time to leave he silently climbed into the back of the minibus and stared out of the window, oblivious to anyone around him. The general consensus was that he was suffering some kind of breakdown and the Americans in particular had all sorts of theories as to what had caused it. Dereck had found a flight home two days before and no one was concerned about him.

At the airport and on the aeroplane James ordered beer after beer and after a few hours dozed off slumped up against the window. He and Rachel exchanged few words the entire journey and by the time they were waiting for their bags at Birmingham airport she had all but given up trying to speak to him.

As they emerged through customs she slipped her arm through his and said "Do you want me to come back to the flat with you? Just to make sure you're okay."

"No, thank you, I appreciate it, but I just need to sleep." He was now hungover on top of everything else and his sunken cheeks made him look as sick as he felt.

"If you're sure," she said. "I'll call you tomorrow, maybe it would be good if you went to see David."

"Maybe, I'll have to see." He tried to inject some life into his voice but failed.

"You need to speak to him about the move and the job," she said, "regardless of what you decide about India."

"I've got nearly a week before then, I'll sort it out. I just need to sleep."

They reached the taxi rank and she said "Okay, don't worry, everything's going to be okay." She lifted her head and kissed him on the mouth and walked over to a waiting taxi. After speaking to the driver she waved to James and a few seconds later she was gone. James stood staring after her for a little while and then found himself a ride. As the Indian driver tried to make conversation James thought about Aditya and the guru, he wanted to stop the small-talk and ask him what he knew about meditation, ask him for reassurance about what he'd gone through, but the questions swirled around in his head and he remained silent.

The sight of his front door was a great comfort and he wasted no time letting himself in and shutting out the world. As he walked through his flat he saw the yoga mat still laid out on the floor and a small pile of books he had been flicking through before the trip. The sight of them made him angry and he took his laptop into the kitchen and made himself a black coffee. There were over two hundred messages sitting in his inbox and as he scanned the names of the senders he decided he didn't want to read any of them. But amongst them he spotted an email from Nick and James opened it knowing it was something safe to read. It was no more than the usual daft comments about a football match and good wishes for the trip. James needed to make contact with someone and Nick fit the bill. He turned on his 'phone and gave him a call.

"Hi James, you back in the country?" It was the comforting sound of his old friend's voice.

"Yea, got back about half an hour ago."

"And you're calling me straight away?" Nick laughed. "You got a decent tan?"

"Yea, very brown." James couldn't think of anything further to add.

"You avoid the Deli belly? What were the women like out there?"

"Yea, I was fine. I'm sorry Nick, I'm gonna have to go. I'll give you another call in a few days."

"Oh, alright then. Is everythin' okay mate?"

"Yea, no problem, I have to go, bye." James ended the call, it had been a mistake. How could he have expected him to understand what was happening? He remembered what Rachel had said and called Munro's number. It rang twice and Munro answered.

"Hello James, I hope you're feeling a little better."

"What? How did you know? What have you been told?" James was caught off guard by the comment.

"Rachel rang me, don't worry, it's not unusual for people to have intense reactions. We can help you work through this. In fact, would you like to meet in a few days? I could come up to the house."

"Where are you now?" James asked.

"I'm down in London for a couple more days, but I can get up there if it would be helpful."

"Yea, that'd be good, thank you." There was no strength in James' voice."

"I'll see you on Friday, how about two o'clock?"

"Right, I'll see you then. Thank you."

Munro hung up and James sipped at his coffee. He felt better knowing Munro would help him, he trusted the older man and the connection they had made meant something to him. James went back to the front door and picked up his mail. He shuffled through the envelopes, ignoring everything with a printed address. Amongst the others was a white envelope in an unfamiliar handwriting. James dropped the rest of the pile on the table and tore it open. It was a single sheet of paper and at the bottom it was signed Jacob. James was in no mood for his gripes and nearly threw it with the others. But he was curious and began reading.

Dear James,

None of this will make sense but I need to speak to you immediately when you get back from India. Don't let what went between us before get in the way, we need to talk, you are in danger. Don't show this letter to anyone, including Rachel – this is absolutely vital. If you do nothing else, please destroy this letter when you have read it. I will be in the café near the hall where we meet for yoga, at midday on Thursday. Please meet me there, it is very important.

Jacob.

James read it through a couple of times before folding it back into its envelope and slipping it into the pocket of his jacket hanging on the back of the bedroom door. Despite the insistence that it was urgent, James couldn't imagine what Jacob could possibly have to say to him and with everything else that was happening wasn't sure whether he would bother meeting him. All he could think of was the way Jacob had reacted to seeing him and Rachel together and it still annoyed him. He caught himself cursing him under his breath and was surprised at the strength of the feelings he still had for him.

He found a tin of beans and heated up some noodles. The stodgy carbohydrates were satisfying and he sat in front of his laptop watching some old episodes of an American comedy he liked and as he began to relax his anxieties began to subside. He couldn't be bothered to go out for milk and settled for black coffees for the rest of the night, confident that even this amount of caffeine couldn't overcome his exhaustion. By ten thirty he'd had enough of the day and went into the bathroom to clean his teeth. In the bright light he could see in the mirror the consequences of everything that had happened in India, the sleepless nights, the poor food, everything that had left him weak and nearly fourteen pounds lighter. The skin was peeling at his forehead and along the length of his nose, giving him a soiled, grubby look that no amount of water could wash away.

He climbed into bed and the familiar smell of his sheets and pillow reminded him of the life he knew before the trip. He pulled the quilt tight around himself, longing for a good night's sleep. There was only one incident in the night. A couple of hours after he had fallen asleep he woke to feel the covers being pulled off him. He snatched at them but they were out of reach and as he leaned over the bed to find them he heard his name being called from outside the room. Pulling the quilt back over himself he heard the calling turn into laughter and he buried his face into the pillow to shut it out.

The following morning he slept in late and as he woke he remembered Jacob's letter. He checked the time and knew he could make it without rushing and for no particular reason decided to meet with him. He gave the events of the night little thought and was happy to be back in the flat. He drank more coffee and then went out to see if the car would start. He turned the key and it kicked into life immediately, and he drove over to the church hall. As he entered the café Jacob was sitting with his back to him, bent forward over the table, deep in thought.

James was prepared for confrontation and said firmly "Hello Jacob, I got your letter."

"Thank you for coming," Jacob stood up and looked around at the door. "Please," he said, "take a seat, do you want a drink?"

"Yea, thanks. I'll have a tea." James could see he was nervous, it was unlike him, and it suggested to him that Jacob had something important to say.

When he returned with the tea he again looked at the door and James asked "Are you expecting someone else?"

"No, not at all," Jacob said, sitting back down in his seat. "I'm glad you came, I need to speak to you. I know what you think of me, I know you think I've behaved badly towards you."

"You haven't been very friendly, Jacob, you have to admit it."

"I know how it seems, but you have to believe me, I was trying to protect you. I tried to stop you going to India, I didn't want you getting any deeper into all of this." Jacob spoke quietly, he didn't want anyone overhearing what he had to say.

"Into what?" James said.

"You must know by now, or maybe you don't. How much have you worked out yet?"

"About what? Just come out and say it." James was becoming impatient.

"I've seen other people go on the pilgrimages, it doesn't always happen, but people get damaged. I could see from what they were saying in the group that they thought you were the sort to respond to it, they knew you could be reached."

"What did they know?" James' voice rose and Jacob looked around again to see if anyone was listening.

"You're no more than an offering James, this isn't about giving you anything. You need to get out. I know you've got a job down in London, for god's sake don't take it. Make some excuse, walk away from it. It isn't what you think it is, you have to believe me."

"I've already given my notice in at my old place, I can't turn it down now."

"To hell with it, what does it matter? It's just a job James, you know there's more at stake than that."

"What did you mean by an offering?" James feared he knew the answer already.

"Have things been happening to you?" Jacob was calm again.

"Yes, a lot of things," James admitted.

"I'm talking about bad things, things you can't explain. Have you been aware of the presence of others with you?"

James stared at him and nodded.

"This isn't Hinduism," Jacob whispered, "you know that."

"I have to speak to Rachel, I don't know what to make of this."

"No, Rachel is part of it, they use her to draw people in. I know how that sounds to you, but you have to believe me."

James could feel his anger rising, "is this just another way of trying to break us up? I don't believe for a minute that Rachel would do that. You don't know how we feel about each other."

"I'm sorry James, I know it's horrible to hear. If you go to London these things you've been experiencing will only get worse. "

"I'm seeing Munro tomorrow," James said, "I'll get the truth from him."

"Don't breath a word of this to them. You have no idea how much I'm risking meeting you like this. If you tell them what I've said, I don't know what they'd do to me. I was with Munro this morning, there's a side to him you haven't seen. Please James, don't betray me to them."

"Where did you meet him?" James asked.

"At the flat."

"When did he come up from London?" James said.

"I don't know, he's been here most of the week, we had a meeting on Monday. Why do you ask?"

"He told me last night that he was still in London. Why would he lie to me like that? I don't understand what the hell's going on."

"That's right James, you don't. Just get out, have nothing more to do with them."

James got to his feet, "I'm going to see him now. If he's here I want to ask him why he lied to me."

As he turned to leave Jacob chased after him and outside the café grabbed his arm. "Don't go there feeling like this. You'll say something you'll regret. Give yourself time to calm down. They mustn't know I've said anything. They're dangerous and powerful people, James, you don't understand what they can do."

James broke away from him, "Don't worry. If Munro's really there then I won't mention you. But if you're lying I'll see to you myself, I promise."

Jacob stood and watched James stride away before turning and disappearing into the crowd of shoppers. James returned to his car and drove quickly across the city. His emotions swung back and forth between confusion and anger towards whoever he suspected was lying. He hoped it was Jacob, everything would be straightforward if all this was just an attempt to take Rachel away from him. As he turned into the wide street outside the flat he found a space a few cars up and parked. Before he could get out of the car the flat door opened and Rachel stepped into the sunshine, buttoning her coat as she descended the steps. James was about to call to her when he saw Munro coming out behind her and walking down to where she was waiting for him. James watched as they embraced and kissed for a long time. Munro's hand slid down her back and held the top of her thigh beneath her dress.

It was too much to see. James was numb with shock and when Munro released her Rachel began walking towards where James was parked. Before she saw him she smiled and swung her arm back and forth like a child. As they locked eyes the smile dropped from her face before she spun round to alert Munro who had already gone back into the building. As she looked back at James he had started his car and was pulling away. She made no attempt to stop or even signal to him, but stood motionless and without reaction as she watched him drive off down the street.

Chapter 40

Back at his flat James sat staring into space, seeing nothing. None of it made sense to him and no matter how he tried to understand what was happening he came up empty. The picture of Munro with his hands on Rachel remained before him and tears of anger and betrayal stung his eyes.

After a while he felt the impulse to do something but he couldn't see a way through. He turned on his 'phone and scrolled through the address book, hoping there might be someone he could turn to. As Rachel's number slid up he looked at the shape of the letters in her name; just a short while ago there had been a pleasure just to look at them, but now they brought bitterness. Without thinking he called her but she didn't answer. He tried again but she wasn't responding. He could feel his anger growing and he selected Munro. After a few rings Munro answered, sounding cautious. "Hello James, where are you?"

"What does it matter where I am? What's going on? You told me you were in London. Why'd you lie to me, Munro?" James' voice shook as he spoke.

"I didn't lie James, I had a change of plans and was able to get away earlier than expected."

"That's another lie, you've been here all week. Why are you treating me like this?"

Munro was silent and then said "Who told you I was here all week?"

There was a calm menace that was unmistakable in his tone and James said "No one had to tell me, I saw you when I drove over to the flat."

"But that makes no sense James, we spoke yesterday and you mentioned nothing about it. Who told you I was here all week?" Munro's voice was slow and deliberate which only exaggerated the loss of control that James was revealing.

"I saw you with Rachel, outside the flat, I saw you together." James was holding back his tears, as he mentioned her name it spiked something within him and his emotions flooded forward.

"That has nothing to do with you. I'll ask you again, who told you where I was, James?"

"Nothing to do with me? What are you talking about? Have you been involved with her all along?"

The line went dead as Munro hung up on him. The tears finally fell from James' eyes in streams of confusion and pain. He tried Rachel's number one last time and slammed the 'phone down when she failed to answer. He stood up and paced around the living room, as he came to the bedroom door he punched his fist through the cheap wood and shouted "Bitch!"

Back at the table he picked up his 'phone and saw Emma's name on the list. For a brief moment he hesitated before ringing her, fearing it would only complicate things further.

"Hello James, it's been a long time." Her voice sounded the same as it always had when they were happy.

"Emma, I'm sorry for calling, I didn't know who to turn to. I need to speak to someone."

"What's wrong James? You sound upset."

"I am, can we meet to talk?"

"I'm sorry James, there isn't any point. I've moved on, we can't go over all this again." Her impatience was clear and James feared she would refuse him.

"Please Emma, it's not about us, I promise. I'm not looking to start things up again, I just need to talk to someone. I couldn't think of anyone else, just for a short while, please."

"We're talking now, why don't you say what you need to tell me?"

"I can't, not over the 'phone. Can I meet you tomorrow? Just for an hour, I promise."

"Where are you?" She asked.

"I'm in Birmingham, I can be there whatever time suits you."

There was a long pause before she answered, "I'm seeing someone else James. I don't think it can do any good us meeting, not after all this time."

"Please, Emma, I'm in a mess, I don't have anyone else to trust. I just need to talk, one hour and then I'll go."

"Alright, but don't come thinking there's anything more to it. I don't want to meet at my flat, where shall we do it?"

"Pick a restaurant or a pub and send me the postcode. I'll find it." He was filled with relief as she spoke.

"Alright, I'll see you at seven, that'll give you time to get home."

"Thank you, Emma, it means a lot to me. Just message me the details."

"Alright, bye." She hung up and James wiped the tears from his eyes. He hadn't planned to try and win her back but still hearing that she was seeing someone felt like bad news. He considered calling Rachel one more time but instead put on his jacket and went out to get some cash from the machine at the local petrol station. He realised he needed to eat something and maybe buy Emma a gift. As he followed the road down to the garage he felt jumpy, his hands were shaking and he was breathless. At the cash machine he pressed his numbers and selected to withdraw money. But the message flashed up that there were insufficient funds in his account. He selected to see his balance and stared in disbelief to discover he was three thousand pounds overdrawn. He stood staring at the screen unable to comprehend how it could be true. He retrieved his card and outside the garage took out his 'phone and searched for the number of his 'phone banking. He eventually got through to a woman with a thick Scottish accent who confirmed that his account was overdrawn.

"But that's not possible, there was over eight grand in there before I went to India."

"I can provide you with a list of debits," she said impassively, "if you think there have been illegal transactions on this account you need to notify us."

"I am notifying you, my money's gone," he shouted.

"I understand you are distressed, James but if you check your account you can tell us which debits you claim were made by someone else. Is there anything else I can help you with today?"

"My money's gone!" He shouted as he ended the call. He felt helpless and couldn't think clearly enough to go back and check his account details. Instead he used his debit card to buy a bottle of brandy from the garage which he opened long before he reached his flat and began gulping as he walked. He wanted nothing except to close everything down, to escape from his own life.

In the flat he lay on his bed and continued to swallow from the bottle. It was quickly gone and he lay groaning out loud, a mindless moan that became a wail. And then he was silent, all his feelings stopped and he lay motionless, his eyes open but blind to everything. James arched forwards and threw the empty bottle against the wall, sending pieces of glass in every direction. He fell back and before he hit the mattress he was out.

Chapter 41

James woke around ten to a room of splintered glass and an overwhelming sense of gloom. He tried to remember the events of the previous night but it was a blur. He checked his 'phone and found a message from Emma confirming where they would meet. This was enough to give him hope and he slid his legs over the edge of the bed and sat up. He tried to reach Jacob but was informed that the number no longer existed. Checking the time he worked out how long he had before he had to set off and then decided to try and sort out his bank account. Even the events from before he had started drinking were now uncertain and he couldn't be sure what had really happened.

As he stood up a slither of glass cut into the ball of his foot and he winced in pain and hopped back to the bed. He inspected the cut and managed to pull out the piece of glass; immediately a heavy flow of blood gushed from beneath the skin which he tried to halt by wrapping a T-shirt around his foot. He carefully stepped across to the door and as he turned on the light thousands of pieces of glass glittered across the carpet. He cursed his stupidity and still mumbling to himself went into the kitchen to make coffee. He found some plasters and covered up the cut in his foot which was still bleeding.

He opened his laptop and went into his banking details. As his account opened he stared in disbelief: there was a quarter of a million pounds. He didn't know how to respond. He considered speaking to someone at the bank but feared the consequences. Instead he decided to go to the cash machine and take out his limit while there were funds. At least he would have enough to get him through the day no matter what else happened. This bizarre error in his funds was more than an accident, he knew it. Someone was sending him a message.

Twenty minutes later he was sliding his card into the cash machine and punching in his code. It seemed to take an age but finally he selected to see his balance, and this time there was exactly what should have been there from the beginning, eight and a half thousand pounds. He was relieved to see it, and took out two hundred and fifty just to feel safe. As he walked back to the flat he considered how the errors could have occurred, and tried to shake off the suspicion that it had been deliberate.

For the rest of the morning he did very little, he couldn't concentrate on anything and he remained preoccupied with Rachel and Munro. Every noise from the street and through the walls from his neighbours irritated him, he found himself fantasising violent responses to anyone he heard and especially at the thought of Munro. He didn't think to wash or shave, and when enough time had passed he went out to his car and typed the postcode Emma had sent him into the sat nav. He didn't notice that he had left his front door open as he drove away, and had he have seen it he wouldn't have bothered going back.

He drove aggressively, he swore at other drivers and every car around him seemed to be trying to swerve at him or cut him off. He kept looking in his rear view mirror, convinced that police cars were about to pull him over, and not for a single moment did he consider what he would say to Emma. There was no pause in his actions, only a relentless urge forwards that was desperate and unthinking. Entering the outskirts of Bath he began to notice people staring at him from the side of the road and as he drew up to a set of traffic lights he wound down his window and began yelling at two young men. They looked at each other in bewilderment as the lights changed and James sped away.

As he approached his destination he noticed the time: he was half an hour late. He was convinced he had left in good time and slapped the palms of his hands hard onto the steering wheel. He spotted the name of the place and found a parking space nearby. He began to panic about whether she would still be there and ran along the street to the entrance. Through the window he saw her sitting at a table near the wall and she waved at the sight of him. She was wearing a dress James had never seen before and it added to the sense of distance between them since he had last seen her. James rushed in to her table, "I'm sorry I'm late, I don't know what happened," he blurted.

"James, what's happened to you? You look terrible."

"What?" He was annoyed at her question, "What do you mean?"

"Look at you, you look like you've not slept for days. What's been going on? You look so thin."

James sat down opposite her, she was as beautiful as he remembered, but now he could see she didn't love him. The way her eyes looked back at him reminded him of when she had left. "Who's this new guy you're with?" He asked.

"What? Why do you want to know that? Is that why you've come? I told you, I can't go back to how we were. It's over James."

"No!" He said in anger, "That's not why I'm here." He looked away from her and then buried his face in his hands.

"James, I'm concerned for you, I've never seen you like this. Has something happened?"

He looked at her again and felt her concern, "I've been to India, I've been meditating, something's happened."

"What? What's happened? Was it in India? Have you done something?"

"No, it's not that. Well. I don't know, maybe I have, I don't know how to explain it."

"Are you in trouble with the police? Is it something like that?"

"No, it's something else. I'm seeing things, something keeps talking to me, like it's with me, or in me. It sounds crazy, I can see in your face, you think I'm crazy."

"No, I promise I don't. I'm going to get you something to eat, then I want you to start at the beginning." She went over to the counter and spoke to the young woman behind the till.

When she returned James said "What did you say to her? Did you say something about me?"

"Of course not, I ordered some tea and a cake. You're being paranoid James, you know you can trust me."

His impulse was to throw the word back in her face, she was with someone else now, she had left him, but he did want to trust her. He nodded, "Thank you."

The waitress brought a tray over and Emma thanked her. As she placed the tea pot before them the young girl glanced at James and frowned. As she walked away she looked back and Emma understood what was going through her head. She poured him a tea and pushed the cake towards him, "I remembered you always liked these." He ignored the food and sipped from the cup, the first drink he had had since that morning.

"How did it start? What exactly has happened?" The kindness in her voice was more than he could bear and he began to cry.

"I'm sorry Emma, you don't need this. I don't know how to explain it."

"It's okay, just say it. Don't dress it up, what is it?"

"There was a guru in India, we were meditating, it's a long story, but there was something else there, something…." His voice trailed off.

"Something spiritual?" Emma said.

"Yea, something different, spiritual, he told me they were guides, they're doing things to me and I can't make it stop."

Emma's face grew more serious, she fell silent and watched his hands shaking as he raised the cup to his lips. "Will you come and see someone?"

"Who?" James snapped.

"My friend, Demetrius, I think he can help."

"Is he your new boyfriend?" James had become sullen and he didn't hide his contempt.

"Yes, but I think he can help. Listen to me, James, I'm worried about you. I think you need help."

"From Demetrius?" James spat.

"Maybe, I don't know, but he'll know what to do." She reached across the table and held his hand, "Trust me James, you need help. I can't give it, I'm not sure what to do. Please."

He looked at her and said "Okay, when?"

"I can give him a call, we might be able to go now." She found her 'phone and James watched and listened as she spoke to her new man. "Hello Demetrius, not so good. Yes, he's right here, can I bring him over to your place?" Emma glanced across at James as Demetrius spoke and forced a smile to console him. "Thank you, we'll be there soon." As she put her 'phone away she said "I came by bus, can you drive me there?"

"He's okay with me coming?" James was wary.

"Yes, he's waiting for us."

James finished his drink and led her out to his car. She commented that she was surprised that it was still running to try and lighten his mood but she couldn't reach him. She directed him about a mile across the city and they left the car outside his flat. It was an old Victorian street with arched windows and wide pavements. The large houses had been divided into flats where many students now lived. Emma knocked at a large green door and it opened to reveal a good looking Greek man about their age. He and Emma exchanged kisses and she said "This is James."

"Hi, I'm Demetrius, I am pleased to meet you, James." He extended his arm and the two men shook hands. "Please, come in." Demetrius led them down a dark hall to his flat which was just two rooms divided by a cheap plaster board. Everything was tidy and there were few possessions except for a set of paintings on a shelf in one corner. James noticed them immediately, they unsettled him and as he tried to turn away and sit in one of the armchairs he couldn't pull his attention away from them.

Emma began explaining why she had come over when James interrupted them, "What are those paintings? I don't like them."

"They are icons," Demetrius explained, "I am Orthodox."

Demetrius looked at Emma as she continued to sum up her reasons for bringing James over and began to wave his hand before her. "No, it's alright, you don't have to explain anymore." He turned back to James and said "I think I know someone who can help you. Do you have to get back to Birmingham for anything tonight?"

James shook his head, "No, nothing."

"Then please stay the night with me. I have a spare bed I can set up. Tomorrow I would like to take you to meet someone who I think can help." He looked at Emma and said "I will give Father Silouan a call."

"Father Silouan!" James repeated. "You mean a priest?"

"Don't be alarmed James, you know yourself that you are suffering from something spiritual. He is a wise man, he will know what to do."

"I've had enough of gurus," James said.

"Father Silouan is no guru, I promise you. He has a lot of experience in these matters, all you have to do is talk to him and explain what you are going through."

James glanced back at the icons and shook his head, "I don't want to sleep in here."

"That's okay," Demetrius assured him, "you can have my bed. I'll sleep on the cot."

James nodded and looked at Emma, she smiled and patted his hand saying "It's going to be okay." She looked at Demetrius and said "Thank you, let me know what time you're going and I'll come round."

"No, I think it's best if we go without you," Demetrius said. "It'll be simpler that way."

She smiled at James once more, "I have to go, I'm expecting my sister round later."

"That's okay, thank you for what you've done. Do you need a lift?" James said.

"No stay here, it's not far."

James remained seated while Demetrius walked Emma to the front door. He was jealous of what they had but didn't blame Demetrius for anything. Alone in the room he moved to the seat furthest from the icons, becoming resentful of their presence. It felt an imposition to have them there, as though Demetrius was trying to provoke him. But he tried to control himself, he knew this stranger was trying to help him and he had to take whatever help he could.

When the Greek returned he offered James some tea and said "I have some food to cook, are you hungry?"

"No thank you," James said, "you go ahead."

"It's no problem, are you sure you've eaten?"

"I can't get anything down, food would make me sick."

Demetrius studied him for a moment, "I will make that call to Father Silouan."

Chapter 42

Demetrius was a generous host and made every effort to accommodate James despite his guest's mood shifts. He told him about Greece and why he had come to England, and by the end of the evening James was a little more relaxed and asked him "Is Emma now Orthodox?"

"No, not yet, she is preparing for baptism at Pascha."

"Pascha?" James repeated.

"Yes, Easter," said Demetrius. She would have to be Orthodox in order for them to be married but Demetrius didn't mention this.

Later Demetrius brought out a folding bed and pushed back the chairs to make room. "I've put a clean sheet on my bed, make yourself at home."

James lay in the dark unable to sleep. His thoughts jumped through the events of the past few weeks and everything he remembered brought him distress. He began to feel ashamed of himself and imagined how everyone would be disgusted with him. This only made him angry and the violent impulses surged through him. He was unable to focus on any single thought, as though he could no longer direct his mind; he felt as though it was being led entirely by the confusion of emotions that randomly possessed him. Around three in the morning he finally fell to sleep and his dreams were as chaotic as had been his waking mind.

When he woke it was still dark and his body was paralysed. A figure was sitting on his chest, its back arched as it pressed itself into him. James felt the scream strangled in his throat as the figure bent forwards so that he could look into its face. It was the same set of eyes he had seen when he had meditated with Aditya, the same distorted features that had rushed him in the little room back in India. James could feel the muscles in his body tense as they struggled for release but he had no control over his body. This realisation brought him a new fear: what if he were to go through and murder Demetrius? What if whatever was holding him still could control his actions? The horror this brought him was too much but before he lost consciousness the presence was gone and his body released. At once every scream that had been suppressed escaped from him, and Demetrius came running into the room.

"What is it James? What's wrong?"

Despite knowing him for only a short time James gripped Demetrius' arm and clung to him. "There was something here, it was on me."

Demetrius turned on the light and James saw him cross himself. "What are you doing?" James yelled. "Why did you do that?"

"Don't worry," Demetrius was trying to stay calm, "I am asking for God's help."

James fell back and twisted away from him. "I don't want your God, take Him away."

"Do you want me to leave?" Demetrius asked.

"Yes, I'm sorry, go away," James cried out.

Demetrius went through to the other room and James noticed the soft glow of candlelight coming through the doorway. He pushed his face down into the sheet and moaned a low guttural groan in an attempt to block out the sound of Demetrius whose voice was barely audible as he prayed.

The following morning Demetrius brought James coffee and encouraged him to take a shower. His demeanour was friendly but serious and he didn't linger too long with his guest. "I have arranged to see Father Silouan at nine, he lives about forty minutes from here," he said.

James felt a reluctance to go along, it struck him that some kind of trap was being set and he began to grow suspicious of the Greek. He tried to conceal the fact that he was now watching his host carefully, convinced he was trying to catch him out. Conversation between the two men dried up and by the time they were heading out they exchanged little more than what was necessary to follow their route. As he drove, James suddenly said "Why are you mumbling? Stop it."

"I'm sorry," Demetrius said, "I was praying."

They drew up outside a semi-detached house in a small cul de sac, and James was unimpressed. "Is this how you keep your priests? I've seen servants live in better places."

"Father Silouan is a servant," Demetrius replied, "he doesn't need a palace."

James parked in the driveway and they walked to the front door. James' suspicions grew and he sensed something terrible was about to happen. His instincts told him to run, whoever lived here intended to harm him, he knew it. But there was nowhere to run, and James understood that he had no one else to turn to. He overcame his fear and stood motionless as Demetrius knocked at the door.

James let out a contemptuous laugh as a small balding man in his late sixties opened the door to them. An old cassock hung from his wiry frame and as Demetrius held out his hands the little priest blessed him. James overcame the urge to challenge them, he wanted to yell and mock them, but managed to remain silent. The priest looked at him, "Hello James, I am Father Silouan. Would you like to come in?"

Despite all his suspicions James nodded and followed him in. Everything was simple and clean in the house and as they went through to the living room James saw another set of icons. Father Silouan noticed him staring at them and said "This is an icon of the Mother of God, have you seen these kinds of images before?"

"Only at Demetrius' flat," said James, "they make me feel…"

His voice trailed off and Father Silouan asked "What? How do they make you feel James?"

"Uneasy I suppose," James said turning away from them. "I don't know why, I don't like to look at them, they…"

Again his words hung in the air and the elderly priest invited his guests to sit. "Now James, Demetrius has given me a few details of what's going on, but it would be useful to hear it from you. Can you tell me what you think is wrong?"

James looked down at his feet for a moment and Demetrius began to suspect that he wasn't going to cooperate. But to his relief James began to speak in a calm voice that was more controlled than at any time since he had met him.

"I am being attacked," James said. "Something spiritual is attacking me. A guru in India told me they were guides and now they're with me all the time. They hate me, I hear them laughing at me, they tell me to kill myself. I'm exhausted, I don't know how much longer I can go on with it. I don't want to die, but I can't see any other way of escaping them."

He stopped and looked at Father Silouan who didn't respond but sat silently listening, slowly running a knotted rope through his fingers. "Is there anything you can do to help me?" James said.

"Yes," Father Silouan said, "you are possessed by demons, the Church can help you." The words struck James like a physical blow and he visibly flinched. He knew it was true but hearing someone say it was a shock.

"The Church?" James said. "Can't you do anything?"

"I will do as the Church teaches us, but you must understand this is not a power I possess. The authority of the Church will act through me, but all that we do will be according to God's will."

"I don't even know if I believe in God," James confessed.

"You may not," Father Silouan said, "but the demons do. And whether you believe or not, God can deliver you from them."

James wiped his mouth with a trembling hand, he felt afraid again and Father Silouan recognised the suspicion in his eyes. "Don't let them scare you, they don't want you free, they like to torment you, they want you as their plaything. Ignore anything they say to you, don't engage in any way. They are liars and nothing they say is to be trusted. Would you consent to me saying the prayers of exorcism? I have made a short fast and can pray with you now if you wish."

At first James didn't answer, he looked back and forth between the two men, an inner voice prompting him to abuse them and leave. "I want you to pray for me," he finally said weakly.

"Good," Father Silouan said, "we must go out to my little chapel in the garden." He stood up and beckoned for them to follow. They went through the kitchen to what looked like a large shed with a cross above the door. It was unlocked and inside there was a wall of icons before them and a small wooden stand on which sat a number of books. "If you don't want to do this stand quietly where you are," Father Silouan instructed, "otherwise you are welcome to venerate the icons with

311

me." He stepped forwards and began making the cross over himself and bowing to touch the floor. As he moved across in front of the images Demetrius did the same while James stood watching. Father Silouan returned to the icon of Christ and began asking for forgiveness, he crossed himself again and once more kissed the image.

He seemed to have forgotten all about James as he walked to the stand and began reading a prayer in an unemotional, monotone voice. There was no hint of theatrics, and James began to wonder if he should stay. Father Silouan went through a doorway in the screen of icons and a few minutes later came out wearing a stole around his neck which reached down to his feet and around his wrists he wore golden cuffs. He resumed his reading of the prayers in the same flat voice which lacked any of the drama James had expected. He indicated to Demetrius to bring James around in front of him and the old priest raised a cross before him as he prayed. He waved the cross over James and Demetrius went through the doorway to light incense, all the time the same monotone recital of prayers continued.

James felt Father Silouan's words become a persistent pulling at him, like a hook was caught in his gut, it tugged at his insides and James thought he was going to be sick. And still the prayers continued, they swirled around James' head so that he felt them physically wrenching at his insides. As Father Silouan uttered the command to depart James was simultaneously pulled in different directions so that he felt his legs giving way and he grabbed the book stand for support.

"When's it going to end?" James cried, but the priest ignored him; his pleas to God continued.

Suddenly James shouted "He invited us in!"

Demetrius looked nervously at the priest who seemed oblivious to everything James said. Finally James heard a loud popping sound and he felt something like a change of pressure in his ears and the sensation of vomiting but nothing physical came out of him. His stomach tightened and he was overcome with weakness so that Demetrius had to catch him before he dropped to the floor. Father Silouan turned the page of his book and read on, his words like canon fire pushing the battle on.

Without warning he fell silent, he looked at Demetrius and said "Give him some water to drink."

Demetrius helped James to a wooden bench at the back of the chapel and poured some water from a plastic bottle. James gulped thirstily, it hurt his throat as he swallowed and as his stomach reacted to the liquid he ached with hunger. He looked up at Father Silouan and smiled, his eyes shone with gratitude and he felt stillness within himself.

"Right let's feed this boy," Father Silouan said, "I need to eat as well."

James stood up and wanted to tell the old priest what he was feeling but Father Silouan said "Not now. You need to rest, have something to eat. We'll talk where it's comfortable." He patted James on the shoulder and said "Well done," and venerated the icons before they left.

Back in the house Father Silouan told Demetrius where to find everything and took James into the living room. This time James noticed the beautiful gold that shimmered around the Mother of God in the icon and he could see a look of compassion in her face.

"Take a seat James, we should talk. First of all, is there anything you want to ask?"

"Will they return?" He said.

"Only if you become involved in anything dangerous again. The sure way to protect yourself is to look at how you're living, you need to put your house in order. You must understand that we are living through a war, all of us participate in it whether we know it or not. The demons attack us constantly, and if we are ignorant of it, we may give ourselves to them."

"Do you mean most people are...possessed?" James said.

"No, not possessed, in His mercy God does not permit this. But most of us do not need to be possessed, we willingly follow their orders without even knowing it. What we have done today is win a battle, but this does not mean we have won the war. Our salvation is always in the balance, any one of us can betray our King at any time; we are all sinful creatures."

"Then how can anyone be saved?"

"No matter how many times we fall, however many times we are beaten, God calls us to stand and fight again."

"I have always known there is something more, I just wanted to find it. I didn't intend to do anything evil."

"Many people, especially the young, are told that to find God they must transcend reality. This is a lie James, we do not find God by escaping reality, we find Him here, in this very world."

"But it all felt so... so spiritual," James said.

Father Silouan nodded, "The demons are cunning. Just because something is spiritual does not mean it is good. There are many spirits in this world, you have encountered some of them. They work tirelessly to destroy us. They will bring us pleasure, comfort, make us feel good in all sorts of ways, and if we are ignorant we may believe that these are signs of spiritual health while in reality they point to our death, our spiritual death."

"What do I do now? Everything has gone."

"I would encourage you to find a church, even if you are not yet convinced of what you believe. God has touched you, it is time for you to come to your senses, seek the truth; there is a door you must knock at, and when you do it will open to you."

"What about my job? I'm supposed to be working for these people."

"Forget about it. Go back to Sheffield, you can get references from your last place, start again. Go home where people know you and have nothing more to do with these occult practices."

"Father Silouan, I wanted more from life, I just didn't know where to look. What can I do now? I know I've been touched by evil. Will God really accept me?"

Father Silouan's eyes were filled with gentleness, "The bones that are humbled, they shall rejoice, a broken and contrite spirit God will not despise." He smiled and said "God's mercy is infinite. He loves us more than the demons hate us."

The old priest looked tired, he stood and excused himself and James looked out at the garden. He went over and tried the French windows and stepped into the fresh air. For the first time since he could remember there was silence within him. Only now that they were gone could he see the evil spirits for what they were and he recognised how close he had come to being lost. He tilted his head back and looked up into the skies through tears of joy and whispered "Forgive me, Lord."

CPSIA information can be obtained
at www.ICGtesting.com
Printed in the USA
LVHW110958150520
655672LV00001B/75